SHADOW
ANGELS

BOOKS BY D.K. HOOD

Her Bleeding Heart

Chase Her Shadow

Now You See Me

Their Wicked Games

Where Hidden Souls Lie

D.K. HOOD
SHADOW
ANGELS

bookouture

Published by Bookouture in 2023

An imprint of Storyfire Ltd.
Carmelite House
50 Victoria Embankment
London EC4Y oDZ

www.bookouture.com

ISBN: 978-1-83525-493-6
eBook ISBN: 978-1-83790-767-0

To my readers. Thank you so much for following me into the thrilling world of Beth Katz.

INTRODUCTION

In this world of equality, why can't I identify as a psychopathic serial killer and be accepted? After all, in the animal kingdom, predators are part of the natural order of things. They're tolerated alongside us, and yet, I'm hunted. Being the daughter of a serial killer changed my life in so many ways. As a child I figured I was normal, but by the time I discovered that being "just like dad" was unlawful... it was too late.

Psychopathic behavior can lie undisturbed, hidden in our genes, until a traumatic event triggers a violent episode, and that may be true for most like me but I'm different from the others. Think of me as a modified, upgraded version. You see, as Special Agent Beth Katz, I must hide the charismatic serial killer side of me and act "normal" to fight crime, but in the guise of the Tarot Killer, I can sneak away to seek vengeance on twisted maniacs who slip through the net of justice.

Working close to crime offers me a smorgasbord of choices, but I must move in the shadows because the law that protects kid murderers, pedophiles, and thrill killers doesn't protect me. Can't they understand I'm just taking out the trash?

PROLOGUE

FRIDAY

Icy fingers of dread walked along the vertebrae of Cassie Burnham's spine under the forbidding stare of the man leaning against the bar. He'd been glaring at her with unnerving intensity each time she took the stage in the Fuzzy Peach bar at the Outlaws Saloon. Not the lustful look most patrons gave her, his contempt for her radiated across the room. Dancing and acting provocative was proving difficult under his judgmental gaze. It happened every night. The moment the music started and she wrapped herself around the glistening silver pole, he emerged from the shadows, eyes narrowed in menace.

Relieved when the final strains of her music ended for her last appearance of the night, Cassie left the stage and slapped away the hands reaching out to touch her. Most of them were miners who flocked to town on weekends, cashed up and ready to party, and apart from booze and gambling, they had nowhere else to spend their pay. Many in the audience ignored the no-touch policy, and the bouncers were too slow or lazy to cross the floor to the stage to protect the dancers. Seeing those leering faces made her skin crawl and she hated her life. Being a stripper in a mining town in the middle of nowhere had become the end of the road for Cassie. Sure, the hourly rate was good and she got to keep her tips, but it was a dead-end job.

Exhausted after hours onstage, Cassie gathered up her costume and an itchy trickle of sweat ran between her shoulder blades. She wanted to be far away from this place and searched for her discarded clothes. After wrestling a bra from one of the men in the crowd and ignoring the grabbing hands, she headed toward the dressing rooms. Outside was below zero but inside the saloon heat rose in clouds of unwashed male and stale beer. She nodded to the next dancer heading for the stage and walked along the passageway and into the dressing room, leaving the loud music, cheers, and suggestive remarks behind her. As she entered the crowded room, a wall of cheap perfume hit her, mixed with the stench of sweat and smelly feet. Women moved around, packed together like sardines, dressing or sitting in front of mirrors touching up their makeup. Stripping was the only gig in town that paid the big bucks, and she would cash in before she got too old, because the next stop would be a bartender or working at the local gas station. Saturday night was always busy, but thankfully, her shift was over. She pushed her sweaty costumes into her backpack, added her makeup bag and long blonde wig, and then made her way to the showers. It was good to wash the sparkling makeup from her body and remove the touch of the men forcing bills down her underwear. She'd set her mind on buying a new pair of boots for the winter and with tonight's tips she'd have more than enough money. The happy thought brightened her mood and she hummed as she dried her long hair.

Ten minutes later, she opened the stage door and looked both ways. It wouldn't be the first time an amorous drunken miner had tried to force himself on her, but the dark alleyway appeared deserted. As she stepped out of the back door it clanged shut behind her and an icy chill blasted her, seeping through the seams of her clothes and sending shivers across her heated flesh. She longed to take a deep breath of cool mountain air, but the alleyway was lined with overflowing dumpsters. Only a single light illuminated the dancers' exit from the building and anything could be hiding in the alleyway. Cats, rats, or bears frequented the area hunting for food.

Fear gripped her as shadows moved and she paused, scanning the way ahead before stepping into the darkness. Watching the deep shadows, she maneuvered carefully through the garbage, trying not to breathe in the stink of stale Chinese takeout and cat pee. At the end of the alleyway, a single streetlight cast an orange glow like a beacon of safety and she headed toward it. The dancers always left their vehicles parked on Quartz, a narrow road that ran behind a number of industrial buildings. As she headed toward the light, she blew out a deep sigh. This area of town could be anywhere in the country. It was hard to believe the Outlaws Saloon was in the outlying areas of the beautiful Rattlesnake Creek. The picturesque center of town seemed to exist in a world of its own. It was as if time had stopped. The main street of Rattlesnake Creek resembled a town in the Old West with most of the buildings constructed decades ago from wood or rock hewn out of the mountains by the miners.

In her periphery, the shadows moved and the shape of a large figure fell across the alleyway. Heart pounding, she slipped one hand inside her purse for the can of bear spray. Man or bear, it would slow him down some and give her time to escape. Unsure if she should move forward or go back, she turned and looked over one shoulder. The dark alleyway loomed behind her frighteningly still, even the cats had deserted it. Ahead, long shadows reached out like witches' fingers, their long nails threatening to tear her apart. She stared into the darkness for long seconds, trying to rationalize her fear. She'd walked along this alleyway one hundred times before and each time something spooked her. Gathering her courage, and taking a strong grip on the bear spray, she walked into the shadows. As she reached the end of the alleyway, she increased her pace and burst out into the light.

Pain slammed into the side of her head and she staggered, falling to her knees. The gritty sidewalk cut deep into her flesh as bright starbursts erupted in her eyes and the metallic taste of blood coated her tongue. What had happened? No one was there. The only sound was the muffled *thump, thump, thump* from the club. She tried to turn her head to look around but moving it hurt so bad. Her mouth refused to open, and only mewing sounds came from between her lips. She'd dropped the can of bear spray and she watched helplessly as it spun on the ground before rolling away into the gutter. On hands and knees, she crawled along the sidewalk trying to get away. Seconds later, denim-clad legs and dark brown work boots came into view. Dizzy and confused, Cassie turned her head to look at her attacker when agony clanged through her temples and the sidewalk blurred. Flat on the bitterly cold ground, she couldn't move. Was she dying?

Strong hands lifted her under the arms and her face slid over plastic. It dragged against her skin in a strange burning sensation. The man grunted behind her and as her knees smashed against metal, only a whimper escaped her lips. He said nothing as he ripped back her arms and brutally applied zip ties. Gaffer tape was wrapped around her head, sealing her mouth. She couldn't breathe. Terror gripped her as doors slammed shut and an engine started. Face down and unable to move, she slid around on the plastic coating the floor as the vehicle accelerated around corners at high speed. Nausea gripped her as the truck swayed and bumped, tossing her around until it finally stopped. The door slid open, washing her with freezing night air. She moved her eyes as moonlight outlined the man. She could hear his heavy breathing and smell his rancid sweat. Unable to feel her arms or legs, she could only grunt as he rolled her onto her back. She flopped over and gazed into his shadowed features. Terrified and unable to fight, she stared at him.

A low chuckle broke the silence as the sharp blade of the knife in his hand reflected in the moonlight.

"Oh, don't look so worried, little lady. We have all night and then some."

ONE

MONDAY

Eagle's Nest Forest was wearing its fall dress in a multitude of golds, browns, and greens as Special Agent Beth Katz walked onto the stoop of the cabin alongside Rattlesnake Creek. It had been one of the five cabins she'd considered buying over the past few weeks as a place for her to use as a retreat. She needed a place away from the office as her home base. After witnessing a brutal murder some months previously, she'd taken the obligatory psych test, and failed. The FBI director had forced her to take time away from the big city and reassigned her to Rattlesnake Creek. In truth, being a wolf in sheep's clothing she'd come too close to becoming the prime suspect in a murder case. Anxious to seek revenge on a serial killer who delighted in raping and killing young girls, she'd allowed her guard to slip a little. Dispatching a monster from one of her cases wasn't her usual MO, but catching the killer in the act, she'd allowed her own dark side to take control. It had taken split-second timing to shift the blame onto the mythical Tarot Killer by leaving a tarot card floating in the murderer's blood.

As a master of disguise and skilled in many types of self-defense, the daughter of a serial killer had become the notorious Tarot Killer—the mythical killer of monsters, who'd never left a trace behind, was also an FBI agent. She worked close to investigations, moved invisibly through the dark web as if it was her home, and hunted down unstoppable killers.

She'd left DC almost three months ago to work with Senior Special Agent Dax Styles in a sprawling mining town that time had left behind. The majority of buildings were from the original settlers way back in the 1800s, although new builds were mixed in to accommodate the growing population of miners. Lucrative mines surrounded the area and included the outlying towns of Rainbow, Serenity, and Spring Grove. Although Rattlesnake Creek appeared from the outside to be isolated, the opposite was true. The mines produced a steady flow of workers and the town had a regular bus service. She'd recently discovered the railroad ran scenic tours alongside the mountains and stopped twice daily.

As the Rattlesnake Creek FBI field office serviced many of the outlying small towns, cases requiring their expertise were few and far between, which usually meant that they assisted the local sheriff, Cash Ryder, in any local incidents. Most times it was on weekends, when the miners came into town causing a ruckus. They usually headed for the local saloons to spend their pay and clashed with workers from other mines. This meant that she would take a few days during the week in lieu of the weekend she spent on the job. This worked well for Beth because she could slip away if necessary and, disguised as the Tarot Killer, could keep her dark side happy. The cabin would make this easier, as would her new silver GMC truck, chosen because of the multitude of the same brand and color in the area. Under the guise of fixing up the old cabin and searching across the country for furniture and other items to make it comfortable, she could slip unnoticed into towns all over

Montana. Once the cabin was complete, she'd take up art and, if she needed to go missing for a time, use the excuse of painting the scenery in the area.

The cabin door creaked as she opened it but inside was a pleasant surprise. The real estate agent had mentioned this cabin was owned by a miner who'd raised a family here and then retired. He'd followed his kids to live in Helena six months previously. The log cabin, like many used for fishing or hunting sleepovers, had rough logs notched together. The roof, she'd been told, had recently been replaced with asphalt shingles. The front door led straight into the family room. It had a separate kitchen and three bedrooms. The bathroom was serviceable and water came from a pump connected directly to the crisp clean mountain-fed river. The kitchen sink had a water purifier that had just been fitted, so she wouldn't need to boil her drinking water. It had a generator, but to her surprise, she discovered one side of the roof had solar panels leading to a storage battery. She turned around in the family room. The place had a good feel to it and it had the added bonus of a shed with a sturdy lock and a meat locker. She smiled and pulled out her phone, glad to see she had five bars, and called the real estate agent. "Mr. Brine. It's Beth Katz. The cabin with the asphalt shingles, I'd like to make an offer." She listened to the man. "Yes, I'll be by in twenty minutes." She disconnected and took one last look before closing and locking the door. "Now all I need is furniture." She grinned. She'd created the perfect alibi for any time she needed to be away.

Her apartment was in the FBI building. It was self-contained but the high security meant being under surveillance twenty-four hours a day. It was nice enough, with a gym and the office an elevator ride away, but she shared the building with Dax Styles, or "Styles" as he preferred to be called. The tough ex-Army MP had his own set of rules and they seemed to work.

He'd been through a messy marriage breakup, so was distant at times, but for some weird reason she liked him and his dog, Bear. He had her back and she could trust him on the job, but she doubted he'd understand her double life. In truth, she'd need to be on her guard. Dax Styles was as sharp as a knife. One slip and he'd see right through her.

TWO

Senior Special Agent Dax Styles checked the contents of his truck. He'd packed his fishing gear, sleeping bag, a few supplies, and a bag of dog food. As he headed for the open door, his phone chimed. It was Cash Ryder, the local sheriff. "Morning, Cash. What can I do for you?"

"It might be nothing. It might be something, but it's not anything I can handle alone." Ryder blew out a breath. *"A woman by the name of Cassie Burnham has gone missing. No one has seen a trace of her since she left Outlaws at around ten on Friday night. She's one of the strippers."*

Sliding in behind the wheel of his truck, Styles leaned back in his seat. "Who called it in?"

"One of the other strippers, Rosie Donohue. She found Cassie's purse and a can of bear spray on Quartz when she left later that evening and figured she dropped it. Apparently, most of them have a ton of things to carry back to their vehicles after their shifts. She said they often find bits and pieces of clothing on the sidewalk belonging to one of them or the other." Ryder cleared his throat. *"Rosie has kids, and it slipped her mind until Sunday. She called Cassie and left a message but hasn't*

heard from her. She dropped by her place this morning to see her, and her neighbor said she hasn't been home, all weekend. I asked Rosie if Cassie entertained any of the customers, and she was adamant that Cassie wouldn't give a miner the time of day."

Frowning, Styles drummed his fingers on the steering wheel. "Did Rosie put in a missing person report?"

"Yeah, mainly because she knows that Cassie hasn't got any family here. She doesn't have a boyfriend and doesn't socialize with anyone outside a few of the girls from Outlaws. Rosie said she'd called her friends, but nobody's heard from her. I'm at a loss to know what to do next."

As Ryder's expertise extended to local brawls, traffic violations, and robbery, he often looked to Styles for assistance. Although during a recent spate of murders covering three counties he had been surprised with Ryder's professionalism under crisis. "Did you collect the purse and bear spray and check them for prints?"

"Yeah, two sets of prints. One set is Rosie's, so I'm assuming the other is Cassie's." Ryder's chair squeaked as it rolled around behind his desk. *"What now?"*

Styles sighed. "What's her address? I'll meet you there and we'll do a welfare check." He thought for a beat. "Are her keys in her purse?"

"Yeah."

Rubbing his chin, Styles stared through the windshield at the clear blue sky. He should be fishing. "So, we have the keys to her home. I assume she has a vehicle? Did you check out Quartz Road? Is her vehicle there? Any evidence of a struggle? Maybe she was abducted?"

"This is why I called you, Styles. I need a second pair of eyes on this."

Rolling his eyes skyward, Styles smothered a groan of regret. "Okay, meet me on Quartz in five. We'll go by her house later. I assume the purse was found near the alleyway leading from Outlaws Saloon?"

"Yeah." Ryder blew out a relieved breath. *"Thanks. I'm leaving now."* He disconnected.

The thought of contacting Beth crossed his mind, but why should he disturb her? She'd assisted in three brawls over the weekend and had made a point of needing at least one personal day to go buy a cabin. It wasn't as if it were an FBI matter, so he started the engine and headed toward Quartz. As he turned the corner, a small lump in the grass caught his attention. He pulled in and slid from behind the wheel. As he got closer, the shape of a backpack came into view. He went back to his vehicle and rummaged through his forensics kit for a pair of examination gloves and a large evidence bag. Returning to the backpack, he pulled on the gloves and recoiled at the sight of blonde tresses spilling out of the top. Concerned at finding body parts, he swallowed hard and then sniffed the air and, smelling no signs of decay, flipped open the top of the backpack to peer inside. He discovered a blonde wig, an assortment of skimpy brightly colored underwear, a makeup bag, and shoes. He shook his head, this likely belonged to Cassie. He closed the backpack and dropped it into the evidence bag before carrying it back to his truck.

After continuing along Quartz, he pulled to the curb opposite a meat-processing plant and nosed his truck up behind Ryder's cruiser. He leaned over the back seat and patted Bear on the head. "Wait here, boy. With luck, I'll have this sewn up in an hour or so and we can be on our way." He headed toward Ryder. "What have we got?"

"Cassie's truck is a metallic blue Ford pickup." Ryder indicated with his phone toward a similar vehicle parked alongside the curb. "Plates match." He walked all around it, peering inside. "It looks fine. Maybe she hooked up with a customer? Some of them do make extra cash on the side."

Styles shook his head. "I don't figure it's fine. I found a back-pack that has to belong to her. You must have driven right past it. It's in an evidence bag in my truck. We'll need to walk the alleyway and look for signs of a struggle."

"Sure." Ryder looked perplexed. "This used to be such a quiet town. I'd go weeks on end without anything happening. Since all the mines expanded operation, our crime rate has gone up five hundred percent."

Following Ryder into the alleyway, Styles shrugged. "It goes with the population increase. I figure it's time you asked the mayor for a deputy. Now I have Beth working with me, we're gonna be away a lot of the time. You can't be expected to handle everything on your own. In your place, I'd ask for two deputies. Serenity is smaller than Rattlesnake Creek and Sheriff Adams has two deputies. You should use him as an example." He pulled out a flashlight and shone it under each of the dump-sters. "Man, this place stinks."

They walked back and forth for a time but found nothing of interest. Ryder even went to the trouble of lifting up the dump-ster lids and peering inside. Styles shook his head. "Nothing happened here. We should look out on the sidewalk opposite the alleyway."

After scanning the sidewalk in both directions, Styles stopped at the entrance to the alleyway to examine the ground. He took a piece of chalk out of his pocket and circled a few dark spots. "We need to get a sample of that. It looks like blood."

"I'm on it." Ryder ran back to his cruiser, returning with a test kit, and carefully took a sample of the spots on the sidewalk. "I'll drop it into Nate." He was referring to Doctor Nate Mace, the only doctor with an office in town. "He'll be able to tell us if it's human or not. If it is, we'll send it over to the medical exam-iner in Black Rock Falls for analysis."

Nodding, Styles walked up and down slowly, searching for any other clues to the woman's disappearance, but found nothing. He turned back to Ryder. "I guess we go check her house, but I think it's a waste of time. This is where Rosie found her purse, and her backpack was thrown into the bushes. I'd say it's pretty clear that someone has abducted Cassie Burnham and we need to find her fast."

THREE

Not sure how to interpret her new feelings, Beth stared at her reflection in the mirror. She'd experienced satisfaction many a time after dispatching a particularly despicable serial killer or solving a difficult case, but this was something new. After signing the documents to complete the sale of the small cabin in the forest, everything around her appeared to be different. The leaves on the trees had become greener and the sun on her flesh warmer, and she even found herself smiling as she walked into Tommy Joe's Bar and Grill to order takeout from TJ. Dumbfounded by the elation, she stared into the refection of her eyes. Could this be what it felt like to be happy? Perhaps it was the new normal as her life had suddenly slotted into place. Buying the cabin would give her the freedom she required, and she needed to move around if she planned to hunt down a particularly nasty serial killer she'd been watching over the last few weeks.

Life in Rattlesnake Creek had been tame, although she had to admit she enjoyed standing back-to-back with Styles behind saloons in the middle of a brawl breaking up fights. Disagreements in town happened with unnerving frequency at least every weekend, with some disputes spilling over to the following week. Although that wasn't usual as the mining companies required their workers on site from Monday to Friday. She could handle herself, but Styles was in a class of his own. Being a military police officer may have had its disadvantages during his time in the Army as he was often despised by the rank and file, but his ability to fight was outstanding. As an MP he had to deal with every situation, including taking down highly skilled operatives, which meant miners didn't so much as ruffle his feathers. Often, their arrival on scene was enough to break up a ruckus, but it usually depended on how much drink was involved.

Beth went back to her laptop. She had a vicious, bloodthirsty serial killer in her sights. This one passed all her self-imposed rules of engagement, but getting to him unnoticed would be a problem. During the downtime between cases, she'd collected files on a number of cold cases. Investigators were always looking for links between cold and current cases, and as she had access to the FBI databases, it gave her an excuse to be scanning current case files. She made sure to follow a number of FBI investigations and to discuss them with Styles to avoid suspicion. It was interesting to see how different investigators who supposedly followed the same procedure made so many mistakes. Most of them seemed to be chasing their tails. Where she could determine a pattern in a murderer's MO almost immediately, it seemed to take some of the others months to apprehend a killer. She'd taken note to keep well away from the Snakeskin Gully field office cases. They had a higher-than-average rate of success, and she put that down to one of the agents, Jo Wells, being a renowned criminal behavioral analyst. She shuddered. That was one person she never wanted to meet. From all accounts she could spot a serial killer a mile away.

The case that really grabbed her interest happened in Eagle
Rock, Montana, recently. It wasn't connected to her current
case but it intrigued her dark side as if calling her to action. The
remains of two women were found dumped behind a strip mall
on a desolate stretch of land, their bodies covered with bushes
and lawn clippings. Six months previously three bodies,
including one of a young child, had been discovered in Last
Hope, a neighboring town. The subsequent autopsy reports
stated that although dumped in the same location, the times of
death occurred approximately a week apart. The murders, by
strangulation or stabbing, had the same MO and resembled the
attempted murder of Natalie Kingsley, who'd escaped a vicious
attack over a year ago. Chilled to the bone by her statement, it
was obvious by reading the autopsy reports that the same man
was responsible for the entire killing spree.

Natalie had arrived in Eagle Rock with little money and
called a number on a flyer at the local bus station offering a
room for a few hours' work on a man's ranch. The guy, who
called himself Bill, had offered to drive by in his van to give her
more information. He looked okay and he'd mentioned being
married with kids. After discussing the deal out in the parking
lot, she'd agreed. The terms he'd offered suited her and she
needed a place to stay, so took the offered ride to his ranch. She
never arrived. He'd driven to an isolated area, raped and strangled her, but somehow she'd survived. She'd regained conscious-
ness as he was dressing and, terrified, had pretended to be dead.
As he'd driven away, she'd become lucid and when he stopped
the van at a gas station and went inside, she'd grabbed up her
clothes and escaped. Her description of the van and the CCTV
footage from the gas station had pointed to one suspect: Levi
Jackson, a drifter handyman. When her purse was discovered in
Jackson's 2016 Chevrolet Express later that same night, he was
arrested and sent to trial.

Beth chewed on her pen as she read through the court transcript. How had he walked? The case against him was solid but his defense was strong. He'd stated he'd picked her up for rough sex. The CCTV footage had her climbing into his van willingly. He'd stated she'd fallen asleep in the back of the van and he'd left her in the van when he stopped for gas. She was gone when he'd returned from the roadhouse and he hadn't seen the need to look for her. Sex workers didn't usually hang around. Once again, the CCTV footage showed him leaving the van and entering the roadhouse. Moments later she slipped away dragging on her coat.

Beth looked into Jackson's background. He might have been a drifter but he wasn't without means, with cash in the bank. Thanks to glowing character statements from a few locals he'd worked for as a handyman and his softly spoken charming manner, his defense won over the jury. It was a slam dunk after they produced a rap sheet of Natalie's priors listing arrests for soliciting.

Intrigued, Beth read and reread the case files again. There was no mention of finding Bill's flyer, and Natalie had called from a pay phone. None of the numbers on the pay phone had been traced to Jackson. In fact, Jackson's phone had never been placed into evidence because he'd admitted to paying Natalie for sex. He also mentioned she'd solicited him, and they'd come to an agreement on a price. In that agreement, he'd made it quite clear what he required from her. The defense made a point of the fact that he left the forest with Natalie in the van. The prosecution had no evidence he tried to kill her, and if there was any suspicion he'd been involved in the other murders, there would be reasonable doubt, because if he thought Natalie was dead, as she claimed, why didn't he dump her and cover her with leaves?

Beth shook her head in dismay. Jackson likely hadn't

finished with her yet or he had a planned dump site in another area. Maybe he knew she wasn't dead? There could be a ton of reasons why he didn't dump her body at the rape scene. She read through the evidence and clicked her tongue in disgust at the lack of basic procedure. The bills in Natalie's purse hadn't been checked for prints. The main mistake was that the van wasn't taken into evidence and given a forensic sweep. In fact, the entire investigation by the local PD was a joke.

She sighed. Three months ago, another murdered woman was found, this time in a town near Billings, followed by a mother and daughter a week later, all with the same MO. She'd noticed the similarities to the Jackson case and the current murder victims involved in the current FBI investigation because one of the victims and her daughter had been seen climbing into a white van. It fit the description of Jackson's 2016 Chevrolet Express right down to the torn sticker on the back bumper.

The case interested Beth because the FBI had disregarded Jackson as a suspect. Why? The MO fit, but without priors and the previous not guilty verdict, she guessed they'd neglected to dig deeper for fear of the double-jeopardy laws. This was a mistake she'd never make because he fit the profile. Although, the six-month gap between the first two sets of murders was a problem. She believed that unless the killer had been incapaci- tated or jailed at the time between murders, it was too long between murders for someone who thrill-killed. There must be more bodies, somewhere. This killer indulged in frenzied kills close together, which made six months between kills unfeasible. It was Jackson, she would swear by it. Beth understood him so well she could almost step into his skin and know his next move. She pulled out a map and scanned the suburbs around Billings. The killer had established a comfort zone. He killed twice and then moved to another town but all within a comfortable radius of Billings. The pattern was clear to see. The next time he murdered, another would follow in the same town within seven days. Now it would be a waiting game before she could predict where he would strike. She ran her finger over the map, making an imaginary circle around Billings. Levi Jackson was out there, waiting for a call from his next victim. Which town was hiding more victims and when would he strike again?

FOUR

After searching Cassie Burnham's house and speaking to a handful of her friends, Styles had nothing further on her disappearance. It was obvious she'd been abducted, but without one shred of evidence to suggest who might have taken her, he returned to the office. It was too late to go fishing but he'd given Bear a run at the local park before heading home and the dog seemed happy enough. He'd grabbed takeout from Tommy Joe's Bar and Grill and returned to the office. Although it was Ryder's case, he needed to create a case file and write it up. Something had happened to Cassie Burnham and when she left the club at that time of night, there wasn't a soul on the street to witness her abduction. All Ryder could do was to follow procedure and put out a BOLO with Cassie's description in the hope that someone may have seen something. If she'd been taken from one of the busier streets in town, her chances of being seen would have been greater, but during the evenings Quartz was rarely used by anyone other than the strippers. The inadequate lighting along the sidewalk was dangerous and Styles had complained to the local council many a time, stating that it wasn't safe for the women leaving the gentlemen's club. Unfortunately, it seemed that even in Rattlesnake Creek, those people living on the edge of acceptable society weren't considered worthy of the expense.

As he filled the coffee machine, the door to the office opened and Beth walked inside. Happy to see her, he waved and smiled. "I gather your day off didn't go as planned like mine?"

"Mine went just fine." Beth leaned one hip against her desk and smiled at him. "I closed the deal on my cabin. Well, it's more like a small house... and I got a really good price. It has a family room, kitchen, bathroom, and three bedrooms, not to mention solar power."

Surprised to find her in such a good mood, Styles grinned. "You haven't bought a place beside a bear's cave, have you?"

"Nope. The area around it is well cleared. It has river frontage, but not close enough for it to be a problem after the melt. I discussed all this with the real estate agent. I also took the time to take a good look around for any bear scat or other signs of wildlife. I believe it's far enough away from the mountain not to cause me any immediate problems. It was built about twenty years ago, and when I checked out the old shed and meat locker, I couldn't see any signs that animals have tried to force their way inside." She walked over to the kitchenette and took down two cups from the shelf. "It's a perfect place for me to fix up. When I'm done, I'll use it for an artist's retreat."

Styles chuckled. "Or maybe a weekend hideaway. I've seen the way you've been looking at Nate."

"Not likely and not Nate. He's nice but a little boring." Beth took out the fixings for the coffee. "Although, if I had any thoughts in that direction, I would more likely be using my apartment. It would be much more comfortable and closer to the local restaurants. Or do you think I'm a cheap date?"

Laughing, Styles shook his head. "Not at all." He moved the

cups over to the coffee machine. "What brings you back into the office this afternoon?"

"I was just about to ask you the same question?" Beth slid the fixings toward him. "You were supposed to be fishing for the next two days. I'd finished my business in town and got bored. You?"

Styles explained about Cassie Burnham. "It's a mystery. Ryder will follow up with the backpack and put out an all-points bulletin and a BOLO with her description." He sighed. "The problem is, all around here is so vast, she could be anywhere, and after so long, she could be across the state line for all we know."

"Like trying to find a needle in a haystack." Beth added fixings to her coffee. "Did you speak to the other dancers at the club? They might know if she had any threats or problems with a customer. Usually, they warn each other if someone in the crowd is a problem."

Impressed by her knowledge, Styles shook his head. "Not yet. The investigation hasn't gotten that far. How do you know so much about exotic dancers?" He dropped into his office chair and took a sip of his coffee.

"Oh, I became friends with a few female dancers during my pole-dancing classes." Beth stared at him her expression deadly serious.

Spraying coffee across his desk, Styles choked. Eyes watering, he stared at her incredulous. "Your what?" He grabbed handfuls of tissues and mopped up the coffee dripping from the edge of his desk.

"That's a typical reaction. I assume that you're not aware that pole dancing is a very intense form of exercise." She let out a long sigh. "When I was working in DC the hours were variable and I needed to keep fit. It was easier to have a pole in my apartment than to risk running around the city in the middle of the night."

Trying without too much success to shift the image of Beth pole dancing from his mind, Styles swiveled in his seat and opened his laptop. "Ah, I see."

"Yeah, well, some of the girls who attended the classes intended to become strippers or were there to hone their skills." Beth cleared her throat. "We often went for drinks afterward and those type of topics came up. I never mentioned I was an FBI agent. I don't think it would have gone down too well."

Hoping the tips of his ears weren't bright red, Styles turned around to face her. "So, you figure we should go and speak to the dancers about any suspicious men hanging around the club? I'll call Ryder, it's his case."

"I'll speak to them." Beth looked at him across her desk. "Maybe you could talk to the security guys. They might have noticed someone acting strange, but I doubt it, only a few of them care about the girls, most of their attention is on the patrons. I gather the crowd gets unruly at times?" Her mouth curled up at the corners and she gave him a knowing smile.

If he'd given her the impression that he spent most of his downtime in strip clubs, she was very much mistaken. "The only time I ever see what goes on inside a gentlemen's club, Beth, is if Ryder gets called out to prevent a ruckus, and I get hauled along too. It's not a place I frequent. If I need a drink and company, I'll drop by TJ's." He shrugged. "Not that there's anything wrong with women removing their clothes for a living, it's just that those types of dives aren't my scene."

"That's good to know, but they're not all dives. Some are very high-class establishments." Beth's attention moved to her computer screen and then slid back to him. "Are we dropping by Outlaws tonight? If so, and we don't want to arouse suspicion, I'll wear something suitable for the occasion and go dressed as a dancer. It is a gentlemen's club after all."

Remembering their previous trip to San Francisco, when

Beth disguised herself as a sex worker, Styles cleared his throat. "Do you have something suitable to wear?"

"I'm sure I can find something. It's not like I'm going onstage, is it?" She chuckled. "Don't worry, I won't sully your reputation."

Snorting, Styles shook his head. "Don't worry about me. I doubt the FBI would take notice of any local complaints and it's not as if I need the townsfolks' vote to keep my job. Just give Ryder a wide birth. Right now the conservative side of town considers him to be the best thing since sliced bread."

"Sure, I'll keep away from him, but you're not expecting him to show at Outlaws tonight, are you?"

Styles shook his head. "Nope." He pulled out his notebook. "I'll write up a case file for Cassie. What are you working on?"

"I'm still sifting through cold cases." Beth let out a long sigh and reached for her cup. "I'm particularly interested in possible serial killer murders with DNA traces. I'm convinced unless a serial killer is dead or in jail, the chances of them reoffending is great. I'm hoping to link them to some of the current cases the FBI has under investigation at the moment."

Styles scratched his chin. "Just don't go stepping on anyone's toes. There are a number of cases we can take on if you're bored."

"Ah, the boring ones that should be handled by the local PD?" Beth shrugged. "I consider them to be a waste of our resources when one of these cold case files could lead to an arrest of a monster."

Styles glanced at his watch. "I agree, and we have all afternoon. Mondays are pretty quiet nights in town. The only time I've ever been called out over a brawl has been Friday through Sunday."

"Well, from the local websites, the gentlemen's clubs open around seven and close around midnight weekdays and two over the weekend." She peered at him over the edge of the screen. "They must attract enough customers through the door to open seven days a week." She stared at her computer. "The meals look good and you can get a private dance at Outlaws. Maybe that's an idea if you want to ask one of the girls a few questions?"

Incredulous, Styles gaped at her. "I admit, at times I don't do things by the book, but having a stranger wiggling around on my lap isn't a style of interrogation process I'd consider—at any time." He narrowed his gaze at her. "Not now, not ever."

"Oh, you're no fun at all." Beth grinned at him as if she was having the time of her life. "Haven't you ever been undercover? It's all about role-playing and getting people to believe you're the character they see. You know if you've read my jacket, I went through training for undercover missions. I'm confident in my ability, and you know darn well I can handle myself. With the right preparation and backup, I figure I could bring down most perps."

Shaking his head, Styles stood to refill his coffee cup. "I don't figure it would take much preparation for me to walk into Outlaws as a customer, Beth. They don't worry about who is coming through the door as long as they pay the cover charge. What makes you think a dancer would spill her guts to me? She doesn't know me, and if I showed her my creds, she'd run for the hills." He returned to his desk and opened his bag of takeout. "Pulled pork and coleslaw on a bun. You want one?"

"No thanks." Beth kept her eyes on the screen. "I had something earlier. What time tonight?"

Thinking for a beat, Styles swallowed a bite of his bun. "Eight. We'll give them an hour or so to get going." He looked at her. "The dancers usually go around back. I'll walk you to the door to make sure you get inside okay. The dancer's entrance is in a dark alleyway lined with dumpsters."

"Okay." Beth was scanning her computer screen. "Oh good. There's a store that sells Halloween and festival supplies in

Rainbow. If we're going to play dress-up, I'm going to stock up. That's the problem with a small town, we don't have a Walmart."

Styles shrugged. "That's what shopping online is for, Beth." He sipped his coffee. "Keep the receipts. If you're planning on using disguises in the future, we'll use our budget."

"Then we'd have to write up the undercover sting in a report." Beth glanced up at him. "Sometimes, protocol goes out of the window when it's necessary to decide on the fly—just like San Francisco. The director would expect a mission plan weeks before we make a move and in my experience by the time he decides it's too late. In most situations, there isn't time to organize a team for backup, especially in the backwoods towns we're assigned to. We'll need to be our own backup. I know you believe I'm reckless and fly by the seat of my pants, but I get the job done." She lifted one shoulder. "I figure we both have our fair share of maverick when it comes to getting justice."

Scratching his head, Styles took in the confident, rebellious woman in front of him. Dammit, she was so much like him it was frightening.

FIVE

In my mind's eye, I see everything. In the daytime, I'm like a golden eagle flying in a thermal current viewing all below me. Mountains, forests, and rivers are part of my domain. As I circle high above, the towns below me form a perfect triangle, each joined by black snakes winding away through forests and alongside rivers. At night I prowl the streets, like a wolf hunting my prey. No one sees me. I blend into the background or hide in the shadows. My plans are set, each perfect place preselected for my darlings.

Excitement shivers in the pit of my stomach. Will she still be there waiting for me? So many times, they're missing. Lately, I experimented with different animal repellants to keep them safe. There is nothing worse than finding one of my darlings torn apart by wildlife. Sweet memories fill my head, speeding my heart. I took my time to enjoy Cassie's company, spending the entire night lying beside her. I loved the way her eyes stared blindly into nothingness and when her skin grew cold, I kept her warm. In the early hours of the morning, I bathed her meticulously, brushed her hair, and applied makeup. She looked so beautiful, and I wanted to stay with her forever, but my time was running short.

Today her stiff limbs will be pliable. It's so important to leave her for the last time looking her best. My heart pounds as I walk through the wheatgrass. Taking a different path to the old building is essential. I can't be discovered, I have so many more darlings to add to my collection. My hands tremble as I push open the door and move inside. The scent of her washes over me in the sweetest perfume. I go to her, and fall on my knees, rejoicing that she is whole, untouched, and as beautiful as ever. "Are you pleased to see me?"

The breeze through the broken window moves her hair as if she's nodding to me. I laugh and cup her smiling face. The old sofa is perfect for her and I spend time arranging her legs just right. Her makeup looks fine, but I can't resist brushing her hair again one last time. I loop a silken strand across my palm, and it seems alive as I draw it through my fingers to attach a pink bow and then cut the strand gently. I need a remembrance of our weekend together. I stand to leave and smile at her. She looks back at me as if begging me not to leave. She's still the seductive little minx I craved, but no longer an obsession. I have so many more on my list. I take one last look to fix her in my mind. "Bye, Cassie. It's been a blast."

SIX

"So, what are you going to wear?" Styles leaned toward Beth over a meal at Tommy Joe's Bar and Grill and raised both eyebrows. "It's getting cold and I don't want you dying of hypothermia."

Amused by the way the tips of his ears pinked, Beth sipped a glass of very good Sauvignon Blanc and stared at him. She couldn't tell him she had a trunk filled with various costumes. She'd gathered a variety of items from charity shops and complemented them with various trinkets to create a perfect disguise whenever she needed one. "You recall the ton of things I purchased in San Francisco when I went undercover as a sex worker?" In truth it hadn't been a ton of things, but "say it and they'll believe it" usually worked.

"Vividly." Styles cleared his throat. "You kinda freaked me out."

Biting back a smile at the memory, Beth shrugged nonchalantly. "Well, I have a variety of wigs and a box of disposable contact lenses in every color of the rainbow, even ones that look like snake eyes." She pulled a slice of Black Forest cake toward her and lifted her fork. "I figured the green contacts and a red wig should be enough. The dancers change into their costumes at the club. They don't parade around the streets wearing them, so I won't get cold. I'll just wear my jeans and sweater and I have an old coat. I'll make sure I'm not recognized." She looked him up and down. "You on the other hand will stand out like a red flag to a bull. The black Stetson with the snakeskin head-band and the buckle on your belt are very distinctive. You'll need to mess yourself up some before you walk me to the door or the game will be up before we start."

"I can do that just fine. I passed as your pimp in San Francisco and I was wearing casual clothes." Styles grinned at her. "That was a night to remember. Hey, did you ever hear any whispers about the drug dealers we took down?"

Shaking her head, Beth savored a mouthful of cake and swallowed. "You look happy now but at the time, you told me I was batshit crazy." She met his gaze. "The local FBI agent who followed up never mentioned them, only the girls they rescued." She shrugged. "I didn't mind them taking the kudos. The end result was the same."

It had been relaxing lingering over dinner and talking shop and about her plans for her cabin, but Beth wished she could go home and fall into bed. As Ryder's BOLO and APB had yielded no response, she'd need to move mountains to find Cassie Burnham. "Getting back to the missing stripper, all we really know is the time she left the club." She finished her cake and emptied her glass of wine. "You know as well as I do in an abduction after forty-eight hours the trail runs cold. The chances of finding her alive are minimal at best."

"You're talking like it's a done deal?" Styles stretched out his legs and stared at her over his coffee cup. "Nate said the marks on the sidewalk were blood, but we don't have Cassie's DNA. People fall over and bleed. It could have been there for weeks."

Nodding, Beth ran her finger over the chocolate frosting on

her plate and when she noticed Styles watching her, wiped it on a paper towel. "It is a done deal." She sighed. "Think about it. It's not a disgruntled boyfriend or a kidnap-for-ransom deal or we'd have received a note or something. It wasn't a drive-by grab and rape or she'd have shown by now. It was organized. Someone knew her shifts and waited for her. He could have attacked her in the alleyway, but from where her purse was found and the blood, which is her blood type, I figure he waited for her to come out of the alleyway and then hit her. Once she was on the ground, she'd be dizzy and easy to overpower. It would be too risky to kill her there, so chances are he dragged her into a vehicle. I've studied these killers. At this point they're high on the rush of the abduction. They have their prize. This is when they're most dangerous. He'd have his killing field planned and go there to do... whatever." She waved a hand toward the door. "There are mineshafts all over. He could have driven in any direction, killed her, and dropped her down one. Our chances of finding her are one in a thousand at best." She met his gaze. "I want to find her alive as much as you do, Styles, but we also need to be looking for signs of a body dumped close by. Once a victim is dead, the thrill is over... Well, it is for most of them."

"You could be right." Styles rubbed the scar on his chin. "I'll send a message to the forest wardens so they're aware she's missing. They might spot a clue to the location of her body."

Beth pushed her plate away and sighed. The chocolate cake was very good. "What type of clue?"

"Crows usually swarm anywhere there's something dead." Styles picked up his Stetson from the chair beside him and pushed it on his head. "They'll call it in if they find anything suspicious." He stood and Bear appeared from under the table. He bent to pat him. "I'll leave him behind tonight as we're going incognito."

Gathering her phone and purse, Beth took bills from her

billfold and dropped them on the table with a smile. "My turn to pay and it was my celebratory dinner for purchasing a cabin."

"I've learned not to argue with you, Beth." Styles shrugged and pulled on his gloves. "Although, TJ noticed the friction between us when it comes to paying the bill. He suggested we run a tab and split it at the end of each week."

Finding his embarrassment charming when she paid the tab, she nodded. "Fine by me."

Mist swirled through the streets as they made their way back to the FBI building. It was a cold evening that held the promise of winter. The crisp night air didn't deter the townsfolk from venturing out to visit the diners or the saloons. Most nodded to them as they passed by and only a few crossed the road to avoid them. The doors to the FBI building clicked open and Beth hurried to her apartment to change. Satisfied her disguise was fitting for the part, she checked her watch and then stepped out into the passageway to wait for Styles by the elevator.

"The red hair suits you." Wearing a Montana State football jersey and a ball cap, Styles flashed her a confident smile and bent closer. "How do you make your lips look all puffy?"

Beth stepped inside the elevator. "Makeup is all. This look I got from YouTube. There are step-by-step instructions on there and a ton of really creepy Halloween makeovers."

"For guys too?" Styles followed her from the elevator and headed for his truck.

Beth waved keys at him. "Sure. Take my ride. Yours is like a neon sign."

"Do you figure the Tarot Killer uses YouTube for his disguises?" He took the keys and slid behind the wheel. As they drove through town, he turned to her. "Some people say he can turn into a woman."

Styles was smart but not quite in her league. She'd joined the undercover team to openly use disguises without drawing suspicion, but those she used as the Tarot Killer were far more sophisticated... In fact, as law enforcement had no idea of her gender, she had to admit her skills went beyond good. Smothering a smug smile, she turned to him. "I've seen male undercover operatives dress as women but they're not very convincing. Everyone's disguise works better used within their gender, so the Tarot Killer has to be a guy. Maybe he's an actor or works in FX?"

"That's something to consider." Styles pulled up behind a line of vehicles on Quartz. "He passes as so many different people all the time or at least we think he does. No one has given us the same description twice."

Looking away, Beth regretted mentioning FBI undercover agents. Allowing that seed to float around in his inquisitive mind could throw the cat among the pigeons. Distracting his thoughts was an option. Smiling as he came to her side, she slid her arm through his and giggled. "I'd like to see him pass as a stripper in a gentlemen's club."

"So would I." Styles grinned. "Then we'd catch him for sure."

SEVEN

The dim alleyway to the stage door of the gentlemen's club gave Beth an insight into Cassie Burnham's last moments. She cast her gaze from one end to the other, taking in the advantages through the eyes of a killer. A security guard or someone else working there could move around without attracting attention, but a security guard might be missed. Hiding in the alleyway didn't make sense for a killer, because the chances of a worker coming out from one of the other buildings to dump garbage and seeing them would be too much of a risk. Waiting at the mouth of the alleyway would be the easiest way and Cassie would have been closer to his vehicle for transport. She glanced at Styles. "It didn't happen here. There are too many variables."

"This is the door." Styles pressed the buzzer and slid into the shadows. "Call me when you plan to leave."

The door swung open and a man looked her over and waved her inside. She stared at him. "Dressing room?"

"Nah." A large imposing man stared down at her. "The boss didn't tell me about anyone new starting tonight."

Undeterred, Beth shrugged. "That's because I haven't

decided if I want to work here yet. Before I start, I need to speak to the other girls and find out if this place is legit."

"Just a minute." The security guy spoke into his radio and waited for a reply. "Okay, you got five minutes. Down the passageway and you'll run right into it." The door shut behind him. "I'm Bruno. If you take the job, you report to me."

Beth pushed past him. "Thanks. You passed the security test." She hurried to the dressing room.

She wrinkled her nose as a miasma of smells wafted along the passageway toward her. Inside the brightly lit room, scantily clad women crowded around the dressing table mirrors, chatting like a gaggle of geese. She edged her way around the room and headed for a woman dressed in strips of sparkling blue latex. "Okay if I sit down?"

"Sure." The woman slid her feet into stiletto heels. "I haven't seen you before. You new here?"

"Yeah, I'm Clarissa. I'm planning on working here. How do you find the conditions?

"Not bad." The woman stood and peered at her reflection in one of the mirrors. "Better than some."

Nodding Beth stared up at her. "Good to know. The last place I worked some creep tried to follow me home. Is there anyone in the crowd I should be watching out for?"

"Just about all of them." The woman turned her heavily made-up eyes toward her. "I'm Val. The miners are fools, all catcalls, but they fill every orifice with bills. There are a few creeps who just stare. They don't smile or anything, just give you the deadeye. I don't know why they bother coming if they resent what we do."

A waft of cheap perfume washed over her, and Beth waved a hand in front of her face. She nodded. "Yeah, I've had those. The guy who followed me home was real creepy. He watched me every night."

A woman wearing a platinum-blonde wig sat down on the arm of the sofa.

"Hi there. I'm Rosie." She frowned. "Funny you should say that because Cassie, one of the dancers, was worried about the same thing and now she's missing."

Beth opened her eyes wide feigning shock. "Missing?"

"Yeah, missing, and I found her purse and bear spray out by the road." Rosie touched Beth's shoulder. "It has everyone on edge."

Beth turned to look at her. "Did she point the perv out to you? Maybe you should tell the cops?"

"No, but I looked for him." Rosie crossed her legs, bouncing one shoe on the tip of her toes. "Cassie said he was always at the bar or in the shadows and came out and glared at her the moment she took the stage. I never saw him, but I've had my fair share of glares as well. I figure some guys feel guilty about being here, like what we do is wrong or something. I often see them have an internal battle with themselves. They are different from the others. They never come up and give us a tip."

Trying to think fast a way to phrase questions without giving away the investigation, she opened her eyes wide as if horrified. "Oh wow! Do you figure he took her right off the street?"

"Maybe." Rosie shook her head. "It's possible. If so, he knew she finished at ten. Our hours are plain to see. As men have favorites, we all dance at the same time and on the same days of each week. It's written outside the main door alongside our photographs, so everyone knows our hours. It would be really easy to work out when we leave."

Beth thought for a beat. "It's too bad you didn't get to see the creep."

"Cassie thinks he was one of the miners because he came Friday through Sunday. He was average, she said, wore a ball cap. Most of them do and average for the miners is around five-ten I guess, so that leaves us with nothing to tell the sheriff. He is doing his best. One man can't work miracles. I guess we'll all need to be careful now. I'm not leaving home without my Glock."

Nodding, Beth looked from one to the other. "Maybe she told one of the other girls and they saw him?"

"Cassie didn't talk to many of us." Rosie smiled. "She did her sets and then left." She looked at her. "I hope we haven't changed your mind about working here. It's not so bad. Although the club in Rainbow is classier. I've heard tell the security there is better and they have someone on the stage door to walk you to your vehicle."

Standing, Beth smiled. "Thanks, I'll keep that in mind. Where's the bathroom?"

"Through that door." Rosie pointed across the room. "It was nice to meet you."

Inside the bathroom, Beth called Styles but couldn't hear him over the noise of the music. She told him she was leaving and backed it up with a message before making her way through the dressing room and along the corridor to the stage door. She pushed open the heavy metal door and peered into the stinking alleyway. The darkness outside was oppressive. Shadows spilled from the dumpsters, closing in the walls around her, and cold wind from the mountains rolled garbage along the alleyway. Pieces of takeout wrappers had piled up around the wheels on the bottom of the dumpsters and flapped in the wind like pinned moths. Nothing moved, and Styles would be heading her way soon. Confident in her own ability to deal with just about anything, she stepped into the alleyway and headed toward Quartz. The heels of her boots made a distinctive sound on the asphalt, which made her more convinced that Cassie had been attacked on the sidewalk. Using the light on her phone to illuminate the way ahead, she walked quickly through the alleyway and out onto Quartz.

Styles had parked the truck about fifty yards from the alley-way. A cold wind blasted through the clothes, chilling her to the bone with each step along the sidewalk. A roar of an engine came from nowhere and the headlights of a truck flooded the dark road as it passed by. In a squeal of brakes, the air was filled with the smell of burning rubber as the vehicle reversed at high speed, the back end swaying from side to side before coming to rest opposite her. A grinning young man hung out the driver's window staring at her, but he wasn't alone. Grinning faces peered at her through the windows and laughter spilled out of the back of the cab. She stopped walking, pulled out her phone, and called Styles. "Nine one one."

Not waiting for his reply, she pushed the phone into her jeans pocket and shoved her purse into the pocket of her jacket. She was unarmed apart from the sharpened hatpin she'd thrust into the wig. Unsure if the security at the gentlemen's club would look kindly at her taking a weapon inside, she had left her sidearm at home. She kept walking, ignoring the men's catcalls, but the truck stuck with her.

"Hey, little lady, you finished early. Do you want to party with us?" The driver maneuvered the truck closer to her side of the road, barely missing the parked vehicles.

Planning a way to get away without causing a ruckus, Beth glanced ahead to the road running into Quartz. She had gone over the plan with Styles a number of times. After dropping her at the stage door, he would walk around the block and enter the club from the front door. The same would be in reverse and she expected him to come around the corner at any second. Her truck was in sight when the vehicle carrying the men slipped into a space alongside her. Her heart rate quickened as they tumbled out of the doors in a cloud of beer stench. Four strong men in their mid-twenties intent on mischief all grinned at her, elbowed each other, and acted like kids. Would these be the same men who took Cassie? If so, she wouldn't have stood a chance against the four of them. Concerned her old coat would restrict her movements, she slowly drew down the zipper, shrugged out of it, and dropped it onto the hood of a GMC pickup.

Her actions received wolf whistles and jeers from the men. She ignored them and stood on the sidewalk facing them down. Only a fool would believe she could take down four young men alone, and she was no fool, but she could do a ton of damage in a short time. Taking short steps backward to avoid them circling her, Beth tried to choreograph an attack in her mind. They wouldn't be expecting someone with her hand-to-hand combat skills. The men looked at each other and nodded and then two of them ran at her. It was like a set football move as one feigned to the left and the other scooped her up and slammed her down on the hood of the GMC pickup. Air rushed from her lungs as his heavy weight pressed against her. A grinning mouth poured alcohol-flavored breath over her face. He grabbed for her arms but wasn't quick enough. Beth slapped at him with both hands. "FBI, stand down."

"Sure, you are. They have strippers in the FBI now, cool." The man turned and a wide smile split his face at his friends' catcalls. "Wait your turn."

Anger raged through her and she lifted both fists and smashed them into the man's ears, his smile vanished but he hadn't moved. Without hesitation, she thrust both thumbs into his eyes. His scream of terror roared in her ears as he staggered back. Breathless, she slid from the hood and landed on her feet just as another man came forward screaming abuse with his two friends flanking him. She ducked a punch, spinning away to land an elbow to his kidney, but off balance, she'd allowed the other two men to grab her. Raking the heel of her boot down the shins of one of them, she twisted and dropped to unbalance them. As they stumbled forward, Beth headbutted one on the nose. Blood rushed down his face coloring his lips ruby red. The other man gaped in surprise as the first man dropped his grip on her arm and cradled his bloody face.

"I'm gonna mess you up real bad." The remaining man grabbed her hair, dragging off her wig, and then landed a short brutal punch to her stomach. "How do you like that, FBI agent?"

Gasping, Beth went to her knees. Winded and in pain, she ducked another blow from the man standing over her, wild eyed. She glared back at him. "I'll make you regret you ever laid hands on me."

The other men recovered fast and ran at her as mad as hell. Grabbed by the hair, dragged along the sidewalk, and unable to get away, Beth reacted on survival instinct when the one holding her telegraphed a knee strike to her head. As he took a step back, she balled up her fist and punched him in the groin. When he howled and went down, rolling into the fetal position, Beth staggered to her feet. The next second, Styles appeared and everything changed real fast. The remaining men shaped up to fight, and adrenaline spiking, Beth flicked Styles a glance. "Oh, look it's the late Dax Styles."

"I've got this." Styles gave her a nonchalant shrug. Without warning, one of the men rushed him, and as if in slow motion, he landed a roundhouse kick to his head. His attacker crumbled to the ground and didn't move. Styles stared at the other two men and shook his head as they raised their fists and advanced. "Enough, okay? Can you really be that stupid? You know I'm FBI." He slid out and aimed his .357 Magnum at them. "Trust me, boys. I don't need this to mess you up real bad, but it must be your lucky day. I don't feel like getting my hands dirty." Styles smiled at them. "Move a muscle. I dare you." He slid Beth a sideways glance. "You, okay?"

Hurting, but not wanting to give her attackers the satisfaction of knowing, she gave a shake of her head. "What? Do you honestly believe these SOBs could hurt me? They're pussycats."

"Good to know." Styles moved toward the men. "FBI. On the ground, hands on your heads." He looked at Beth. "Do you have zip ties in your vehicle?" He fished the keys from his pocket and handed them to her.

When Beth collected the zip ties from the truck and cuffed the men, Styles patted them down, relieving them of knives and handguns. She pulled out her phone and called Ryder. "Four men attacked me on Quartz. They could be involved in the disappearance of Cassie Burnham. We have them in custody. I want them arrested for attacking a federal officer."

"You got it. I'll be there in five." Ryder disconnected.

EIGHT

Beth shivered as freezing mountain air chilled her cheeks. It blasted through her sweater, raising goosebumps on her flesh. She cast her attention over the men sitting at the curb with their backs against their truck and then turned to Styles. "I'm going to wait in the truck. When we're done here, I need you to drive me to see Nate."

"Nate?" Styles rolled his eyes to the sky. "Ah, I see." He looked away.

Annoyed by his assumption that she had something going with the local doctor, Beth moved into his line of sight and dropped her voice to just above a whisper so the perps couldn't overhear her. "I don't think you do see, Styles. The guy in the red ball cap punched me in the stomach. If we intend to prosecute these men for attacking me, I'll need medical proof and the sooner the better."

"He punched you?" Styles turned slowly toward her eyebrows raised. "Darn it, I'm sorry, Beth. Are you hurt bad? I should have been here. It was just so noisy in the club. I heard you saying you were planning to leave soon and when you called again I was just leaving."

Shaking her head, Beth collected her things from the hood of the GMC pickup and stared at him. "I'm bruised is all, but did it slip your mind Cassie Burnham vanished from this area and I'm dressed like a stripper?"

"Nope. I ran the moment you said, nine one one. Cross my heart. It would have taken an Olympian sprinter to get here faster." Styles glanced at the men. "Maybe I'll have a little man-to-man chat with the guy in the red baseball cap before Cash gets here?" He turned back to look at her. "I don't like that he laid hands on you, Beth."

Shrugging into her coat, Beth waved a hand at him in dismissal. "Don't. Trust me, they'll have us suspended for police brutality if you do." She smiled at him. "But I do appreciate the offer. I can't recall the last person who actually cared about my well-being."

"I care." Styles frowned and his eyes held true compassion. "We're partners and watch each other's back, right?"

Dependable, trustworthy Dax Styles was more than she'd bargained for. It would take some getting used to. Beth nodded slowly. "I'd like that, thanks." She indicated toward her vehicle. "I'll wait in the truck."

She climbed into the passenger seat of her truck. She tossed the wig on the back seat and, using wipes from a packet in the glove box, removed her makeup and then ran both hands through her hair, releasing it from the tie at the nape of her neck. The next moment, Ryder pulled up behind her in his cruiser and she watched with interest as he shoved three men into the back seat. The fourth man, coincidentally the one with the red baseball cap, was escorted to her truck by Styles. The door opened letting in a blast of freezing air. In these cases, where a regular truck was used in the arrest, it was protocol for law enforcement to sit beside the prisoner, but whatever Styles had said to the guy in the red cap must have made an impression, as he sat there subdued with his head hanging down.

"They'll all be sharing the same jail cell tonight." Styles slid behind the wheel frowning. "I must have told Ryder a hundred times to ask the mayor to build a second cell in his office."

The cabin quickly filled with a stench of stale beer and onions. Beth waved a hand in front of her nose. "I'll never get the stink of him out of my truck."

After dropping the prisoner at the sheriff's office, they headed to see Nate. He lived above his practice and was apparently used to being disturbed in the evenings. Ushered into his examination room, Beth explained what had happened.

"Okay." Nate pulled on a pair of examination gloves. "Do you need any help getting onto the gurney?" He kicked a small step toward it and offered his hand.

Waving his hand away, Beth climbed onto the gurney and laid down to allow him to examine her stomach. He was very professional and thorough, with a gentle touch and good bedside manner. She looked at his concerned face. "I don't feel like anything is broken. He got me under the ribs."

"Hmm, bruising mostly, but come back if you have any blood loss at all." He put one hand behind her back to help her sit up. "Do you need pain meds?"

Shaking her head, Beth pulled down her sweater. "I'll be fine. I just need a record of the injury in case the local DA wants to proceed with charges"

"Okay." Nate's brow wrinkled. "I'm surprised you're still on your feet. A blow like that would normally have felled most people. I couldn't help noticing the other scars on your body. Did you get them in the line of duty?"

Not wanting to discuss her past life with him, she shrugged. "Nothing I can talk about."

"You can always talk to me, Beth, inside these rooms." Nate went to his desk, sat down, and looked at her. "I take patient-doctor confidentiality very seriously. If ever there's anything you need to talk about, I'm here for you."

Any thought of getting closer to this man fled in that moment. He was just too darn inquisitive. One slip and he'd discover her secret, and that could never happen. She'd need to choose her friends wisely to keep safe. She zipped up her coat and smiled at him. "Thanks for the offer."

"That's okay." Nate stood. "My receptionist will email you first thing for your insurance details, and we'll bill them direct. Don't forget, any other symptoms—cramping, bleeding—call me or go straight to the hospital."

Beth nodded. "Sure." She walked through the door to where Styles was waiting. "I'm good to go."

"Is she?" Styles looked at Nate. "Beth will never admit she's hurting."

"I'd be calling the paramedics to take her to the hospital if there were a problem." Nate shrugged. "She knows her body, is all."

"Okay." Styles opened the door for her and stood back. "From that look, Beth, I figure you plan to interview the prisoners, but it's not going to happen. It's a conflict of interest. We'll have to trust Ryder with this one."

Agreeing, Beth tried to push down the anger of being beaten. If she'd been armed, it would have been a different story. "Call him and tell him to tape the interview. I want to know their whereabouts on Friday night. I figure they'll lawyer up because most of it is my word against the four of them. You saw me on the ground. You didn't see what happened before or hear me identify myself. They'll walk and might come after me for fighting back."

"Nah." Styles shook his head. "You were on the ground when I came around the corner. It was self-defense. There were four of them and one of you, but I can see your point."

On the way back to the office they discussed the information they'd obtained from Outlaws. Beth listened with interest. "I hadn't realized miners came into the club during the week. I figured they worked Monday to Friday. Well, that was the information I received when I called Longhorn Peak Mine."

"Not all mines operate the same hours." Styles turned into the FBI parking lot. "Twelve hours on and twelve hours off is usual, five days a week, but some do alternate shifts, as in night shift and day shift, with days off during the week. This means that miners could be in any of the strip clubs across the three towns any day of the week. Believe it or not, this actually gives us an advantage, because if it does happen to be one of the miners, we'll be able to track his whereabouts without too much trouble." He gave her a long considering look. "You look all in. I'm happy to keep discussing this case, but it can wait for the morning."

Beth picked up her purse and grabbed the wig from the back seat. She needed a long hot shower and some rest. Her mind was working overtime on the other case and sometimes sleeping on it was the best solution. "Okay, what are your plans for the morning?"

"We'll follow up on tonight's events, I guess." He sighed. "I do have another idea. As nothing has come in about Cassie Burnham, I could take the chopper up and we'll do a search of our own? She has to be out there somewhere, and if she is dead, as you assume, and thrown down one of the old mine shafts, there will be signs. A dead body attracts wildlife from all over. We'd spot something unusual down there. I have a list of the current hunting areas, so we can dismiss them for now."

Frowning, Beth stared at him. In the dark she seemed to be speaking to his silhouette. It was surreal. "How so?"

"Because hunters field-dress their kills and leave a bunch of crap behind that attracts wildlife, and a local would avoid those areas or risk running into someone." Styles shrugged and turned to face her. "If this killer is as organized as you say, he wouldn't risk being seen. We'll search outside of the hunting areas and look for crows swarming. They're a good indication something is dead."

NINE

TUESDAY

Alone in the office the following morning, Beth spent her time waiting for Styles to do his preflight check on the chopper by following the updated information on the case that interested her in Eagle Rock. As predicted, another body had been found. She read the autopsy report on the woman. The injuries sustained and the method of disposal were exactly the same as the cold case victims found in Eagle Rock and New Hope. Convinced that Levi Jackson had established a comfort zone, she predicted the next murder would be in a nearby town. If he continued in this pattern, she believed she'd be able to anticipate his next move. However, his kills were usually at least one week apart, so she'd need to be patient.

She searched through the FBI files, surprised that not one of the investigations had included Levi Jackson's whereabouts at the time of the recent crimes. It would seem that the local FBI agents on the case had completely dismissed Levi Jackson as a possible suspect. She'd need to spend valuable time hunting him down and following his digital trail. It was illegal to track his purchases, but no one could trace anything she did on the dark web. Convinced Jackson would be feeling confident since the acquittal for the other kidnapping, he'd no doubt own a regular phone for his handyman business. The fact he placed notices on community boards for work and also got jobs by word of mouth was mentioned in his trial. A phone could be traced as well, but getting a list of calls would be too risky. The credit card trace would just have to do. The investigation never mentioned a second phone, the one he would have used for the abduction of Natalie Kingsley. It only made sense that the phone number he used on the flyers advertising a cheap room for rent came from a burner and he destroyed it the moment he lured a woman into his van.

Convinced Jackson moved in a regular pattern, she knew that tracing his movements wouldn't be too difficult once she had a starting point. Finding one of his notices would be her prime objective, but as he was known around town, she assumed, speaking to people in the lumber yard or general store would achieve a result. The only problem would be getting away from Styles for a day to investigate. Once she had enough information, she'd use the dark web to track him. On there, no one would ever suspect her involvement. Jackson needed to be stopped. He was smart and as slippery as an eel. She would bring him to justice, but in the meantime, how many more women and children would die by his hand?

Forcing her mind back to the Cassie Burnham case, Beth saved her secret research files on Jackson to a special folder hidden on the dark web just as the door rattled and Styles entered the office. She quickly changed the page to her email and smiled as a link to an audio file dropped in her mailbox. It was Ryder's interview with the four men taken into custody the previous evening. She looked up at Styles and smiled. "The audio files have just arrived. Do you want to listen to them now or later?"

"Did Ryder send any notes?" Styles went to the coffee machine and filled a Thermos. "If so, copy them to your phone.

If we don't find anything, we'll discuss them in the chopper."
He turned to look at her. "The light is good at the moment, but
cloud cover is expected this afternoon. If we have a chance of
finding any trace of Cassie Burnham we need to leave now."

Beth sent the notes to her phone and when it chimed a
message, she closed her computer and stood to grab her coat.
"Okay, done."

"While I was refueling the chopper, I had a call from one of
the forest wardens." Styles followed her into the elevator and
they headed for the roof. "He hasn't noticed any great increase
in birds over the forest and suggested searching the lowlands.
Apparently one of the hunters mentioned seeing a few murders
of crows around, so I figured we'll circle around and see what
we can find."

Beth followed him onto the roof and walked into a blast of
arctic wind. "It's freezing up here."

"Tell me about it." Styles pulled gloves from his pocket.
"I've been up here for almost an hour. It's going to be a difficult
takeoff in the high wind, but we'll be okay."

After climbing inside and shutting the door, Beth attached
her seatbelt and pulled on headphones. It had taken a few trips
for her to get used to riding in the chopper. Styles was a good
pilot but fearless, and sometimes he scared her a little when
they traveled through the mountains, barely missing the trees or
the rocky outcrops at high speed. The lowlands sounded much
better. She sat back to enjoy the scenery, searching all around
for flocks of birds. "Over there to the right. I think that's crows
just above the wheatgrass."

"I see them." Styles moved the chopper around in an arc
and they swooped over the crows scattering them like buckshot.
"I'll take her down."

They landed and she turned to Styles. "I'll go."

Jumping down from the chopper, she ran through the
golden wheatgrass. The smell of death crawled up her

nostrils, making her gag. She pulled up her sweater to cover her mouth and, heart pounding, she moved closer. The tall grass was restricting her view and she pushed past it and stopped dead at the half-eaten carcass of what looked like a deer. She turned and followed her path back to the chopper. Breathing hard, she climbed back inside and dropped into her seat. "Animal."

"Okay." Styles took the chopper up again and they circled for a time before he headed west. "There are some ranches over this way. We might as well check them as well. Some of them are deserted. The land was purchased by the mining companies years ago and never mined."

It took a few minutes before Beth realized a cabin's black roof was moving. "I see crows on the roof of a cabin. All just sitting there like they're waiting for something."

The chopper landed and Styles climbed out, leaving the rotor blades spinning. Beth ducked low and followed him to the house. She didn't have to sniff the air to smell death. "Well, something around here has died, that's for sure."

They circled the cabin and finding nothing, Beth followed Styles to the front door. The place was deserted, dusty rags hung from the windows. The gutters overflowed with grass and at one end a sapling had taken root. Beth looked all around, scanning the dirt road. "It looks like someone has been here. Nothing distinctive but the grass is bent over like a truck has driven over it recently more than once."

"This place is old." Styles indicated to the front door. "The paint is flaking off all over. I figure it's been deserted for over twenty years, but the stink sure leads here. There's no animal damage, but there's evidence someone was here recently. I figure we've found Cassie Burnham." He switched on his flashlight. "Can you cope with a decomposed body?"

A shiver of apprehension slid down Beth's spine. He had to be joking and she stared at him frowning. "Hmm. Let me see.

Maybe you need to carry me over the threshold as it's our first in-house murder?"

"Ah, no." Styles snorted. He stared at her over the top of his sunglasses before he removed them and slowly pushed them into his top pocket. He gave her the killer stare he had, the one that would stop most people in their tracks, as if evaluating the situation and then suddenly burst out laughing. "Oh, no." He wiped at his face. "I haven't laughed in a situation like this for years. It makes me feel guilty." He shook his head. "You have the weirdest sense of humor." He raised one eyebrow. "I'm used to people being serious all the time. In the Army, people don't joke around the dead."

Concerned she might have given him the wrong impression, she shook her head. "Oh, I'm sorry. I didn't mean to be insensitive toward the victim, not at all. Mac always said my filter is faulty in situations like this."

"I know what you mean." Styles waved her toward the door. "Let's get at it and I'll tell you a story about me on the way home. What happened was totally inappropriate at the time. I later discovered that nervous laughter or bad jokes are a psychological response to anxiety and tension. So, if this is an outlet for stress, Beth, I understand." He tried the door. "It's open. Keep back. Just in case someone is inside."

Pressing the flat of her left hand on the weathered wooden door, Beth pushed it open. A blast of disgusting smell leaked out and she suppressed a gag. "FBI. Is anyone inside? Call out."

Nothing.

A loud bang came from inside, the noise echoing like a ricochet through the house. In the same second a blast of foul air shot out the door. Expecting someone to come out blasting, Beth ducked and ran alongside the house. Heart hammering, with her back to the wall, she drew her weapon as Styles flattened himself against the outside of the house beside her. "What was that?"

"I hope it was just a door slamming inside. Or we've got company." Styles leaned against the wall beside her, his .357 Magnum hanging down at his side. "Wait and listen. If someone is in there, chances are they'll shoot again. If nothing happens, we'll go inside and take a look."

They waited in silence listening, but it was only the whoosh of wind as it brushed the top of the wheatgrass and the squawks as crows once again descended on the house that broke the silence. Five long minutes passed before Beth turned to Styles. "Ready?"

"Yeah." Styles rubbed the tip of his nose. "Although I'm not looking forward to it."

Pulling face masks from her pocket, Beth thrust one at Styles before placing one over her face and then searched her pockets for examination gloves. She passed him a pair. "Here. Want me to go first?"

"Nope and we follow procedure to the letter here, Beth. I don't figure anyone needs our help right now, and we won't be able to breathe in there. We'll go round back." Styles waved her toward the back of the house. "If the front door is unlocked, the back one will be as well. I'll open it. If we hear anything, I'll go high, you go low."

Beth nodded. "Sounds like a plan."

They headed to the back of the cabin. The stench of decomposition oozed through the cracks between the dilapidated logs and hung there in a wall of nasty. Beth coughed and could taste death in the back of her throat. "How many bodies do you figure are in there?"

"Oh, man, it stinks on ice but one can smell that bad." Styles stopped alongside the house and, walking to the shade of a nearby tree, removed his Stetson and hung it on a branch along with his coat. "If you're wearing anything you want to keep. I suggest shucking it now. That stink never washes out and I'm not sacrificing my hat or good coat for what might be a dead animal."

Beth nodded and tossed her coat over a branch. The wind chilled her warm skin as she gathered up her long hair and tucked it inside a woolen cap. She recalled trying to get the stink from her hair once before. Death odors had a way of sticking like gum. "Okay, let's do this."

She followed Styles to the back of the house and stood to one side as he opened the back door, pushing it wide. They blinked into the dim interior. The door opened up to a dusty litter-strewn kitchen and she could see through an open door and along a hallway straight into the family room. Startled by a figure reclining on a sofa, she jumped back and pressed her back to the wall. "I see someone."

"Yeah, me too." Styles pulled out a flashlight and aimed through the doorway. He held one hand up to her. "Ah, there's a dead woman in there, posed on a sofa." He pulled the door shut and frowned. "It's nasty."

Frowning, Beth took the flashlight from him. "I need to see, Styles."

Pushing the door open, she moved the flashlight beam over the corpse. Sickened and shocked to the core when a smiling face with wide open eyes stared back at her, she fumbled the flashlight. The scene was impossible. No one retained an expression like that when they died. Heavy makeup covered the face. Cherry-red lips smiled a gruesome welcome, and bright blue eyeshadow highlighted her staring eyes. The long dark hair was fashioned around the face and moved eerily in the breeze from the front door. The dead woman sat with her arms along the back of the dilapidated sofa in a lewd pose. The killer had created the scene to shock and it had hit its mark. Her stomach clenched and she swallowed hard trying not to spew. "Well, she's obviously dead. I figure we stay outside to avoid contaminating evidence." She pulled the door shut and coughed. "What do you say?"

"My thoughts exactly. Get your coat on, you're turning blue. You won't have stink on you." Styles walked slowly back to the pile of clothes and shrugged into his coat. He pulled out his phone. "I'll call it in to Ryder." He made the call. After a time explaining and giving coordinates, he sighed. "There's nothing you can do, Cash. Just call the ME and get him out here."

"Do you figure it's Cassie Burnham?" Ryder cleared his throat. *"Can you make out what happened to her?"*

"I don't know if it's Cassie. She's kinda messed up." Styles dusted off his hat by slapping it against his thigh. "We decided to remain outside. We didn't want to contaminate the crime scene but we'll leave the front door open to clear out the stink."

"Okay. She is dead, right? You sure?" Ryder's chair squeaked and Beth could imagine him getting to his feet. *"You don't need me to send the paramedics?"*

Staring at Styles, Beth raised both eyebrows. She leaned closer to him. "Hi, Cash, Beth here. She's very dead. The smell is real bad and it's a gruesome crime scene, so you'll need to prepare yourself. It's one of those murders you'll never forget. Bring masks and plenty of gloves. If you're coming with Dr. Wolfe, you might need to wear an old uniform. The stink of a body this ripe tends to hang around some and you'll need to burn your clothes unless you have forensic coveralls."

"Yeah, Dr. Wolfe advised me to order some after the last case. I'll bring some for you too but they're all my size. They might swamp you."

Impressed Beth nodded. "That would be great. Thanks. We'll trade. We have a ton of them back at the office."

"I'm sending you the coordinates now." Styles took the phone off speaker and pressed it to his ear. "Call Wolfe now. It will take him an hour to get here. You'll need to meet him at the hospital helipad. He won't have access to the roof at the FBI building. We'll scout around and search the area for evidence." He waited a beat and then disconnected. "We'll take the bird up and see if we can make out a track leading to anywhere. On foot and level to the ground, all we'll be able to see is grass."

Excitement shivered through Beth at the thought of meeting Dr. Shane Wolfe again. The last time, the man who resembled a Viking marauder—tall, white-blond hair with gray eyes—had looked straight through her as if he had X-ray vision. He had the experience to analyze a murder scene on the fly and no wonder. He worked alongside one of the best teams in Montana: Sheriff Jenna Alton and her husband, Deputy David Kane, along with a team of highly trained professionals, lived in Black Rock Falls. In recent years the expanding town had come to be known as Serial Killer Central. Beth had been drawn to a case there and, heavily disguised as the Tarot Killer, had gotten involved. It had taken all her skill to complete her task and then vanish into thin air. She'd left the sheriff scratching her head, but Jenna Alton would never have been able to stop the man who murdered for profit. He'd have killed again and then vanished if Beth hadn't stopped him. She smiled to herself. Wolfe made a worthy adversary and keeping one step ahead of him would ensure she remained at the top of her game.

"What are you smiling at?" Styles gave her an inquisitive stare as he climbed into the chopper. "After looking inside that cabin, I'm finding it hard to keep down my breakfast."

Shaking her head, Beth shrugged and grabbed at anything for an excuse. "Oh, nothing. I was just thinking how Bear would have loved to tear around in this long grass. It's miles of wide-open spaces here. Dogs love to run, don't they?" She climbed in beside him and shrugged. "I don't dwell on scenes like that. I try to think about something nice. There'll be time to worry about it once Wolfe arrives." She smiled at him. "How about you take our minds away from the crimes scene and tell me your inappropriate-behavior story. I'm intrigued."

"Okay, but first put these on." Styles handed her a set of headphones. "It's not something I'm proud to admit to, but at the time, my brother and I could see the funny side of it. I was still a kid, sixteen or so, and attended the funeral of a very beloved great-aunt with my brother. We stood to the back of a large crowd of mourners. It was held in California and in the graveyard was a bunch of pineapple palms. They look like giant pineapples." He stared at her.

Beth nodded. "Yeah, I know what they are, so why were they so funny?"

"During the service, my brother leaned toward me all serious and pointed to the trees. He said, "Bodies must make dang good fertilizer if the size of them pineapples is any indication. Now, I know how old Mr. Digby wins the pumpkin competition each year. He must have bodies buried all over." Styles grinned at her. "We broke up laughing... well snorting and covering our faces."

Surprised he'd told her, she smiled. "I'd have laughed too. Did you get into trouble with your folks?"

"Nope, they thought we were sobbing." He shrugged. "I still feel guilty about it. I loved my aunt."

Fastening her seatbelt, Beth glanced at him. "Don't beat yourself up about it. Your aunt was probably looking down on you and laughing with you. I'd hate people to cry at my funeral. Not that I have anyone who'd attend."

"God forbid something might happen to you, but I'd be there." He flicked her a glance. "You have my word."

Taken aback, Beth stared at him. "Really? Thank you so much."

There he goes again, making me like him. He's always ready to fight and bends the rules, but he never crosses the line, like I do. I need to be more like him. I hate to admit it, but he's becoming my hero. I'd love to come clean and tell him about the real me. Maybe one day, when he gets to know how I tick, he'll understand I'm here to put things right. The phone in her pocket vibrated, breaking her thoughts, and she pulled it out and opened the message. "It's from Ryder. He forgot to mention he released the men. They can't be held for Cassie Burnham's murder, if that is her in the cabin, because they were all working on Friday night."

"They should have been held for attacking you." Styles took the chopper straight up and then began a low sweep of the immediate area.

Beth thumbed in a reply and waited for a response. "He says it's my word against the four of them. They said I was dressed like a stripper and removed my coat in a seductive manner as if inviting them. When they came over to speak with me, they said I went crazy and attacked them. They were only defending themselves and the only time they knew we were FBI is when you arrived. He spoke to the DA and we can't make a case against them without witnesses, so they walked."

"Wonderful." Styles took the chopper in another sweep. "Look below at the dirt track. It's been used recently. It runs to the highway. It's too dry to pick up any tracks but he came here and more than one time." He took the chopper down lower.

A chill ran down Beth's spine and she stared at the sea of golden wheatgrass moving like turbulent waves under the wind from the chopper. "Then he's an organized killer." She shuddered. "I hope he didn't come back for visits. Those guys are beyond creepy."

"I just wonder how they get rid of the stink." Styles shot her a glance. "It's not something you can cover with cologne."

Beth shook her head. "Maybe we're looking for a killer in a hazmat suit?"

TEN

Serenity, Montana

Disoriented and unable to move, Vicki Strauss wiggled her fingers, touching a coarse fabric. Her nose pressed against a prickly surface, and when she inhaled, the distinctive smell of an old carpet filled her nostrils. Panic gripped her and she tried to scream but the filthy rag pressing against her tongue muted any noise. Someone had wrapped her in a carpet so tight she could hardly take a breath. A dull ache throbbed in her temples. Desperately fighting to get free without success, she lay panting. A voice, smooth and cajoling, drifted through the stifling fabric surrounding her. She forced out a reply but only a muffled grunt escaped the gag.

"You'll need to keep quiet, my lovely." It was a man's voice. "I'll have to move you now. Be good and I won't hurt you."

Dragged and then lifted, her head tipped down and bent almost double, she appeared to hang in the air. The carpet unrolled. She spun and fell hard onto a dirt floor. Trying to get onto hands and knees as a dank dim space surrounded her, she glanced over one shoulder to see the man who'd captured her, but only shadows moved through the open space above her. She dragged the gag from her mouth, and as the smell of rotting potatoes crawled up her nose, she realized she'd been dumped in a small root cellar. Footsteps came from above and something thumped onto the floor beside her and hit her hand. In the half-light she made out a large plastic bottle of water. She closed her fist around it just as a squeaking trapdoor slammed shut above her head, thrusting her into darkness. The next second a bolt slid shut. "Let me out of here. What do you want with me?"

Nothing.

She screamed long and loud until footsteps came again. "Let me out of here. I won't tell anyone."

"Later." A low sinister chuckle leaked through the wooden trap above her head. The way out was high enough to be out of reach, but she could hear his muffled voice. "We'll be taking a little ride to my special place. I have a friend you might like to meet and maybe I'll get you to strip just for me. I'd like that. Just the three of us, darlin'."

An uncontrollable shudder of revulsion wracked her body. It was one of the creeps from the club. She'd taken on private dances to make some extra cash and being so close to sweating fast-breathing old men made her want to spew. She'd vowed to never do it again—but at someone's mercy, how far would she be prepared to go to get out of this tomb?

The footsteps, slow and methodical, walked away. Alone and trapped, she let out a long sob. What had happened? How had she gotten into this terrible situation? She tried to push through the ringing in her ears to think straight. Most of it was blank but she pushed back her memory. It must still be Tuesday. She'd arrived around nine at the Silver Nugget Saloon to collect her pay. Friday was normally pay night for the dancers, but she'd been unwell with food poisoning and missed an entire weekend's work. After leaving the club, she'd headed to the landfill to dump the garbage she'd accumulated during the week. It was something that she did regularly every Tuesday morning. As she reached the outskirts of Serenity, she'd been sure a pickup was following her, and frequently checked her rearview mirror. Panic gripped her when she'd made a number of turns, and the vehicle had stuck with her, but when she took the dirt road to the landfill, the pickup had driven by as if heading toward the highway. She'd dumped her garbage and headed for the recycling area when the pickup had suddenly emerged and backed in beside her... then nothing. She couldn't recall a darn thing.

Unsteady, she pushed to her feet. Above light filtered through the floorboards, making strange shapes across the packed dirt floor. She moved a few steps one way, hands stretched out. Her fingers touched rough-cut wooden shelves coated with dirt. Cobwebs stuck to her fingers and cold shivers slid over her at the threat of spiders, rats, and other cellar dwellers occupying the small space. She shuffled around and tripped over something. It was a chair, and she ran her fingers all over it and then dragged it under the trapdoor. Wobbly, she climbed unsteadily onto the chair and pushed hard at the trapdoor but it barely moved. Panic gripped her. There was no way out. No escape. She flopped onto the chair and reached for the bottle of water. It was cold and she drank deeply. Tears streamed down her face and her shoulders shook. She drank again as the room tilted. Her vision blurred and the bottle tumbled from her palm. She slid from the chair and her face scraped along the dirt floor. She couldn't move. As the room moved in and out of focus, she gasped, trying to suck in one more breath. *Oh, no, he drugged the water.*

ELEVEN

Dr. Shane Wolfe started his career in the Marines as a chopper pilot. He'd flown medivac choppers during many conflicts and had seen his fair share of carnage, but nothing really prepared a person for the horrific cruelty one human could inflict on another. During the flight, Styles had brought him up to speed with the situation in Serenity. He glanced at his daughter, Emily, a medical examiner in training, and wondered if she was ready to experience this type of crime scene. His other assistant, Colt Webber, a badge-holding deputy from Black Rock Falls, was practically bombproof. Wolfe had worked with agents Styles and Katz previously and found them to be very professional. The young sheriff, Cash Ryder, was inexperienced in murder cases. Whoever expected him to keep law and order in more than one county without a deputy had no thought for him or the townsfolk. The crime rate was increasing all over and he'd come to realize since living in Black Rock Falls that remote mountainous regions were a haven for anyone who wanted to live off the grid. People could hide or go missing and never be found. It was often by dumb luck they'd discovered the bodies of murder victims before the wildlife had cleaned the area.

He dropped the chopper into an open space close to the cabin and waited for Ryder and Webber to climb down and collect the gurney and body bags. He needed to speak to Emily. He pulled off his headset and turned to her. "This is a particularly gruesome crime scene. The victim is badly decomposed and posed with makeup. The body has been tampered with, as in the facial features may be disturbing, clownlike, according to Agent Styles. It's fine if you'd rather remain outside this time."

"Oh, Dad." Emily shook her head. "I've seen corpses at the body farm riddled with maggots and victims of many horrendous crimes. It's all part of the job. I know I'll always be your little girl, but I'd be in the wrong profession if death in all its unimaginable facets worried me." She squeezed his arm. "I love that you care about me and please don't ever stop protecting me from the maniacs who commit the crimes. Those are the people who keep me awake at night. The dead can't hurt me and they need us to tell their story, right?"

Always impressed by his intelligent daughter, Wolfe smiled. "They sure do. Come on then. Let's get at it. Suit up. Styles mentioned it stinks in there."

As he climbed down from the chopper, the smell of death came on a gust of wind. He grimaced and walked toward Beth Katz and Styles. "You didn't go inside?"

"Nope." Styles wiped mentholated salve under his nose before fitting a face mask. "We didn't want to contaminate the crime scene. It's obvious the victim is deceased and we didn't have any coveralls. It's only by luck we found her. I did a fly-by searching for murders of crows in the area or gathering predators. We noticed the crows swarming over the roof and came down to take a look."

"Someone has been coming here frequently." Beth waved a hand toward a dirt road leading away from the dilapidated log cabin. "We followed it back to the highway and it's obvious from the way the grass is bent over that someone's been using it over the last few days. We searched around some but couldn't find any tire tracks or indication of the vehicle used." She cleared her throat. "We believe the victim might be Cassie Burnham. She went missing from Rattlesnake Creek Friday last. She is an exotic dancer who works at Outlaws gentlemen's club. Her purse and phone were found on Quartz by another dancer, who reported her missing."

Nodding, Wolfe looked from one to the other. "So y'all have no idea if there's more than one body inside the house?"

"Nope." Styles took a pair of blue coveralls from Ryder and put them on. "We don't have anyone else missing, so had no reason to believe there'd be anyone else inside."

After witnessing what serial killers were capable of, Wolfe never took anything for granted. "Maybe not missing from this county, but you don't know who you're dealing with. The cabin could be the dumping ground for a serial killer." He waved a hand around him, encompassing the whole area. "Look how isolated this place is. Y'all know serial killers can travel all over, and if this is a collector who enjoys visiting his kills, this place would be perfect." He looked from one to the other. "If you're coming inside the cabin with me, get suited up. I want you to keep to the perimeter of the room. If the killer spent time with the victim, I would expect to find trace evidence all over. There are powerful flashlights in my kit. Why don't y'all grab them. We'll need as much light as possible inside." He turned to Webber and Emily. "Full suit, cover everything, and use the face shields. When a body like this is so advanced in decomposition, it can ooze bodily fluids." He turned back to Beth and Styles. "I suggest you do the same." He glanced at Ryder. "You too. As sheriff, you'll need to be present. If any of y'all need to spew, go outside, got it?"

"Yes, sir." Ryder's face paled.

After suiting up, Wolfe led the way to the front door and peered inside. The smell was overpowering even with the mentholated salve. He checked the floor, noting the footprints in the dust-covered floorboards. He held out a hand to prevent anyone from following. "Webber, get some shots of these prints. They're not conclusive but we'll have an idea of the size of boots the killer was wearing." He moved back outside to allow Webber to do his job.

Looking at the others, he indicated toward the door. "Y'all see how easy it is to trample over evidence? I know this isn't your first crime scene, but if you're planning on catching this killer, we'll need all the evidence we can find. This cabin could be a goldmine of information."

"You're preaching to the choir." Styles smiled at him and held up evidence bags. "I'm hoping to fill these."

Wolfe nodded. "Okay, as soon as Webber is done, we'll go inside."

Noticing Beth had walked over to speak to Emily, he lowered his voice. "Is Beth settling in okay?"

"Better than okay." Styles rubbed the scar on his chin and met his gaze. "She's kinda out there, you know. She skirts around the rules some like me. She's not afraid of anything and can fight like a wildcat. I'll tell you about her encounter with a group of drunken louts over a drink sometime." He winked. "She is one of the best investigators I've had the pleasure to work with. I'm not sure what Mac's true intention was for sending her here. I'm starting to believe it was to keep an eye on me. She's a good agent and I hope she remains here for a long time."

Pleasantly surprised, Wolfe nodded. "She's not backing away from crime scenes? Acting depressed or withdrawn?"

"The opposite." Styles frowned. "I have to rein her in. It's all good." He slapped Wolfe on the back. "Best partner I've ever had."

"Shane, I'm done with the footprints." Webber appeared in the doorway. "I'll go ahead and record the scene."

Steeling himself, Wolfe followed him inside. Crime scenes didn't keep him awake at night but his compassion for the victims often knotted his stomach. Using his flashlight, he moved through a small mudroom. Pegs along one wall held a very old slicker. On a bench sat a pair of leather gloves covered in cobwebs. They still held the shape of the last hands that had worn them. Taking the lead, he moved inside the family room. A dust-covered sofa had been turned to face the hallway running through the cabin to the back door. Long glossy hair tumbled over the back of the chair, moving in the breeze from the door. Long bare arms discolored by livor mortis stretched out along the top of the sofa. He stepped closer and bent to look at the hands and then turned to Webber. "Get a close-up of the arms."

He waved everyone closer. "The arms are stitched to the sofa using embroidery floss." He frowned staring at it. "The sutures have bled." He lifted his gaze to the shocked faces. "She was alive when he did this."

"This killer is sadistic." Beth shook her head and anger flashed in her eyes.

Checking out the floor before he moved, Wolfe stepped around the sofa. Even after being forewarned, the distorted clownlike face startled him. The naked woman was posed indecently and he pushed down the need to cover her. He always maintained a victim's dignity, but in this case, it was vital evidence of a seriously deranged mind. He examined the body, took the temperature, and shook his head. There was no obvious cause of death. He'd discovered some discoloration of the scalp and superficial grazes on her knees and palms. He moved the victim's head. The neck wasn't broken. His attention moved to a silver glint in one of her ears. He bent closer and exhaled. He glanced at Beth. "I figure that's a spike in her ear. I'll know more during the autopsy but that might be the cause of death."

"He was a busy boy." Beth shook her head and followed

him around the chair and stood beside him. "The behavioral analyst you work with, Jo Wells, would be very interested in this case. Posing a woman like that means something special to him. I figured I knew how a psychopath's mind works, but this one beats all." She glanced at Styles. "He must have had some crazy childhood."

"That is nothing like Cassie Burnham." Ryder shook his head. "Well, apart from the hair."

"I figure the killer changed the features to fit his fantasy." Styles glanced at Beth. "You've always said these killers are acting out a fantasy. He's made her fit, is all."

Intrigued, Wolfe examined the victim's face. Crude stitches had lifted the mouth and held open the eyes. The makeup was thick and applied without care, yet the hair was immaculate. He leaned forward. "He's taken a trophy. There's a chunk of hair missing." He looked at the others. "Spread out and do a grid search." He shook his head. "I do have one concern about this homicide."

"Which is?" Beth stared at him.

Wolfe turned back to the body and indicated to Emily to bag the victim's hands. He looked over one shoulder at Beth. She was composed and interested in what was happening. "This isn't his first kill. From the planning, posing, and returning. He's done this before, and I'd say many times."

TWELVE

Intrigued by the mind of the killer, and the extent this one went to complete their fantasy, Beth walked around the body a number of times, taking in every intricate detail. This killer had been so careful not to leave any trace of himself behind, and once the body was bagged and on the gurney, she meticulously examined every inch of the sofa looking for evidence. She removed the cushions and searched underneath. She found a thin leather strip, like a hair tie, and a coin before holding out each cushion for Webber to allow him to collect any hairs with a handheld vacuum cleaner. All around her people were searching every inch of the cabin. She replaced the cushions and followed the footprints to the back door, turning to look back into the family room. Had he placed the body to shock anyone who stumbled over it—or was it there as a greeting? She beckoned Styles. "Look at this through my eyes for a minute. We were shocked, right, when we saw the victim, but what if he arranged her that way to greet him when he came to visit?"

"You saying that seeing a naked dead woman smiling at him was a turn on?" Styles stared at her for a long time and then moved his attention back to the family room. "Oh, that's real sick." He blew out a long breath. "Necrophiliacs are real, so it's possible. I agree with you. The agent out at Snakeskin Gully, Jo Wells, would be interested in this killer. Maybe we should speak to her and think about taking this case. I figure Ryder is way out of his depth on this one. I'll ask him if he wants to call us in officially. Do you agree?"

Nodding, Beth looked around, avoiding Styles' penetrating gaze. Calling in Special Agent Jo Wells would be a double-edged sword. If she was as good as everyone said, she might be placing her own head in a noose. Then again, they didn't have to invite her to Rattlesnake Creek, a phone call would suffice. "Yeah, I do want this case and we can contact Jo Wells when we get back to the office."

"Okay, I'll go speak to Ryder now." Styles headed in his direction.

An inquisitive itch jumped around inside Beth's brain. There was a spike in the victim's ear and she'd used a hatpin in the same way many a time to dispose of a killer, and the idea of someone else copying her seemed to be having a strange effect on her. On the one hand, the idea intrigued her, on the other it made her vulnerable in ways only she could understand. Over the years she'd varied the method of her executions, mainly to confuse the cops working on the case, but the hatpin was a favorite. She'd also discovered since working in the FBI that most law enforcement officers didn't exactly bust a gut chasing down the murderer of a serial killer. In fact, the FBI hadn't formed a taskforce to hunt down the Tarot Killer. Although, they had issued a shoot-to-kill order for her, no one was actually looking for her. She guessed that not being the only serial killer in the USA meant that there were many taskforces across the country hunting down other psychopaths with far less kills.

Dragging her mind back to the case at hand, she walked back through the kitchen and into the family room. The rest of the team was collecting evidence bags and placing them all in a plastic container. She walked over to Wolfe. "We want to take over this case, once we've cleared it with Ryder. I agree with you. I think this guy has killed before and will likely do again very soon." She sighed. "When are you doing the autopsy?"

"I usually complete the autopsy in the morgue at Black Rock Falls." Wolfe stared at her over his face mask. "If you could collect DNA samples from Cassie Burnham's residence, I'd be able to make a positive ID. With or without a positive ID, as it's a homicide, I'll be conducting the autopsy at ten in the morning. Are you planning on attending?"

"I think we should." Styles had moved up beside her and turned to Wolfe. "Will I be able to drop our chopper down on the roof of the medical examiner's building?"

"Yeah, sure." Wolfe nodded. "I have room for four of them up there. If you mention it to Jo Wells, she might be interested in attending as well. She has Agent Ty Carter to fly her and an FBI chopper at her disposal. They're a great team. I'm sure you'll get along just fine."

Beth's stomach went into freefall but she found herself nodding at his suggestion. "Sure, we need all the help we can get with this case right now."

"I'm done here." Wolfe glanced around at his team. "I'll see y'all in the morning. Don't forget those DNA samples, now. Bring them along and I'll process them. I can get a result in a couple of hours. You know what I need, right? Toothbrush, hairbrush, used tissues, underwear are all great sources of DNA."

"We'll go and check out her place now." Styles followed him to the door. "Her personal belongings, including her house keys, are at Ryder's office." He glanced over at Ryder. "We'll give you a ride back to town so Wolfe doesn't need to make a stop."

"Thanks." Ryder nodded and turned to Beth. "I appreciate you coming in on the case with me." He glanced toward the sofa and shook his head. "I sure hope I never see a murder like this one again."

"Hmm." Beth didn't want to sugarcoat the situation for him, but she already knew where the investigation was headed—she'd seen it so many times before. "Well buckle up, because this guy has only started. From what I'm seeing, he does this all over, so he'll do it again. This is why we asked to take the case. This killer won't be stopped until we stop him. He isn't someone you should try to tackle alone." She narrowed her gaze. "He is enjoying himself right now and you'll be a threat to him. Remember that if he ever has you cornered, don't hesitate to take him down or you'll be his next victim."

THIRTEEN

TUESDAY AFTERNOON

Rattlesnake Creek

Time stopped ticking by for Vicki Strauss. No longer the minutes, seconds, hours, days, or weeks sped by. Instead her life had become a series of agonizing breaths. The naked, masked monster who held her captive had subjected her to every indecency known to man. This time she'd woken in screaming pain from a drugged sleep. Something terrible had happened to her face, and she couldn't move her lips or close her eyes. Trembling and so cold, even with the fire roaring in the hearth of the old dilapidated cabin, she turned her head and gaped in horror at the crude stitches attaching her arms to the back of a large sofa. Shock grasped her, swimming her head and making her limbs jerk. So much pain but she couldn't close her eyes to block it out. What had he done to her this time? The sofa dipped as he sat beside her, staring at her and then running a brush through her long hair. Shuddering, she tried to speak to him but with her lips drawn back in a wide smile, the words came out strange.

"You don't need to thank me." The man smiled at her. His mouth showing through the hideous, zombie mask. She wondered why he wore the mask now. When he'd kidnapped her, she'd recognized him as one of the men she'd performed a private dance for just last week. "We've had so much fun together it would be a shame to spoil it. I want to remember you just like this, smiling and welcoming me like you did at the club. I know you didn't want to leave me and now you can stay. I'll never have to share you with anyone again. You've become one of my darlings. Are you happy, Vicki?"

With the feeling of hot needles running through her, Vicki screamed. She had to get away and if tearing her flesh from the sofa was her only escape, so be it. She wrenched at her arms, but they were fixed so tight she couldn't move. Sobbing in extreme agony, she stared at the amused expression of the disgusting excuse for a human in front of her. "Nooooo."

Tears ran down her cheeks and the man jumped to his feet. "Stop crying, you'll ruin your makeup." He paced up and down before the sofa. "I'll come by and visit you every night. You'd like that, right? We're so good together. You won't leave me like Cassie. She was so ungrateful. I leave her alone for one night and she just vanishes."

Heedless of the pain, Vicki shook her head. She tried to form words but without the use of her lips only nonsense came out. He was mumbling now as if talking to himself or an imaginary friend. Terrified, she watched as he paced up and down as if trying to control the situation. When he stopped and turned to look at her, she cringed. How much more torture must she endure?

"I figured you'd be different." He stared at her. "You were nice to me at the saloon. I know you wanted to be with me, I could see it in your eyes." He chuckled. "I've been watching you for a long time. I've seen the way you looked at me when you danced. Why did you suddenly start looking at the other guys? They don't love you like I do."

Unable to reply, Vicki could only stare into his wild crazy

eyes. She'd been warned about private dances and how some men became fixated on a dancer as if they'd become his girl-friend. She'd performed her dance but had never allowed him or any of the others to touch her. She shook her head again, making the pain level spike, and then groaned.

"When you came to me and danced real sexy, I knew right then that no one else could have you. The thought of you smiling at another man like the way you smiled at me, just drove me darn right crazy." He bent to stare into her eyes and then smiled. "You told me you wanted to leave that place someday and I've made your wish come true. You belong to me now." He walked out of eyeshot behind the sofa. "Now we'll always be together." He chuckled. "I can see by your 'come get me' smile that you agree."

Terror gripped her as he moved out of sight. What horrific torture did he have planned for her this time? Something cold touched her ears. A burst of red-hot pain screamed through her head and then time stopped forever.

FOURTEEN

The *eau de death* lingered and when they arrived back from searching Cassie Burnham's home, Beth excused herself and took a shower and changed before returning to the office. They'd collected possible DNA samples for Wolfe and packed them away securely for the morning's trip. Intrigued by the killer's MO, she went straight to her laptop to search for any similar cases. The killer's method of stitching the victim to the sofa and changing her face was unusual but something in the back of her mind triggered a memory, not specifically the same but close. In one case a killer had placed a mask over the victims' faces, making them all appear the same. Another had changed the appearance using superglue. She scanned the psychological profiles on the killers, the conclusions being what she'd known to be true. The psychopath had changed the victim to fit his fantasy. The trigger factor that made them kill was usually centered on the victim. *Just like him.*

Her father's face lingered in her mind and she slapped it away, but the memories of him never left her. Cutthroat Jack was serving multiple life sentences for murder and she hated him. Having a notorious serial killer as a father was bad enough, but his victims looked just like her. Had she been his motive for killing? Were all those deaths her fault? Had he lusted after her and his sick depraved mind pushed him to murder? He'd killed her mother to keep her quiet. She'd been there unable to do a thing to help her. That terrible night, she'd heard maniacal ramblings dribbling from his twisted mind as he plunged the knife deep.

Horrified, confused, but with the deep-seated knowledge that some part of her understood him had terrified her. She'd ran and kept on running but she carried his genes, and a legacy to be just like him. The thought left her sick to her stomach. She'd fought her dark side with all her being but had no control over what she'd become. Realization she had compassion for the victims of crime had given her hope. From that day on, she'd used her dark side to stop men like him.

With effort, she smothered the living nightmares running rampant though her head and forced her mind to concentrate on the screen. Her best source of weird and unusual behavior was the dark web. After running a few lines of code to access the forbidden zones, she slid into the world used by the "depraved for pay" society that lived in streams of data. This was the place anything and everything was for sale. Teasers were posted like advertisements for specials at the mall. These posts often led to auctions of children, photographs, or movies. Many people had specific tastes and using certain words or phrases often got results. She hunted for "embroidery floss" and had gotten a few hits when an alert came in about another murder victim found in a shallow grave in Running Water, Montana. She pushed back her chair and walked to the coffee machine to clear the current case from her mind.

For her it was like changing channels on the TV. Most people watched more than one show or followed a number of series, moving from one to the other without a problem. It was the same for her. She could move from one case to another and keep each case clear in her mind. The Levi Jackson case may not have held her center of attention, but it was there lurking in the background. She'd been waiting for him to make his next move and he'd just made it. As she'd predicted, he'd also moved to another town in his comfort zone. The recent murder in Running Water fit his MO. A woman found raped and strangled in a shallow grave in Jackson's favorite dumping ground had been covered with lawn clippings. She shook her head. No arrests had been made and no suspects according to the case files. Because of his acquittal, Jackson had been dismissed as a possible suspect when his MO was as good as a fingerprint.

"Is everything okay?" Styles joined her at the kitchenette and filled a cup from the coffee pot. His hair was still damp from the shower. "You look miles away."

Acting nonchalant, Beth shrugged and dragged her thoughts back to the Cassie Burnham case. "The dark web is usually a font of information, but I must be off my game. I can't find anything about creeps who use embroidery floss as a torture weapon and nothing of real significance in any other cases. I've only searched Montana. I figure we need to look in other states."

"I have a theory about our killer." Styles sipped his coffee, moaned in appreciation, and then leaned against the counter. "One, he's a miner because they have access to maps covering the entire state on a regular basis. Secondly, on the maps he'd know what areas had been purchased by the mines and who owned the mining leases. It's public record."

Confused, Beth stared at him over the rim of her cup. "Okay but I'm not following why this is significant to the case."

"Well, if he discovered where the land was purchased, he'd know where to find the deserted cabins." Styles grinned. "I've been searching through them and there's a ton of them, even ghost towns. No one goes there because it's owned by the mines. You know, blasting dangers and the like. Most are posted with NO TRESPASSING signs."

Uncomprehending, Beth pushed her long hair behind one ear and shrugged. "So?"

"We found Cassie Burnham only by following a forest warden's hunch. We searched for a murder of crows, right?" Styles looked animated. "This guy could have been stowing bodies all over in deserted cabins and no one would have found them."

Beth sipped her coffee. "So you figure he's been doing this for a time and no one has discovered a body?"

"Darn sure." Styles nodded. "You figure his fantasy is centered around strippers, exotic dancers, or whatever the correct term is this week. The problem is often gentlemen's club dancers are transient. They come and go, so maybe if they didn't show for work, nobody reported them missing... or nobody cared. I figure it's worth searching the databases and seeing if there's been any unsolved missing persons cases hereabouts."

The possibilities were endless. Beth sighed. "The problem with people in the high-risk categories is that most times they don't have anyone in their lives who cares about them. Most don't have a place to sleep. Some are just scraping out an exis-tence. Nine times out of ten, the local PD doesn't put in the time to look for them when they discover they're missing. If they're found dead, most of them are just another John or Jane Doe. They are a serial killer's smorgasbord because nobody cares."

"True." Styles scratched his head. "You mentioned that psychopathic serial killers are all different but the one thing they all have is the need to kill, right?"

Wondering where this was going, Beth avoided his pene-trating gaze by bending to grab a sandwich from the refrigerator under the counter. "Yeah, from my studies of Jo Wells' books and others, it certainly seems to be true. Why?"

"So, if it's easier to murder high-risk people to fill the need to kill, why does the Tarot Killer kill dangerous serial killers and advertise his involvement by leaving a tarot card behind? Does he want to be caught or is he thumbing his nose at law enforcement?"

Impressed by his insight, Beth blew out a breath. "He is an atypical serial killer that's for sure. It's something you need to discuss with Jo Wells. She's the expert."

"But you must have an opinion." Styles went to the refrigerator and collected a pile of food. "He can't have a fantasy, can he? All his victims are different."

Refilling her cup from the pot, Beth turned to look at him. "It depends on how you look at them as a whole. Maybe the Tarot Killer's trigger is vengeance. From what I'm seeing, he only takes out those killers who can't be stopped. He watches the cops running in circles while the killings keep on happening and then says, 'enough is enough' and takes them out himself. The card is him saying, 'I did this for humanity.' I don't think it's a snub. Some of the killers he took down were killing kids. I know I shouldn't say this, but I'm glad he stopped them killing—someone had to."

FIFTEEN

Leaving Styles to hunt down missing persons cases, Beth went back to her desk. Her reply to his question had received a nod without a comment. She'd seen a spark of amusement in his eyes, and figured he liked her speaking her mind. Her attention went back to the Levi Jackson case. She'd found killers' whereabouts from various sources over the time she'd started her vigilante quest, but one message board hidden on the dark web contained stories from released prisoners. She had visited it many a time to discover the whereabouts of serial killers. She scanned the message board, flying past posts that were irrelevant to her search. There were a few interesting posts. One in particular caught her eye. Levi Jackson didn't have much of an imagination as it seemed he always referred to himself as Bill to his victims, so when this name came up in one of the posts, Beth's attention went straight to it. It was from a cellmate who mentioned while being held in county awaiting trial that he'd shared a cell with someone he would refer to as Bill. He mentioned how exciting it was speaking to him. Bill had crowed about getting women inside his van on the pretense of renting a room at his ranch. He'd driven them to a secluded area and then raped and murdered them.

The description of the murders fit Levi Jackson's MO. Beth wanted to punch the air when she noticed a link. She clicked on it and found the page titled Bill's Kills. The description rambled on about how he loved to sleep with the bodies and how he reluctantly took them to a remote location to bury them in shallow graves, covering each of them with tree branches and cuttings taken from his own front yard. She looked deeper, going through the code line by line until she discovered another link to Jackson's posts. After bypassing a number of encryptions, she found the photo gallery. Suddenly glad she was facing Styles' desk and he couldn't see over her shoulder, she opened each image file. Shocked to the core, she moved from one file to the next. The sickening images seemed endless. Jackson had murdered at least thirty victims. Her pulse raced and her dark side rose up determined to prevent this maniac from killing vulnerable women and kids again.

Calm down. Trying hard to control her rage, Beth meticulously backtracked on the site, leaving no trace of her being there or leaving a history on her hard drive. She needed to think straight. Right now, she couldn't get away to hunt down Levi Jackson, but she could anticipate his next move. From the evidence he moved from state to state, county to county, establishing a comfort zone between two or three neighboring towns. He spread out his kills between the towns and had become as predictable as the sun rising the following day. Unfortunately, due to her situation at the moment, he would keep on killing until she could stop him, but it was only a matter of time. She stared at her computer screen. *I'm coming for you, Levi.*

Beth used the time finishing her lunch to pull her emotions back under control. After washing her cup and dumping her garbage, she went to Styles' desk. "Find any missing persons?"

"Nope. No women. There is a kid missing in Helena and the two girls from our last case are still missing." He looked at her. "Find anything interesting?"

Leaning one hip on his desk, Beth shook her head. "Nothing we can use. We'll need to hunt down possible suspects if we plan to move forward. I figure we go and visit Outlaws and ask them really nicely if they would allow us to see the list of people who hold tabs there. It would give us some idea who might be a suspect in the Cassie Burnham case. We need to know who was there on Friday night, when she went missing. I don't think it was a random thrill kill. It was too well planned. He must have organized the cabin to stash her body and he knew her movements. He also knew she left alone, and as she worked the same shift on the same days each week, it's either one of the men working there, a security guard or one of the staff, or a regular at the club. Nothing else makes sense."

"Hmm, that would be a ton of people. Although maybe not so many in Outlaws. We'll need to get a warrant. The privacy laws in Montana won't allow a club to just hand over information." He rubbed the scar on his chin. "Do we have probable cause or a darn good reason for obtaining the information?"

Thinking for a beat, Beth sighed. "We have reason to believe that the killer is one of the patrons, due to witnesses statements saying that a number of men acted hostile toward Cassie during her performances. If we could narrow it down to what men were at the club the night she disappeared, including the staff, it would give us a list of suspects to interview." She sucked in a breath. "That's all I've got. You?"

"That might work, especially if we show the judge a photograph of the crime scene. I'll type it up. Being FBI, we're in with a chance." Styles set to work and five minutes later the printer whirred. "Okay, we'll take it over now." He stood and grabbed his jacket from the back of his chair. "Maybe I'll make it clear we need to stop this guy before he kills again."

A shiver walked down Beth's spine as she grabbed her coat. "I just hope he hasn't already struck again."

SIXTEEN

With Bear on their heels, they headed down to the parking lot and climbed into Styles' truck. The icy chill of winter still lingered through spring and as the afternoon closed around them the temperature dropped considerably. People walked along the sidewalk on Main, heads bent against the blustery wind gusts, bundled up in thick coats, some with brightly colored scarfs wrapped around their faces. Beth would have preferred remaining inside the warm truck with Bear. As Styles cranked up the heating for him, Beth pulled her woolen cap over her ears and slid from the seat. An arctic blast lifted Beth's coat and Styles held his hat to prevent losing it as they walked up the steps into the courthouse. The courthouse was an old building built from granite hewn from the mountainside. From the metal plaque attached to the building proclaiming its long history, it had been built during early settlement and for many years had been used as a courthouse and jail. Inside was quiet and their footsteps echoed through deserted hallways. Beth peered down corridors, seeing no one. The building smelled like a library, old books, and printing ink. "It's like a morgue in here."

"The action happens on Thursdays and Fridays unless the judge decides otherwise." Styles smiled at her. "Not that there's much crime in Rattlesnake Creek, but the judge and lawyers still keep office hours."

Beth snorted. "It sounds like a waste of taxpayers' money. Maybe he should be a circuit judge and travel around."

"I figure people think that about law enforcement." Styles grinned at her. "Sometimes we're out fishing between cases and Ryder watches TV most days but we're there when needed."

Beth shrugged. "I guess, but we do travel to other counties and states some of the time."

They reached the judge's office and entered the small room. After speaking to the secretary, they were shown into the judge's office. He held the paperwork in one hand and peered at them over half-moon glasses. The overhead light glistened on his balding pate between the carefully combed wisps of hair. His eyebrows reminded Beth of an owl, black and at least an inch long sticking out like feathers. She had a moment of inappropriate hilarity as she wondered if he'd grown them to brush over his bald head. She quickly glanced away.

"If you were Ryder, I'd deny this request without hesitation, but I figure you have something you're not telling me or don't want on the public record." The judge leaned back in his stuffed leather chair and eyed them like a raptor.

"Yeah, we need to catch this killer before he kills again." Styles accessed his image files and held out his phone. "I don't want to cause a panic if this information gets out, Your Honor. Right now, we have no solid evidence apart from what the other dancers have told us, and we need to narrow down a list of suspects. Knowing who was at the club on Friday night is crucial."

"I see." The judge took the phone and scrolled through the images. The color drained from his face. "To think this animal is walking our streets. I'm going to add an addendum to the request. I'll add credit card receipts. When you have a list of suspects, give me the names and I'll make out a warrant for their bank accounts. I had a case some years ago involving the gentlemen's club. I discovered that some of the patrons use their credit cards to obtain a stack of bills to give to the dancers as tips or whatever. The cash withdrawals are via an ATM and don't show as coming from the club on their bank records. They also pay in cash for a private dance. These men are up close and personal with the dancers, so someone you should consider. If you need anything else, my door is always open." He made notes on the document and signed it. He handed it to Styles. "Do your best to catch this menace, son." He waved him away.

Outside in the hallway, Beth grinned at him. "That was easy. He likes you."

"His son died in action." Styles' expression was solemn. "I guess I remind him of him." He shrugged. "We'll head over to Outlaws and get the information. It's going to take us forever to go through everything."

Smiling, Beth turned to him. "All we need are the names of everyone who was at the club on Friday night and the regular customers who dropped by over the time Cassie was working. It can't be that many people. We'll shoot the names over to the judge and once we have a warrant for their bank accounts, I'll run them through a search program, adding the perimeters, times, and date, and we'll get a list. The only drawback is if he used cash." She met his gaze as they walked back to the truck. "The club would know the regulars; we can push for their names and the staff. A court order like ours is powerful. Clubs don't want any trouble. I'm sure they'll fold and give us the information. I figure there are the regular townsfolk and groups of miners who work the same shifts. It will be easy to confirm who was or wasn't working Friday night."

"After seeing what happened to you, my bet is on a miner or

a group of miners." Styles shook his head slowly. "I sure hope Wolfe finds evidence to nail this guy."

Beth pulled her coat around her as an arctic gale almost lifted her from her feet. "Me too."

SEVENTEEN

The *thump, thump, thump* of loud music trembled the floor and vibrated through Beth's boots as they stepped inside the entrance to Outlaws Saloon. At the back of the room, the door to the gentlemen's club was lit with flashing lights depicting a dancer and a flashing red arrow. It was different this time, walking inside as an FBI agent. With each step she gathered her hard-nosed cop persona around her like a protective cloak. Leading the way, she walked past the bar, ignoring the interested looks from the men on stools hunched over glasses of beer. One of them reached out to touch her arm. Surprised as Styles wasn't far behind her that she'd be bothered by a bar hugger, she stopped walking and glared at him. "Did you want to speak to me?"

"Uh-huh." The man tipped up the brim of his Stetson and his gaze traveled over her. "You shouldn't be heading that way. Can't you read the sign? It says GENTLEMEN'S CLUB. That ain't no place for a fine-looking little gal like you, maybe you should stay here with me." His fingers closed around her wrist and he smiled, displaying discolored front teeth.

Lifting her chin and peering down her nose at him, Beth

moved her gaze slowly to the hand and then back to his face. Behind her, Styles swore under his breath and the power of his menace raised goosebumps on her flesh. It was exhilarating having a partner who walked the thin line between right and wrong like her. It was as if all her senses were tuned to him as he readied himself to fight, but she didn't need him to protect her. She needed *him* to protect the man gripping her arm—*from* her. "Maybe you should take your hands off me."

"Oh, a feisty one." The man dropped his hand with a reluctant sigh, but the grin remained. His attention moved to Styles. "Ah, is she with you?"

"Yeah. Don't mess with her." Styles cleared his throat and moved to her side. "Or you mess with me."

"I sure wouldn't want to go upsetting the FBI." He waved them toward the gentlemen's club door. "Anytime you want a drink, honey, come see me. I'm always here at this time."

She didn't look at Styles but as her dark side reared its ugly head, she directed the full force of it toward the man. "Be careful what you wish for. If I hunt you down, it will be your worst nightmare."

As Beth moved toward the gentlemen's club, Styles barked a laugh. She looked at him. "What?"

"I sure wouldn't want to face you in a dark alleyway." Styles grinned at her.

Laughing, Beth met his gaze. "I'll take that as a compliment."

"I like that about you. I can speak my mind and you don't jump down my throat." Styles kept in step beside her as they walked through the saloon. "I know you're fearless and don't back down but don't underestimate the people in this town. That guy was carrying. Here, if a person feels threatened, they can use lethal force."

Amused, Beth smiled. "I know the law, but he'd never live it

down, would he? I mean, do I really look like a threat to a big
guy like him?"

"No, but neither does a prairie rattlesnake until it bites
you." Styles shrugged.

Out front of the club entrance, a large man wearing a black
suit stretched tightly over the bulging muscles in his arms sat at
a red velvet-covered table. As she approached him the overpowering smell of cologne burned the inside of her nostrils. She
opened her mouth to speak to him when Styles came up
beside her.

"Where's your boss?" Styles pulled the search warrant out
of the inside of his jacket and let it unfold as he held it up in one
hand. "We have a search warrant."

The man with a name plate badge saying WARREN stood
and lifted a two-way to speak to his boss, but Styles ignored him
and pushed through the door. Beth followed close behind and
into the dimly lit club. Nobody noticed their arrival as all eyes
were on the stage and the three cavorting half-naked women. As
Styles seemed to know his way around, she followed him.
Standing in the doorway of a room marked PRIVATE, a tall
skinny man eyed them with suspicion.

"Agents Dax Styles and Beth Katz. We have a warrant to
seize documents." Styles flashed his creds, but it was obvious
that the man knew him. "Credit card receipts and your
employees work schedule for the last two weeks." He waved the
warrant in front of the man's eyes and then pocketed it.

"I don't have anything to hide from the feds. My taxes are
paid up." He stared at Styles. "What am I being set up for,
Styles?"

"Nothing as long as you cooperate, and you know darn well
that I'm not with the IRS." Styles turned to Beth. "This is Hal
Brook, the owner of Outlaws."

Nodding, Beth took out her notebook and handed it to him.
"We need a list of all the customers who visited the gentlemen's

club over the last two weeks. I'm sure you recognize your regular patrons." She waved him into the office. "Give me a list and then we'll start on the other things we need."

"Okay, it's not that I have a choice, is it?" Brook turned and walked into his office.

Styles followed and then Beth moved into the office, closing the door behind her. She stood leaning against it as Brook sat down at his desk and made a list, adding days of the week beside the names. Once he'd finished writing and handed the notebook back to her, she scanned a list of names. "Do you know how many of these men work for the mines?"

"Yeah." Brook held out his hand for the notebook. "I'll mark each name with an asterisk."

"Now the credit card receipts." Styles dropped into the office chair in front of the desk and leaned on the table. "I'll need to know which men on this list received a private dance from Cassie Burnham this week." He gave him a long hard stare. "Don't tell me you don't know, because I know darn well you take a percentage of the cash payments."

"Okay, okay." Brook reached for the notebook on the table. "Cassie has only been doing private dances for the last few months, but she is a favorite with a few of the men. I'll underline their names in the book." He looked up at them and frowned. "I'm assuming that she's still missing? Do you think one of these guys could have taken her?"

Not reading anything sinister from Brook, but not willing to give out any information, Beth shrugged. "We're just following leads, is all. Can you give us a printout of the work schedules?"

"Yeah, sure." Brook tapped away at his computer and behind him a printer jumped into action. He reached around collected the document and handed it to her. "The credit card receipts are all digital now and there's a ton of them. Do you have a stick I can put them on?"

Having worked in cybercrime, Beth never left home

without a few flash drives and pulled one from her pocket. "Here you go." She crossed her arms over her chest and leaned against the wall.

"Two of the men on this list come by regular every Tuesday." Styles glanced up from the notebook. "Are they here now?"

"Yeah, they come by after four, regular as clockwork every Tuesday." Brook smiled at him. "They drop by on Friday as well, same time. I've known them for years. They work day and night shifts out at the Lost Gem Mine. They work Wednesday night, and Thursday and Friday daytime. They're always here Friday night, then work Sunday through Tuesday and finish at three."

"So, you know the shifts the miners usually work?" Styles ran his gaze down the list of frequent customers. "How so?"

"Not all, because they change shifts from time to time. It's good business for me to know when to put more girls on the schedule. We only have one or two working on the slow days." Brook straightened some papers on his desk, knocking them into a pile and slipping them into a drawer. "The men around these parts work unusual hours in the mines and they're all different. Some are one week on and one week off. Others work days one week and nights the next. They often work odd hours. It suits me fine. It means we always have customers walking in the door." He leaned back in his chair, staring at the screen for a few seconds before pulling the flash drive out and handing it to Beth. "There you go." He looked at Styles. "Anything else I can do for you?"

"Yeah, you can point out the men you mentioned." Styles stood. "We can interview them out there in front of everyone, or we can use your office. It's up to you."

"I don't really have a choice, do I?" Brook pushed to his feet and sighed. "I'll bring them to you one at a time. I don't want everyone running out of the club believing we're in the middle of a raid."

Beth took her notebook from Styles. "What are their names?"

"Steve Smith and Jace Conan." Brook moved past her to the door. "I'll bring Steve in first. Please don't scare the heck out of them. They're good customers and tip the girls real well. They're close by. I won't be long."

After making notes, Beth turned to Styles. "You speak to these men. I'm not sure what happens to them when they walk into a strip club. They turn into sexist pigs like it's their right or something to act that way. It took all my willpower out there to stop myself from bending back that man's fingers and breaking them." She shook her head. "A woman should be able to walk into a bar without being touched by someone she doesn't know and then subjected to indecent suggestions."

"I agree." Styles scratched his cheek, concern etched over his face. "Touching you was a mistake. I wasn't going to stand by and watch it either. I figure you handled yourself pretty well in there and kept control of the situation."

Turning around to face him, Beth frowned. "I never lose my temper, Styles. I'm always in control. I don't care where I'm living, but wherever it is, I do expect to be respected as a human being and not an object. I did feel threatened, especially surrounded by an entire room of men mostly under the influence of alcohol, and by Montana law if I considered my life was in danger, I could have drawn down on him... but I didn't, did I?" She chuckled. "Although, when you swore under your breath, I figured you were going to hit him for sure."

"It was on my mind." Styles gave her a slow smile. "I must admit fighting back-to-back with you scratches an itch I get from time to time."

Amused, Beth's concern dissipated like a sun-shower on the

hot blacktop and she relaxed. "Have you always been a brawler?"

"Since grade school." Styles rubbed the scar on his chin as if it reminded him of something long ago. "I was bigger than most of the other kids, and I didn't like bullies picking on the younger ones. So, I spent most of my time in detention or being suspended. It seems I've always been able to hit hard. That's the main reason I went into the Army. I needed self-discipline and an outlet for my aggression. It didn't help. I haven't changed. Agreed, I do have self-control now, but I prefer using my fists to settle a problem rather than shooting people." He grinned. "That's why working here suits me just fine."

"Ha." Amused, Beth shook her head. "And you figured I was the rattlesnake."

EIGHTEEN

As Beth waited to start the interview, she looked at Styles. "Maybe we shouldn't mention that we believe Cassie is dead?"

"Okay." Styles pulled out a notebook from his inside pocket. "We'll just mention she's missing and see what happens." He looked toward the door as it swung open and Brook walked in with a young burly man. "Thanks, Mr. Brook, we'll take it from here."

The strong smell of cologne surrounded the newcomer and Beth stepped back. The men around these parts must bathe in the stuff. If they really believed walking around in a cloud of cheap splash-on was attractive to women, they needed their heads read. Surely she wasn't the only woman who appreciated a more subtle aroma when it came to men's store-bought fragrances.

"What's this all about?" The young man looked from one to the other. "Hal said the FBI wanted to speak to me."

"I'm Agent Styles and this is Agent Katz. We're speaking to anyone who interacted with Cassie Burnham, one of the dancers who works here, over the last week or so." Styles sat on the edge of Brook's desk acting casual. "I believe you're one of her regulars and had a private dance Friday night?"

"So what?" Smith folded his arms across his chest. "I'm not the only one. She's a good-looking girl and dances real fine. It's really none of your business if I enjoy her company for a few minutes once a week. It's not like I'm dating her or anything."

"I agree." Styles shrugged. "I don't give a darn what you do inside the club. I need information on what happened when she left. What time did you leave here Friday last?"

"I don't rightly recall, ten maybe eleven." Smith rubbed the back of his neck. "Me and Jace usually stay over at the motel, like most of the guys who come here. It's an easy walk. We don't spend all our time in the club, we often finish up the night playing pool in the bar."

A thought came to Beth. "Do any of the guys who hang out here take women back to the motel? I'm not looking to charge anyone for soliciting or anything like that. I just want to find out the way of things in town."

"Some do, yeah." Smith's forehead creased into a frown. "Why, has something happened to Cassie? She's not here tonight and I'd hoped to see her dance."

"Did you see her leave the club on Friday night?" Styles ignored his question and just stared at him.

"Nope." Smith smiled. "She breaks up her sessions onstage. Some of them stay up there for an hour, just slow dancing, but Cassie, she gives us a show. On the pole, you know what I mean, and then crawls around the edge of the stage, so we can tuck—"

"Yeah, I get the picture." Styles flicked Beth a glance, rolled his eyes skyward and then turned his attention back to Smith. "So, what did you talk about during her private session with you. I know you talk."

Intrigued, Beth listened intently. This side of gentlemen's clubs were like secret men's business and being a fly on the wall was golden.

"Plenty." Smith swiped at the tip of his nose with the back of his hand. "I've been asking her out since she first danced for me and I don't give up easy." He shrugged. "The dancers make up the majority of available women in town, you know. They do date miners. I'm not sayin' they sell themselves either."

"What did she say?" Styles straightened, his expression alert.

"She always refused." Smith's shoulders slumped. "I didn't want to pester her. She already mentioned she had enough of those types, and she liked me, so she wanted us to remain friends. I figured that was a start and offered to buy her lunch one day, you know, away from the club, like normal people."

Beth moved away from the wall into his line of sight. "Did she ever mention being concerned about anyone in particular?"

"Yeah." Smith blinked as if just realizing she was there. "She told me one guy constantly stared at her, like he hated what she was doing. It creeped her out some. I asked her to point him out to me, but she refused. She didn't want to cause trouble or Hal would fire her."

"Okay, Mr. Smith." Styles handed him a card. "If you think of anything else, or hear anything about Cassie, call me. She's missing and we mean to find her."

"Missing?" Smith frowned. "Since Friday?"

"So it seems." Styles cleared his throat. "Did she mention where she came from, a family, or friends she might visit?"

"Nope, but I'll ask around." Smith tucked the card into his pocket. "If I find out anything, I'll call." He headed for the door.

Beth stared after him. "Send in Jace Conan." She looked at Styles. "What do you think?"

"He was here and has motive. He admitted he wanted her and she brushed him aside. That would be enough to set him off if he is a psychopath. They don't take rejection too well, do they?" Styles nodded slowly. "He's one for the list."

A few minutes later, Jace Conan walked in, hat in hand and

cheeks ruddy. He was dressed in denim jeans, jacket, and a white shirt. He looked like a kid and kept his attention on the ground refusing to meet Beth's eyes. She exchanged a look with Styles and made a motion with her hand to start the questioning.

"Jace Conan?" Styles introduced them and cleared his throat when Conan lifted his face, displaying scratches down one side of his neck.

"Yeah, what's the problem?" Conan moved his gaze over Beth and then dropped it back to his boots.

Beth blinked and then snapped her fingers. "Hey, look at me, not the floor." This was one of the men who'd attacked her the previous evening. With her wig dragged off in the fight and her hair down, she'd had no option but to identify herself as an FBI agent. She wouldn't be able to go undercover in Outlaws again. "You know why we're here, right?"

"I've been cleared of any wrongdoing." Conan stared at her, his eyes narrowed. "You came on to us, taking off your coat all sexy like and wearing jeans so tight they could have been sprayed on. Don't go blaming me, lady. You advertise and men will come running."

Not moving from her place against the wall, Beth shrugged. "That's Agent Katz to you. I'm not a member of the English aristocracy."

"I know you were here on Friday night." Styles moved into the conversation so smoothly Beth blinked at him. "You paid for a private dance with Cassie Burnham."

"Look, there's nothing wrong about paying a girl for a dance." Conan grinned. "I picked Cassie because it drives Steve crazy when she dances for me. Well, dance is what they call it, right? She slides onto my lap and sends me to heaven."

"How did you get the scratches on your neck?" Styles took out his phone and took a picture before Conan could react.

"She did it." Conan indicated with his chin toward Beth.

Shaking her head, Beth pushed off the wall. "Not me. I was wearing gloves. It was way too cold to be out without them and I don't claw people who attack me. I usually break something."

"Where were you around ten on Friday night?" Styles slipped his phone inside his pocket. "After Cassie finished for the night."

"I was here, playing pool in the bar until around eleven and then I walked back to the motel with Steve." He glanced at his watch. "You going to be much longer? I'm missing all my favorite dancers."

"Was anyone at the desk when you returned to the motel?" Styles made a few notes and looked up at him. "I'll need to verify when you returned."

"I don't know." He pulled a key from the pocket of his jeans and dangled it in front of Styles face. "We don't need to check in. We all have keys."

"When did you last see Cassie?" Styles stared at him.

"Last time she was onstage. My dance was earlier, around eight." Conan turned his hat around in his hands. "I didn't see her leave. We were in the bar by then."

"So, you know what time she leaves?" Styles smiled. "She must be a favorite."

"Kinda." Conan's cheeks blushed crimson. "She likes me and gives me extra time with her. We had a drink after the dance last Friday. She sat beside me, all nice like, and we talked. I was her last dance and she had some spare time."

"What did you talk about?" Styles' penetrating gaze was fixed on him.

"Stuff." Conan dropped his gaze to the floor. "I don't recall."

"Okay." Styles handed him a card. "If you think of anything else, or hear any mention of Cassie, call me. If I find out you're withholding information about her disappearance, I'll be coming for you. Understand?"

"Disappearance?" Conan's head snapped up. "She's missing?"

"It seems that way." Styles waved him toward the door. "That's all for now, Mr. Conan."

Shutting the door behind him, Beth turned to Styles. "Oh, those two are up to their necks in this. Those scratches didn't come from me. He's hiding something."

"He sure is." Styles pushed his Stetson firmly on his head. "I don't trust either of them."

NINETEEN

Running Water, Montana

A blast of freezing rain swirled around Tina Simmons as she stepped from the bus. All around her people walked purposely in all directions, some climbing into vehicles, others heading for the roadhouse. She turned around in a circle, unsure of which direction to take. The warm glow from the roadhouse lights looked inviting as if beckoning her. The aroma of burgers and fries drifted on the breeze toward her each time the door opened. Her stomach rumbled as a reminder she hadn't eaten for hours. She pulled her purse from her pocket and checked her billfold. She would need to be careful if she was going to survive on the small amount she had, but where was she going to get a job in Running Water? She made her way into the roadhouse and joined the line at the counter. After waiting for a time, she ordered a burger and fries, took a number, and went to sit at one of the tables by a noticeboard.

Her attention was drawn to a handwritten notice offering a room, meals, and a small wage for a ranch hand. Interested, she stood and plucked the notice from the board. Taking it back to her table, she pulled out her phone and called the number on the page. "Is that Bill? I'm calling about the notice regarding the ranch hand job. Is it still available?"

"*Yeah, I'm Bill.*" The man at the end of the line sounded pleasant. "*My last ranch hand moved on and my wife just made up the room, so you're in luck if you're interested in taking the job. Do you have any experience working on a ranch? I hope you haven't run away from home, like the last kid that applied? I don't need no trouble.*"

Tina sipped her coffee, searching her mind for a decent reply. "Yeah, I've worked with animals before. We had horses when I was a kid. I learn fast and I haven't run away from home. I'm nineteen."

"*Okay, I'll give you a trial for a couple of weeks to see how you go. Go along the highway heading toward town and my place is the third gate on the left.*"

Stifling a yawn, Tina nodded as if the man were in the room. "Unfortunately, I don't have a vehicle. I'm stuck at the roadhouse. That's where I saw your notice about the job. I just got in from Helena."

A waitress came by with her meal and she nibbled on a fry. She heard a sound as if he was covering up the mouthpiece and speaking to someone.

"*That's okay. My ranch isn't too far away. I'll come get you and show you the room.*" Bill sounded breathless. "*I'll be about twenty minutes. What do you look like?*"

Surprised he hadn't asked her name, Tina frowned. "I'm wearing a blue puffy jacket and blue jeans. I have blonde hair and I'm wearing a yellow knitted hat with a bobble on the top. My name is Tina, by the way."

"*Okay, Tina, I'll see you soon. I'll be driving a white Chevrolet Express van. Come out to the parking lot when you see me drive in.*" Bill disconnected.

After checking the time on her phone, Tina finished her meal and went to the restroom to freshen up. When she returned to the dining room, the white van was parked a short distance from the roadhouse, engine running and billowing white steam from the exhaust. She pulled on her backpack and hurried outside to greet it. Rain dashed against her cheeks as she ran across the gravel toward the van. The window buzzed down and the man inside stared at her. She moved closer. "Are you Bill?"

"Yeah, and you must be Tina." He gave her a slow smile. "Jump in."

His window buzzed back up and, with rain running down the back of her neck, she ran around the front of the van. She removed her backpack, tossed it inside, and climbed in behind it. Bill looked normal enough, handsome in a rugged way, clean, and dressed in a thick winter jacket and leather gloves. His Levis were worn at the knees and a little damp around the ankles. She stowed her backpack at her feet and fastened her seatbelt. "You mentioned a wife? Do you have kids?"

"Yeah, a whole bunch." Bill grinned at her. "You'll meet everyone in the morning. I'll drop you at the cabin so you can get settled. It's clean, warm, and private. If you stayed in the house, my kids would drive you crazy, so we put all our hands in cabins." He held out his hand. "Give me your backpack. I'll stow it in back."

Reluctantly, Tina handed it over. The backpack contained all her possessions, and she winced as he tossed it into the back of the van. He took off slowly, the wipers swished through the rain, and he glanced at her as they headed onto the highway.

"So what brings you to Running Water?" He indicated to the rain. "It doesn't rain all the time. It's named after the river, is all."

Shrugging, Tina turned to look at him. "I'm looking for work."

"It's dangerous for a young woman to travel in these parts without a place to stay." Bill accelerated, swishing through puddles. "Where were you planning on staying tonight, if you hadn't seen my flyer?"

"I'm not sure." She stared out of the window. A sense of foreboding tormented her over how long they'd driven. They'd passed many roads on the left since leaving the roadhouse. He'd mentioned only three. She pushed the concern away. He seemed nice enough. "Maybe I'd take the next bus out of here. I can always sleep on the bus."

"Did you pin the flyer back on the board?" Bill shot her a glance.

Searching her pockets, Tina pulled out the flyer and handed it to him. "No, sorry. I didn't want anyone else to take the job."

"It's all good." Bill pulled off the road and followed a dirt track into a wooded area. "The cabin is just through there. I came in the back way." He opened the door and slammed it behind him. "Grab your backpack and I'll show you the way."

The side door to the van slid open as Tina circled the hood. The scent of cut pine branches and grass clippings wafted from inside. "Have you been gardening?"

"Yeah, I'll drop it at the landfill when it stops raining." He smiled at her and shrugged.

A light came on inside displaying a fat black plastic bag. It spilled leaves over a mattress complete with blankets and pillows. Suddenly afraid, Tina hesitated. This had been a huge mistake. They were in the middle of nowhere and only a fool would walk into a dark forest with a stranger. Panic gripped her. She needed a plan fast and glanced around searching for a solution. Her backpack was close to the open door and the highway was maybe only a mile away. She could grab the bag and run. He wouldn't be expecting her to bolt into the forest. She'd be away through the trees in seconds. Heart thundering in her chest, she stepped closer to the door. As her hand closed around the handle of her backpack, pain slammed into the back of her head. She bit her tongue and the metallic taste of blood filled her mouth. Dizzy, the van appeared to tip as he lifted her up as if she weighed nothing and tossed her inside. Her back hit the mattress and he was on top of her, grabbing at her hands. Terror had her by the throat and she bucked, but pinned under the weight of him, she couldn't move. Gasping for air, she aimed her head for his nose, but he moved away as if expecting it and smiled down at her.

"Keep wiggling, Tina." Bill chuckled. "It feels so good."

Fighting for her life, Tina slapped at him. "Get off me."

"Sorry, this is all part of the fun." He kneeled on one arm pinning it down. "You'll see."

The weight of his knee numbed her fingers and parted the bones in her forearm. She couldn't move and was suffocating under him. Seconds later cold handcuffs snapped around one wrist and then the other, attaching her arms to chains on each side of the van. Stretched out, she stared at his grinning face. The weight of him pinned her to the mattress, making it hard to breathe.

"Let me go. I won't tell anyone, I promise."

"No can do." He slid down her body, staring at her with a wild look in his eyes.

Screaming, Tina kicked and bucked, but he was so strong and had her legs secured in seconds. There was nothing she could do. Tears spilled down her face and she trembled at the sight of a knife. It glistened under the overhead light, the edge honed until it was deadly sharp. Begging was her only choice. "Please, don't cut me. I'll be good. I promise."

"You don't really have a choice, do you, Tina? No one can hear you and no one cares what happens to you. It's just you and me. We have all night." Bill slowly pulled down the zipper on her jacket and spread it wide. "Look at you all bundled up in pretty things like a gift." He bent to sniff her neck. "You smell so good." He slid the knife under the edge of her shirt. "Let me see what's inside..."

TWENTY

Rattlesnake Creek

Styles placed two more glasses of red wine on the table and then slid into the booth at Tommy Joe's Bar and Grill opposite Beth. "The steaks are on the grill." He smiled at her. "This wine is very good. I don't mind beer but it's way too cold outside right now. Wine warms, don't you think?"

"I guess. What did Ryder say?" Beth indicated with her chin to the sheriff standing at the counter. "Has he made any headway in the case, or is he leaving everything to us?"

Sipping his wine, Styles smiled. "Oh, he's working the case. He dropped by Lost Gem Mine and spoke to the manager. He's obtained copies of the shifts for the last month or so and to the end of the month. We can use them to cross-reference the info we obtained from Outlaws."

"Why just that mine?" Beth leaned back in her chair looking at him. "You mentioned a few mines in the area."

Nodding, Styles turned the stem of his glass around in his fingers. "That's true but Lost Gem works twenty-four hours, seven days a week, so they have unusual shifts. Two of our suspects work there and he figured it would be a good place to hunt down others who visit Outlaws." He cleared his throat. "As he knows the barman at Outlaws, he was able to call him and ask if he'd noticed any locals dropping by regular, especially on Friday nights, and now he has a list."

"And what are his plans?" Beth stared at him. "We need to be at the autopsy in the morning. Is he planning to hunt down any potential leads?"

It seemed that Beth still hadn't gotten into the slower way of doing things in Rattlesnake Creek, and she wanted everything done yesterday. Styles rubbed his chin. "Do you really want him out there alone stirring up a wasp's nest with a serial killer on the loose? He only has us for backup. It's a little dangerous."

"You'd do it alone, right?" Beth gave him a quizzical stare. "I know he's inexperienced but you gotta stop treating him like a kid. He must be thirty and he can use his service weapon, can't he?"

"He can." Styles regarded her for a long minute. "And yeah, I'd go it alone but I'm different and you know it. Why are you giving him such a hard time? He's following normal procedure and it's what I would do."

"I'm sorry. I didn't mean to." Beth blew out a long breath and her frown melted. She leaned back and shook her head. A sweet smile curled her lips and she shrugged. "It's hard to take out the DC in me. I had superiors snapping at my heels all the time. I know I need to chill and realize that life is slower here. I'm aware Ryder doesn't have the resources to get things done faster." She met his gaze. "I'm finding it hard to find my niche and being laid-back isn't usually my style. I guess I need to unwind some in my downtime."

Nodding, Styles returned the smile, glad to see her relax. She'd been wound up tight for days but suddenly the ice maiden had melted and he could see the well-hidden charming side to her. Her smile lit up her eyes and it was like looking at a different person. Maybe it was the wine? "Laid-back, like now, suits you. I understand the need to be the professional iron lady on the job but it's just you and me here, Beth. I'm not your superior. You can relax with me. You must know that by now, right?"

"Yeah." Beth sipped her wine and shrugged. "I've never really trusted anyone, so making friends in the agency has been difficult."

Her situation dawned on him, like someone turning on a switch. He face-palmed his forehead and peered at her between his fingers. Of course, anyone who worked with her would have known her father was a serial killer. Although the details were redacted, it was still there. He'd read it: *Father a convicted serial killer, currently in Washington State Pen.* She'd have been treated like a pariah. "Oh darn. You know, I've never considered the implications of your background. I should apologize for being an ass." He dropped his hand. "I must admit, I'm curious to know who your father is and who he murdered, but that's just the cop in me." He smiled. "It doesn't make any difference to me. I take people on face value. At first, I thought you were a little strange, let's say, by your interpretation of the law, but when I look at myself I'm the same." He indicated between them. "We're alike. I push boundaries and so do you. If you'd been a stickler for the rules, we'd have clashed big-time."

Their conversation was interrupted when Tommy Joe arrived with the meals.

"There you go." TJ slid the plates onto the table and handed them silverware wrapped in paper napkins. "Enjoy and there's fresh baked apple pie if you're still hungry. More wine?"

"Not for me." Beth smiled. "Although it is very good. We have an early start in the morning."

"Okay." TJ nodded. "If you want pie, give me a wave." He turned to go.

"Do you really want to know about my dad?" Beth slowly

unwrapped her silverware. "I don't usually discuss him, mainly because so much information was blocked out when my mom died." She gave him a long, considering look. "I know what he did, and I've read the court documents. The unredacted copies. I had a right to know and I obtained a court order to view them and they were released to me from the lawyer who represented him in court."

Surprised she was discussing her father, Styles cut into his steak and nodded, hoping that she would continue. He'd often wondered how much being the daughter of a serial killer had affected her on the job. It couldn't have been easy trying to prove herself to her superiors. Perhaps she just needed someone to listen to her. "It must have been some time after he was jailed?"

"Yeah, it wasn't until I joined the FBI." Beth chewed a mouthful of food, swallowed, and then looked at him. "Being in cybercrime meant I had access to everyone's files, but I couldn't find out what had really happened until I received the court transcripts. The problem was after my father murdered my mother, I blocked out everything. He'd been killing for years, and it's obvious now my mother knew about it. You see, he only killed at night and she must have noticed him missing."

Intrigued, Styles listened with interest. "Maybe not. I've read about many cases where men are married, although personally I would imagine there would be some smell about them or bloodstained clothes." He raised one shoulder, considering his ex. "I find it hard to imagine a wife wouldn't notice something unusual about a husband who's been murdering people. Perhaps if your mom did know, she didn't do anything because she was in fear of her life?"

"Well, she'd have gotten it right then, wouldn't she?" Beth cut her steak into small pieces. "He messed her up real bad, attacked her face and cut her breasts. He made her suffer." She gave him a long look. "Why do you think I hate him so much? He caused everything bad in my life. Being in foster care was a nightmare. I was moved from place to place every few months. Some of the places I lived were worse than being in jail in an undeveloped country." She continued to eat as if thinking what next to say.

Styles paused eating and looked at her. "I think I'll have another glass of wine. It's not like we're driving. Want another? We don't have to leave until nine and it's still early."

"Okay." Beth finished her glass and waved at TJ. "I think I'll have a slice of pie, if we're staying." She smiled at him. "I'm enjoying our talk. It's good to be able to speak to someone about my dad. It's kinda bottled up inside me."

Styles smiled at TJ when he came to the table. "You've twisted our arms. We'll have more wine and the pie."

"I'll be right back." TJ collected the plates and went back to the kitchen. Five minutes later, he returned with two glasses of wine and two slices of pie. "Coffee is on the house, if you want to finish off your meal with a cup."

"Maybe later." Beth nodded. "Thanks, TJ, the meal was delicious."

Keeping her conversation in the front of his mind, Styles took his time, eating pie and sipping wine before looking at her again. He didn't want to appear too eager, but in truth, if she unburdened herself, it might make her feel better. "You can speak to me anytime. I'm never going to discuss what you tell me with anyone. Yeah, I'm required to give updates to Mac on how you're doing, but what we discuss between us is private. I figure your old boss is only concerned about your well-being."

"Yeah, he believes I'm reckless and dangerous as a partner." Beth narrowed her gaze. "He never took the time to get to know me." She sighed. "Do you want me to go on, about my dad, I mean?"

Nodding Styles dug into his pie. "Sure."

"The media called my dad Cutthroat Jack." She slid a hand inside her jacket and produced a straight razor. It was old, maybe from the early nineteen hundreds, silver, highly decorated with a horn handle. "This was his weapon of choice."

Familiar with the name and the case, Styles swallowed a sip of wine and stared at her. Cutthroat Jack had murdered thirty women they knew about and could possibly have killed another twenty or so. He stared at the razor and shook his head. "That's a fine piece of history, but there's no way you got that out of evidence."

"Not this one, no." Beth slowly closed the razor and slid it back inside her pocket. "Maybe he used it, maybe not. It was one of a collection of eleven and I figure no DNA was discovered on it. I found them in a storage locker with the rest of the things from the house. The house was sold and the money placed in trust for me when I turned twenty-one. The possessions are still in the locker, paid for each month. Anything of interest was examined by the ME at the time of his arrest, but only one or two things were taken into evidence. He never committed crimes at home before my mother's murder. They found his trophy hoard behind a false wall in the garage. He collected fingernails." She patted the side of her jacket. "This razor and a few others belonged to my grandfather. They're mentioned in his estate documents." She leaned back in her chair. "Before you ask, I carry it as a constant reminder to take down everyone like him." She shuddered. "He was a perverted excuse for a human being and I'm ashamed of him."

Aware speaking about her father was stressful, Styles nodded. "I would be too. So unless you need to discuss him with me again, we'll keep him out of our topic of conversation. Tell me about your cabin."

"It's beautiful and will be more so when I get the time to fix it up." Beth sipped her wine and her eyes danced. "I'm hanging out for some downtime, so I can hit the stores."

Grinning, Styles leaned back in his seat and chuckled. "There's a new fishing rod in my cabin and I've a bunch of new flies I'm hankering to try. Trust me, after a tough case there is nothing better than a week in tranquility."

"Amen to that." Beth held up her glass.

TWENTY-ONE
WEDNESDAY

In the chopper on the way to Black Rock Falls, the conversation Beth had with Styles the previous night ran through her mind. It hadn't been the wine loosening her tongue. She'd allowed her dark side to peek through for a few minutes. It was the charismatic serial killer sitting with Styles, not the FBI agent. Being able to relax with someone had been invigorating, although she'd always been on her guard not to be too likable. Too many psychopathic serial killers came under suspicion by profilers by being too nice. She'd keep her edge on the job and maybe from time to time relax some with Styles. It would be interesting to see if she could manage the switch in a social environment without it being obvious. Most times, her "I'm your best friend, you can trust me" side emerged right before she took out a particularly vicious murdering monster. Although she followed the same ideals as Styles when it came to crime, her definition of justice had a slight twist.

"Autopsies are always difficult and this one will be horrific." Styles' voice came through her headset. "I'll go it alone if it's a problem."

Blinking, Beth turned to look at him. "Thanks, but I'll be

fine." She folded her arms across her chest. "I've already seen the body. How much more horrific can it be?"

"Whoa." Styles shot her a quick glance. "Don't confuse being considerate with overprotectiveness. You haven't said a word to me since we got into the chopper and I figured maybe you were contemplating the autopsy." He drew in a deep sigh. "What the heck happened to you to make you so defensive?"

Memories of her time in foster care flooded her mind. It was a time she wished she could forget but it sat there like a festering wound. A constant reminder of why she needed to remove monsters from society. She shook her head, ignoring him.

"Don't shut me out, Beth." Styles cleared his throat. "You trust me, I know it. Maybe I can help?"

She didn't like recalling the memories, some were too painful. "You can't help me. It's too late."

"It's never too late." Styles took the chopper high over the snowcapped mountains. "I need to know how to deal with your mood swings. I know being caustic isn't the real you. Fine if you want to be like that on the job but I'd like to think we're friends."

She'd never had a friend she could trust or wanted to trust. No one could possibly understand her own personal demons, although Styles had bared his soul about his coercive ex-wife and the damage he'd suffered because of her. She could maybe hint at what happened to her and use it as an excuse. It's not as if she could tell him she killed people. "I mentioned I was in foster care, and although I know there are some really caring people in the system, I didn't meet any of them. Things happened that shouldn't happen to any child, and if I cried or made a fuss they moved me to another home, usually worse than the one previously. It was a vicious cycle and one I don't want to discuss with you."

"Ah, okay, I see." Styles rubbed the scar on his chin. "I know it's not the same, but believe it or not, I was little as a kid. I grew like crazy when I hit ten and I've told you about that time in my life, but between six and ten was a nightmare. Kids bullied me and that's how I got this scar. A kid hit me with a bottle." He shrugged. "I never told anyone because it only made things worse. My folks thought I was clumsy."

Imagining anyone bullying the self-confident Styles was impossible and Beth shook her head. "So you became a brawler? The Army must have been tough. They insist on discipline and I figure you've always been a rogue. How did you rise in the ranks with that attitude?"

"Because I'm good at what I do." Styles shrugged. "I had a hunger to be the best and worked hard, is all, no magic pill." He flicked her a glance as Black Rock Falls came into view. "The thing is, Beth, it's in the past and I leave it there. I can't change what happened, so I move forward. Same with dealing with my divorce. I don't like to fail but there was no other solution."

Staring at the beautiful scenery, Beth rubbed both hands down her face. Oh, she had a solution but not one she could ever share with him. She sighed. "You have a scar where everyone can see it. Mine are on the inside."

"I see." Styles guided the chopper down to the medical examiner's helipad.

Beth unstrapped her seatbelt and turned to look at him as he powered down the chopper. "No, you don't see, because I don't understand why I'm like this either. Like you said, it's a defense mechanism, just like laughing at funerals or whatever. Mac figures I don't have a filter and he's probably right." She collected her things and then glanced at him. "You know, the doctors tested me to see if I was bipolar but I'm not. I guess acting tough is part of my professional persona."

"Well, I won't take it to heart when you bark at me." Styles smiled at her. "Come on, let's get this done so we can get back and help Ryder."

TWENTY-TWO

A cold blast of air hit Beth as she stepped inside the medical examiner's building. She followed Styles and Bear through electronic doorways, pausing each time for Styles to slide his card through the scanner. The odor of death crawled along the passageways, vaguely disguised by disinfectant, as they headed toward Wolfe's office. In front of her, Styles stopped abruptly. She peered around him. Outside the office door sat a Doberman growling and baring his teeth. One loud bark split the silence and echoed along the corridors. The door whooshed open and a man wearing a Stetson, with shaggy blond hair over his collar, jeans, an FBI jacket, and snakeskin cowboy boots stuck his head out and smiled at them. Beth glanced at Styles and nodded to the man. "Agents Beth Katz and Dax Styles out of Rattlesnake Creek field office to see Dr. Wolfe."

"Hi there." The man stood to one side. "Agent Ty Carter out of Snakeskin Gully. Don't mind Zorro. He figures he owns the place." He looked at the dog. "Stand down."

A woman walked out, and Beth instantly recognized her from the image on the back of her books. A wave of panic hit her and her stomach flip-flopped. It was behavioral analyst Agent Jo Wells. She'd dressed casual, blue jeans and a sweater under her FBI jacket. Her hiking boots were a popular Montana brand and the same style as her own. She, it seemed, had embraced the West after living in DC much like herself.

"This is Agent Jo Wells." Carter smiled. "Wolfe figured y'all would want to discuss your current case with her, so as we were in town we dropped by."

"We sure would." Styles grinned. "We had planned to call you, so this is great."

Everyone shook hands. Heart pounding, Beth forced a smile. "I've read your books. The interviews with serial killers are mind-blowing."

"Thanks." Jo pushed a strand of hair behind one ear. "You're welcome to come with me the next time I arrange an interview." She glanced at Styles and her gaze slid over him, assessing him. "Dax too, of course."

Beth flicked a glance at Styles and lowered her voice, leaning in confidentially. "That's just Styles, he never uses his name. I figure it's an Army thing."

"Okay." Jo chuckled. "I call Ty *Carter* most of the time. He's a SEAL."

"When y'all have finished jawing, I'm ready." Wolfe appeared at the door of an examination room. "Lock the dogs in my office and suit up."

"Okay." Styles rubbed Bear's ears and led him inside the office. "Stay."

"I'm guessing he's K-9? What's his name?" Carter looked at Bear.

"Bear, and yeah, K-9. He served in Afghanistan, was wounded, his handler was KIA. I was offered him when I was discharged." Styles indicated with his chin toward Zorro. "It's unusual to see a Doberman as a K-9. What's his story?"

"Bomb squad. He can sniff out an IED in seconds. I raised him from a pup and when I left the SEALs, he came with me. He refuses to eat unless I give him the order." Carter waved his fingers and Zorro walked into the room. "You get along with Bear, now."

Interested in the conversation, Beth took Jo's lead and suited up in scrubs, face mask, and gloves, plus the obligatory swipe of mentholated salve under her nose, before entering the examination room. She recognized the people inside—Emily, Wolfe's daughter, and his assistant, Colt Webber—and nodded a greeting. She joined the others lined up along one side of the room leaning against the counter. The drop in temperature raised goosebumps as she stared at the flat screens on the wall depicting the crime scene and other data. The gurney was rolled out and placed under a huge aluminum light. Wolfe pulled down a microphone to record the session and turned to look at them.

"I've completed the preliminary examination, taken swabs, and examined the body for trace evidence and collected the stomach contents, all of which were required to be collected immediately to avoid contamination or deterioration. Whoever did this was careful, which as I mentioned at the scene indicates this isn't his first time. I found no trace evidence and the body was washed with diluted bleach, removing any latent DNA." Wolfe glanced at them over his face mask. "I've estimated her time of death as late Friday night to Sunday morning, taking into account the low temperature and rate of decomposition. I believe she was murdered not long after her abduction, not more than twelve hours." Wolfe indicated to results on the screen. "She had no alcohol in her system but I found traces of fentanyl in her stomach contents and believe it may have been used to subdue her or put her to sleep. She hadn't eaten for four to six hours prior to her abduction." He pulled back the sheet covering the body of Cassie Burnham. "We have a female approximately twenty-five years of age, average height and weight, in good physical condition. She has breast implants, piercings to her ears and navel, a tattoo of a red rose on the lumbar region of her spine."

Intrigued, Beth held up her hand and Wolfe stopped the recording. She looked at him over her mask. "Have you established a cause of death?"

"I have a question too, as we are pausing for a second." Jo moved closer to the body. "I can see by the bruises on her inner thighs she was likely raped. Is there any evidence he interfered with the body post-mortem?"

"I'll need to complete the autopsy before coming to a cause conclusion but the sharp force trauma to the base of her skull would indicate he severed her spinal cord." Wolfe looked at Jo. "She was alive when he stitched her arms to the sofa and sewed her face. There is hematoma and swelling that would indicate this happened six to twelve hours before death. There is indication of sexual activity prior to death and post-mortem. I found bleach inside her cavities, so it seems he wasn't taking any chances of leaving any trace DNA. No seminal fluid was discovered." He cleared his throat. "She was posed post-mortem and makeup applied and hair brushed."

"She was posed facing the door, so she could be seen by anyone walking inside." Jo stared at the images of the crime scene. "Do you think he went back to visit her more than once?"

"Yeah, the damage to the body would suggest at least three times." Wolfe raised blond eyebrows and his gray eyes held deep concern. "This is one sick puppy."

Beth exchanged a glance with Styles, who nodded at her. She took a step closer and stared at Cassie Burnham. "Does she have other significant injuries? I don't see defense wounds. This would indicate she didn't have time to fight back."

"Good pickup." Wolfe nodded to her. "She has bruising to the left side of her head, consistent with being struck by a right-handed assailant. The grazes on her knees and palms would suggest she fell onto the sidewalk, I found grit and dirt embedded in the flesh. So attacked from the side, fell to the ground, and then probably thrown into a vehicle. She must have been confined and given water laced with the fentanyl. The neat stitching tells me she didn't fight when he stitched her to the sofa or moved when he stitched her face."

Making her own conclusions, Beth could see everything clearly, all the killer's motives, but she needed to act dumb. "Why the smile and open eyes?" Beth looked at Jo. "It's clown-like, horrific not alluring."

"It's the same reason he posed her." Jo shook her head. "She represents a lover or someone he yearned for and couldn't have. He made her look seductive, eyes wide open and smiling a greeting. He faced her toward the door to welcome him each time he visited. To him she was beautiful."

"Oh, Lord." Carter shook his head. "How did someone get so twisted?"

"I can complete the finer details of the autopsy in your absence but I need to examine the sharp force trauma incision to establish cause of death." Wolfe indicated to Webber to assist him and they turned over the body.

Captivated, Beth watched closely as Wolfe went to work, expanding the incision and exposing the base of the skull. It was clear how the woman had died. One plunge with a sharp blade in the right place and death would be instantaneous. She waited for the verdict.

"Yeah, cause of death is a severed brain stem." Wolfe looked at them. "Any more questions? If not, I'll continue and send you a full report, so y'all can get back to hunting down this maniac."

A light flashed above the door and Emily left the room. She returned again shortly, frowning.

"Sorry to interrupt, Dad." Emily turned to Beth her expression grave. "That was your sheriff. There's been another murder."

TWENTY-THREE

Dazzled by the speed Wolfe put everything into motion, Beth slowly removed her gloves, face mask, and scrubs. In the hallway, Wolfe was issuing orders to his staff. She listened with interest.

"Em, put Cassie Burnham back on ice. We'll finish her later. Webber, make sure we have the casket with the cooler loaded into the chopper." He walked over to Beth. "Call Ryder and get him to send everyone coordinates. I'll go and do my preflight."

Nodding, Beth pulled out her phone and as she placed the call Jo came to her side.

"Do you mind if we observe?" Jo tossed her scrubs down a laundry chute. "If it's the same MO, we'll be able to help you with the grunt work. I believe Sheriff Ryder is all alone in Rattlesnake Creek?"

Holding the phone to her ear, Beth held up a finger. "Give me a second."

"We'd love to have you along." Styles came to her side. "I'll be topside with the guys doing a preflight check. Come up when you're ready to leave." He looked at Beth. "Wolfe has a

coffee machine in his office. Grab some to go." He whistled to
Bear and then headed for the stairs to the roof.

Beth stared after him as Ryder answered his phone. "It's
Beth. What do you have for me?"

*"It's an exact replica of the previous murder, right down to
the woman on the sofa staring at the back door."* Clearly
agitated, Ryder cleared his throat. *"It's darn-right creepy out
here. What's your ETA?"*

Beth checked her watch. "I'll message you when we're in
the air. Styles is doing his preflight check. We'll need an open
space to land three choppers. Where are you?"

"It's the same place as before." Ryder sounded incredulous.
*"The forest warden noticed the crows from the fire lookout and
called it in, so I came by and found her."*

Concerned, Beth chewed on her fingers and then dropped
her hand at Jo's inquisitive stare. "The same place, well that's a
first. Lock yourself inside your cruiser and park where you have
a three-sixty-degree view all around. If someone comes, take
images and then get the hell out of Dodge. Don't be a hero."

"Got it." He disconnected.

Shaking her head, Beth looked at Jo and gave her the details.
"He's taking 'returning to the scene of the crime' to a whole new
level. What do you make of his behavior?"

"Hmm, I figure he's done this before and we'll probably
be looking for mummified remains if we want to discover the
rest of his kills." Jo collected her purse from Wolfe's office,
took out a hairbrush, and brushed her hair, securing it with a
rubber band from around her wrist. She headed for the
counter at the back of Wolfe's office. "I'll set up the coffee
machine. It's a pod system, so it takes a little longer. Wolfe
has a ton of Thermoses in that closet over there. We'll need
two for each team. There are boxes of energy bars under the
counter. Grab a ton of those as well. We don't know how long
we'll be away, and if Styles is anything like Carter, he'll

appreciate something to eat. It's been a long morning for all of us."

Nodding, Beth went to work. Jo's expression of a ton of Thermoses wasn't a joke, nor were the boxes of energy bars stacked high under the counter alongside to-go cups. "Does he really need all this stuff?"

"He travels all over at a moment's notice and rarely stops to eat." Jo smiled at her. "So yeah, he does."

Contemplating Jo's assessment of the killer, she removed the lids from the containers and lined them up for Jo to fill. "In my experience, most serial killers work within a comfort zone. This kind of throws that theory out of the window."

"Not necessarily." Jo fed pods into the machine. "This might be his comfort zone for now. He most likely has others spread all over. Remember that these guys are smart and he would figure the cops wouldn't return to the scene anytime soon." She filled one Thermos and screwed on the lid before standing it on the counter beside Beth. "I imagine he's been watching and knew when you took away the body. You live in a mountainous area, so it would be easy enough to find a plateau and keep watch. He probably headed out the moment he noticed the sheriff leaving town or the FBI chopper."

Beth nodded and piled energy bars into three plastic carry bags. She already had a good idea of why he was reusing the cabin. "As Wolfe has determined, he returned a number of times to visit the corpse. I figure he couldn't give up Cassie Burnham and when we took her away, he replaced her immediately. That cabin has become his Shangri-la. It must fit perfectly into one of his fantasies. Wolfe mentioned at the crime scene that he'd taken a lock of hair as a trophy. I figure his fantasy involves a woman with long hair. If this latest one is another stripper, then knowing what triggers him will help narrow the search for suspects."

"I agree. We should include sex workers in our search for

similar crimes. The amount of makeup and the posing screams sex worker to me." Jo smiled at her. "You have a good handle on profiling. What's your specialty?"

Packing two Thermoses in each bag, she turned to meet Jo's gaze. The woman had a penetrating stare that reminded her of Wolfe. He had a way of seeing straight through people and she could almost feel Jo dissecting her psyche. "Cybercrime, but I've always been interested in profiling, especially serial killers. Psychopaths are both varied and interesting with their possible multiple psychoses. We can never really tell what we're dealing with."

"Oh, cybercrime. How interesting. You'd get along with Bobby Kalo." Jo took the bag Beth offered her. "We recruited him when he was a young kid. He'd gotten into trouble hacking the Pentagon. He's super smart, and although he has a few problems keeping within the law at times, he's worth his weight in gold."

Recalling the name, Beth left the bags on the table and pulled on her coat. "Yeah, I've heard of him. He's good." *But not as good as me.*

TWENTY-FOUR

Styles entered the coordinates from Beth's phone and then took the chopper high into the air, taking the lead back to Rattlesnake Creek. He glanced at Beth. "How did you get along with Jo Wells?"

"To be honest, I'm a little in awe of her." Beth poured coffee into two to-go cups and rested one in the cup holder for him. She ripped open an energy bar and rested it on the console. "Eat something. We won't be stopping for hours and after processing another crime scene we'll be exhausted. I don't want you falling asleep flying this thing."

Surprised by her concern, he smiled at her. "You care? This is a side of you I like. I figured you'd tear me a new one after I invited Jo and Carter into our case without discussing it with you first."

"We discussed calling Jo last night over dinner. I don't mind having them to consult with occasionally, but I figure we can handle this one alone. Don't you?" Beth opened an energy bar and took a bite. "And making sure you stay awake is self-preservation." She smiled at him. "Unless you plan to teach me how to fly this thing anytime soon."

Considering her request, Styles shrugged. "I can teach you in our downtime once you get the required license. That's if you have any downtime once you start messing around with that cabin."

"Probably not." Beth sipped her coffee. "When I'm done. I'm planning on doing some landscape painting. There is so much incredible scenery and, like fishing, painting can be very relaxing, no rushing around. I'll use the cabin as a base and chill out for a couple of days at a time between cases." She shot him a glance. "Unless you're planning on hanging around the office?"

Laughing, Styles shook his head. "Nope, I'll have my phone with me if anything happens." He shrugged. "We do have the money for a receptionist in our budget or an assistant. The bureau will arrange someone with the clearance to work with us. Then when we're away or taking some owed downtime, they can run the office in our absence." He flicked her a glance. "There are two empty apartments on the second floor they could use."

"You've never mentioned them before." Beth turned in her seat to stare at him. "I figured the second floor was locked and filled with eyes-only files. The elevator goes right past it."

Styles nodded. "Yeah, it doesn't have lighting. I turned everything off and programed the elevator to bypass it. It's the same footprint as our floor."

"Ah, I see." Beth thought for a beat and then shrugged. "I guess they could sort out the domestic nonsense that Ryder comes to you for assistance with all the time. I figure a secretary/management assistant would be very useful. We get calls all day from stupid people—they could handle them, our budget, and deal with emergencies. I think it's a good idea and I guess if we don't get along with them, they'll be reassigned."

After scanning the area and sending a murder of crows settled on the cabin roof scattering like buckshot, Styles dropped the chopper down as close to the front door as possible.

Ryder's cruiser was parked way out in the middle of the open area on the dry dirt, and it started heading toward them as he landed. "Okay, I'll put in a request." He powered down the engine and looked at her. "Don't hold your breath. It's difficult getting anyone out here. If we do, be prepared to make changes because they might not appreciate the way we skirt the rules. Allowing an outsider to join us might upset the applecart."

"On second thoughts, hold that request." Beth cleared her throat. "I figure we can handle the office alone." She grabbed a forensics kit from behind her seat. "I'm suiting up before we go near the cabin this time."

In a cloud of dust and noise, Carter and then Wolfe dropped down from the sky. Styles waited for the dust to settle and then climbed out. He suited up and wiped a large dollop of mentholated salve under his nose. He stood beside Beth and waited for the teams to arrive. As they headed toward him, they looked like a swarm of aliens all dressed in blue from head to foot and wearing face shields. He turned to Beth. "Maybe I'll take the front door this time."

"Good idea." Beth fell into step beside him as they walked slowly toward the cabin.

Crows circled above in a great cloud of black. It seemed that even the choppers wouldn't deter them from a potential meal. It was déjà vu all over again. They all stood back as Wolfe pushed open the front door and peered inside. Carter and Jo went around back after explaining that Jo wanted to get the full impact of the scene. He looked at Beth. "Is she for real?"

"Yeah, she likes to immerse herself in the killer and get inside their head to imagine what they're thinking." Beth shrugged. "Seems to me, it's kinda obvious." She turned to Ryder, who'd come to her side. "Any clue to who the victim is?"

"Yeah, a maybe at least." Ryder frowned behind his mask. "When I found the body, I called you and while I waited I called every saloon with a gentlemen's club in four counties and asked if any of their girls hadn't showed for work. Seems that Vicki Strauss didn't show Tuesday night. She's an exotic dancer who works at the Silver Nugget Saloon and lives on Riversedge. I called Sheriff Caleb Addams out of Serenity to do a welfare check on Vicki Strauss. Her neighbor informed him that every Tuesday she takes her garbage to the landfill and always takes her neighbor's recyclable as well, but she hasn't seen her return. He went and checked out the landfill and found her vehicle. No sign of Vicki." He indicated toward the cabin. "She has long blonde hair, slight build... just like the victim."

Running the cases through his mind, Styles turned to Beth. "He's widened his comfort zone."

"Maybe." Beth's eyes narrowed over the top of her mask. "Jo has the same theory as you. She also figures he stashed bodies all over. If he's collecting women from different counties, he's moving through his comfort zone. We have three towns in close proximity. All have gentlemen's clubs. What's the bet, he'll hit Rainbow next?"

TWENTY-FIVE

The decomposition of a body has its own distinct smell and it made Beth gag. Human or animal, the stench is the same and acts as a deterrent for the majority of carnivores coming close by, in a warning the remains are not fit for consumption. The built-in warning is ever present for most people, obviously not for the killer of Vicki Strauss. If the woman had been seen on Tuesday morning, the body was fresher than the previous victim, which would indicate that they had disturbed the killer midway through his fantasy. The medical examiner had found evidence to prove that the killer had returned at least three times to visit the last victim. The hairs on the back of her neck prickled a warning. Someone was watching her. Beth moved to the door and scanned the immediate area. As the lowlands bordered the forest, the only clear view would be from above. She tugged on Styles' arm and beckoned him outside. "This guy likes to come back and visit the bodies, so right now he would be angry with us. Someone like him would be keeping a close eye on his victim. He regards her as his property to do with as he wishes."

"He wouldn't be sitting around waiting all day for someone

to show." Styles stood hands on hips and scanned the area. "He wouldn't be able to walk this far from town, and I didn't see any vehicles apart from Ryder's in the vicinity."

Unable to shake the feeling of being watched, Beth shook her head. "Maybe he's perched up in the mountains somewhere?"

"Maybe, but there's still the timing." Styles shrugged. "It's not feasible unless he suspected we'd be here and from all accounts he believed we wouldn't search here again. If it hadn't been for the crows no one would have disturbed him. It's just as well the forest warden is on the ball."

Having a sudden thought, Beth pulled out her phone and checked the bars. "I have a strong signal here. If he's set up a motion detector camera and it goes straight to his phone, he'd be able to see everything we're doing and be able to hear everything we're saying." She stared at him. "They run on a tiny solar power panel. He could set it up and leave it. Plus, if he wanted to check out the victim, he'd be able to access the camera via his phone." She stared at him. "He wouldn't risk uploading to a computer or the cloud. It would be too risky, and anyone can hack it. He'd use a storage chip in the camera, or on a phone."

"Yeah, I agree." Styles shuddered and shook his head. "So, for him, he could look at his handiwork anytime it pleased him. He might have cameras set up all over and enjoys watching his victims decay." He turned to her. "If we find the camera, would you be able to trace the feed back to the phone?"

Beth shook her head. "Unlikely because the moment he knows we're onto him, he'll destroy the phone. He'll know because the phone will alert him we're here." She sighed. "It won't be his regular phone either. No one is that stupid. It will be a phone he'd picked up from somewhere, or from one of the victims, but if it's on a memory card, he'd be changing that regularly." She shrugged. "Security cameras are easily hacked and controlled. He'd know that, so I'm thinking wireless and the video is stored on his phone or it could be in the camera. If we find it, we can take a look, but leaving a memory card in a camera is reckless and from what we've seen so far, he's the opposite."

"Well, I'll be." Styles shielded his eyes from the sun. "This place has a loft." He pointed to the roof. "With a window." He turned to her. "Do solar panels work through glass?"

Nodding Beth followed him to the door. "Yeah, if the window is clean but if dirty, it diminishes the efficiency to some extent, although a camera doesn't use much power." She glanced at him. "The camera will have a rechargeable battery, so it will work twenty-four hours."

"So, do you figure he filmed the murder?" Styles' eyes flashed with interest.

Excitement shivered through Beth. "Yeah, I bet he did. He's sick enough and so darn sure he can't be caught he probably shares the images on the dark web. Many of them do. It's like a snuff movie club and there's a ton of them on there."

"If we find the memory card, and he's on the video, we'll be able to identify him." Styles headed away from the cabin. "I'm going to hunt down a solar panel."

Excited, Beth hurried after him. "The problem is, if he's sharing the footage, he'll be covering his face." She moved to his side and stared at the roof. "I've seen plenty of terrible images on the dark web and it's very rare for the perpetrator to show his face. They know law enforcement keeps it under surveillance and it would only take a trace of code to catch them. They're not that stupid."

Inside the cabin, Beth skirted around Wolfe's team and followed Styles. She stood to one side as he checked the ceilings in the hallway. The cord was hanging down between the bedroom doors and the steps to the loft came down smoothly when Styles pulled on it. "Hold up. What if he's hiding up there?"

"Hmm." Styles pulled his .357 Magnum from the shoulder holster and headed up the steps. "FBI, don't do anything stupid."

Heart pounding, Beth followed and, hearing Carter and Jo running toward them, she turned. "Look for a camera. It will be very small. We think the solar panel is in the loft."

"Gotcha." Carter turned on his heel and headed back to the family room with Jo close behind.

"No one is up here." Styles peered back down the steps. "It's a very small loft. I've found the solar panel right where you figured it would be under the window. I'll disconnect it and feed the wire back through the hole in the floor. Go back to the family room and I'll wiggle the wire. You should be able to locate the camera by backtracking the wiring."

Beth hurried back down the steps and went to the family room and joined the others. Everyone was staring around the room. Having used many surveillance cameras, she went to the front of the sofa. This area was the killer's main point of focus. Any device would be centered on the victim and would be placed to catch every movement, so high on the wall or set at an angle. Her gaze went to an old clock hanging above the door to the family room. "Look up there." She pointed and Carter stretched up and pulled down the clock. The long wire behind it moved as Styles pushed it from above. "That's it. That isn't a keyhole in the face, it's the camera lens." She took the clock and turned it over. She removed the backing and set in the back was a tiny camera. She pulled out the camera, turned it over, flipped open the back, and stared in surprise. "We have a memory card." She looked at Wolfe. "Have you a small bag I can use to transport it and tweezers to remove it? I don't want to touch it."

"Sure, I'll get one for you, but let me look at it first." Wolfe nodded to her and held out his hand. "Ah, it's a common card. I'll be able to read it on my laptop." He looked at his daughter.

"Bring the laptop over here." He removed the chip with care and slotted it into the microcard reader.

The video started to run and everyone stood transfixed as a naked man carried a woman through the front door and into the family room. The killer was a tall man wearing boots and a hideous mask. Beth stared at him, searching for any distinguishing marks, but he had none. The mask covered his head. Only a section of his mouth and eyes could be seen. The eye color was hidden in shadows. There was no way to identify the man on the screen.

"Just a minute." Wolfe paused the playback and zoomed in on the victim. "Her thighs are bruised. He's been holed up with her in another place. Look at her. She's dirty and there's ligature marks on her wrists." He turned and looked at the body, moving around to examine the victim's hands. "They're not so defined as in the video, so he held her here long enough for the marks to subside prior to death. She's been washed post-mortem as well. Even her nails have been cleaned. From the video she's been on a dirt floor. In a root cellar maybe?"

"So, he has a nice little hideaway somewhere close by to keep them before he brings them here to kill." Jo raised both eyebrows. "He obviously needs time to set up the camera before he risks bringing the victims here. You mentioned being drugged using fentanyl. Well that's a powerful drug used in surgery. It's no wonder they don't wake up and escape."

As the video played, Beth watched in morbid fascination as the naked man sewed the victim to the sofa and made the facial changes. When he was done, he used smelling salts to revive her and the horror went up a notch. There was no sound but she could imagine the woman's terrified screams. Beside her, Ryder heaved and ran outside. After a few more minutes of violent depravity, Beth glanced at the stony expressions around her. Jo was shaking her head but hadn't averted her eyes from the small screen. She cleared her throat. "I think we've seen enough. We can analyze it later."

"There are hours of footage here." Wolfe stopped the playback and removed the card. He dropped it into a small plastic container, sealed it, and offered it to Beth. "Send me a copy. It will clarify my autopsy findings and I figure Jo and Carter will want to see it. I think we're done here."

Beth waved away the container. "You take it. It's evidence."

"I'll send you a copy." He stared at Beth. "I'll get the victim back to the morgue. This is an exact copy of the first murder. I'll do an autopsy, and if I find anything new, I'll call you. Unless you want to observe?" His phone rang. "Wolfe." He listened for a while. "I'm in Rattlesnake Creek. I can be there in twenty minutes. Is there a place to land the chopper? Send me the coordinates." He disconnected and looked at the team. "I have another homicide out of Running Water. They believe it's connected to the recent murders around Billings. Same MO: a young woman, suspected rape and torture. Her body was covered with branches and grass clippings like the others." He looked at Webber. "We'll get Vicki Strauss into a body bag and into the casket. I have everything I need from the scene. Pack everything up. Get at it, people."

A tingle of awareness raced up Beth's spine. Her next victim, Bill, aka Levi Jackson, had been a busy boy.

TWENTY-SIX

Outside the cabin, Beth stripped off her face protector and took a few deep breaths. She turned as Jo Wells came to her side. "So what do you think?"

"I have the same conclusions as before." Jo removed her gloves with a snap. "The main problem is he likes to enjoy his victims over time. Now that's been interrupted, he'll escalate and become careless. You'll need to be careful."

"Call us if you need backup." Carter tossed a toothpick into his mouth and smiled around it. "We can be here in half an hour or so. Day or night."

Liking Carter, Beth smiled. He wasn't a threat to her and she didn't feel like he was probing her mind. She hoped her mask hadn't slipped in front of Jo, but she doubted it. Right now, she only wanted to help. "Thanks, we appreciate the assistance. It was good to meet you."

"Likewise." Carter tipped his hat and strolled back to his chopper.

"See you next time." Jo gave her a wave and followed.

Seeing Ryder looking shaken and leaning against a tree, she went to his side. "You okay?"

"Yeah." He looked at her, his eyes red-rimmed. "I can't understand how you can all stand around watching a woman being brutalized and it doesn't affect you?"

Beth shrugged and peeled off her coveralls. "It's because we've seen it so many times before that we become desensitized. It's not that we don't care. It's just that we need to see what's happening so we can prevent it happening again. Can you understand that?"

"I guess." Ryder waved toward the cabin. "When I took the position of sheriff, I wasn't expecting to deal with brutal murders. It's unimaginable to believe that someone who could do that is walking around town."

Pushing her mind past the images on the screen, Beth stared into his bewildered expression. "When you were hunting down miners with certain shifts, did you consider miners from different towns?"

"Not for the Cassie Burnham murder but I made a list." Ryder pulled out his phone. "Gold Rush Mine has a variety of shifts available. I'll hunt down miners who were free Friday through Wednesday. If we add being free on Tuesday to the suspects list, we can cut it down some." He shrugged. "It's going to take time going through it because we can't haul them out of the mines to interview them."

Styles had Bear out of the chopper and was throwing a toy for him as he checked over the chopper once more. Beth headed in his direction with Ryder at her side. "We're concentrating on miners but who else moves around the three towns on a regular basis?"

"Delivery drivers, mail, doctors, nurses, cattlemen, produce." Ryder shook his head. "A ton of people but not all of them visit the clubs."

Beth nodded. "We need to discover which ones of them do. We also need to inform the clubs that their dancers are being murdered so they can pass on the information. It will make them more aware that there's a predator out there."

"I can do that, no worries." Ryder opened his cruiser door and took out his hat. "I'm not a rookie. I'll do my share of interviews. I won't walk into a situation. I'm not stupid and we'll need to split up and find this guy before another woman is murdered."

"You've seen what this man is capable of, Cash." Styles walked up behind them. "Is there anyone you trust you can deputize for a couple of days?"

"Yeah, I guess." Ryder smiled at Styles. "I'll see what I can do."

"Okay." Styles slapped him on the back. "We're heading back to the office now. Send me your list of possible suspects and we'll remove anyone who doesn't fit the general description of the guy in the video. I'm thinking you don't want to sit in on the screening?"

"No thanks." Ryder messed with his phone. "I've emailed it. I'll hunt down the other possibles Beth suggested when I get back to the office." He slid inside his vehicle. "Catch you later."

Beth climbed into the chopper and attached her headset. She had been considering long and hard about catching the killer. "Jo figures we've disturbed the killer's fantasy. We've found the body before he's had time to come back and visit it. We removed Cassie from the house and he struck again. Jo figures he's going to take another woman in the next couple of days. It makes sense to me that Rainbow is possibly the next place he'll hit. It's in his comfort zone and he'll feel safe there. We'll need a plan to stop him. I'm not convinced this perp is a miner. Ryder mentioned a variety of people who regularly move from town to town and although the miners are more likely to frequent the gentlemen's clubs, they're not the only people interested in watching women dancing."

"What are you getting at, Beth?" Styles flicked her a

concerned stare. "Seems to me you're giving us a mountain of suspects to investigate. The most logical are the miners—they fit into the timeline and visited the club—so why deviate from the plan?"

Beth poured coffee into the to-go cups, glad to see it was still hot. "I think we need to cut corners and get moving on this investigation before he kills again. There's only the three of us working this case, so we need to take drastic action."

"I'm all for drastic action." Styles took the coffee she handed him. "What have you conjured up now? Is it legal?"

Shaking her head in disbelief, Beth snorted. "Of course, it's legal. I'm thinking a sting operation. I figure I should go under-cover as a dancer. I've already told you I know how to pole dance, so it wouldn't be difficult for me. I'd slip in just fine. Of course, we'd just have to clear it with the management of the club. It's the only way we'll catch this guy."

"What about all the men staring at you?" Styles took the chopper high over the snowcapped mountains. "I've seen your reaction when men give you unwanted attention. I don't think you would be able to handle it inside a club for a couple of days and you've already said that this man plans everything ahead of time."

Beth nodded. "I'm convinced he does, and just for the record, when I went undercover in the brothel I handled it just fine." She shrugged. "I got the job done fast and saved lives. This is no different and this time I'll have you watching my back. You figure you can mix with the locals without being noticed, so I'll have you in the room with me all the time I'm onstage." She thought for a beat. "Think about it. We've taken away the killer's prize, so he'll grab whoever he can find. I mean to make him come for me."

"And how exactly do you intend to do that?" Styles headed the chopper toward Rattlesnake Creek.

Smiling Beth sipped her coffee. "When I've watched the

video, I'll let you know. This killer has specific tastes. From looking at the victims after he's done with them, he wants big eyes with plenty of makeup and red lips. I can make my eyes big and totally different. I have a variety of contact lenses I can use, wigs, and I'll attach long red nails. Trust me, he won't be able to resist me."

"You're batshit crazy." Styles chuckled as he landed on the roof of the FBI building.

Unconcerned, Beth shrugged. "You've mentioned that before. Maybe that's what it takes to catch this guy."

"Look. I know you're darn good at undercover work but it's risky." Styles turned to her. "Before we consider it as a last resort, at least interview the other two possible suspects first. We have a wider timeframe now and one might slip up. We'll need time to set up the sting with the club in Rainbow anyway. If we don't find more possibles tomorrow, I'll greenlight your idea."

"Okay, fine, but we don't have much time to get things rolling." Beth blew out a long breath. "He's escalating and we might miss our chance and some other poor woman will be killed. We could easily get everything set up and people inter-viewed this afternoon and tomorrow. I could go under tomorrow night, then I'll be there Thursday and Friday nights. It will fit into the killer's schedule."

"Okay but this time, we take all precautions." Styles nodded slowly as he considered her idea. "I'll be hiding close by when you leave the club and we'll have Ryder as backup. He's a fine marksman. Don't underestimate him." He sighed. "I know people in Rainbow. There are plenty of empty miners' cabins we can use. To appear legit, you'll need to have a place to stay. If you do manage to get the killer's attention, I figure he'll follow you to see where you live. Do you think he'll grab you when you leave the club or wait until you reach the cabin?"

Thinking the plan through, Beth collected the bag with the

Thermoses and energy bars and tossed the empty to-go cups inside. "He's anxious and that will make him reckless. He might follow me home to see if I live alone and attack me at once. Or he'll wait and grab me the next night. By then he'll know when I leave the club and when I arrive home alone. If you find me a secluded little cottage, he'll probably be waiting in my yard for when I get home. He'll be watching closely, so if you plan on keeping me alive, you'll need to be one step ahead of him."

TWENTY-SEVEN

Anger trembles through me as I stare at the black screen on my phone. It's a useless object now the cops have discovered my surveillance camera. I rip open the phone, tear out the SIM, and scratch it with my knife, and then after wiping the phone clean, toss it into the fast-flowing river. I have many more stashed in a secret place, so it's no great loss. The camera, on the other hand, will be difficult to replace, mainly because the cops would be watching to see if anyone purchases a replacement. It's just as well, I have another set up in a cabin in the forest out at Rainbow. The cops are generally stupid. After finding two bodies in the same cabin, they'll assume I'm going to take another girl from Rattlesnake Creek. Although maybe they'll change their mind when they discover Vicki Strauss was out of Serenity, but they'll never consider Rainbow.

Tempters, the sweet little club set on the back of the Little Gem Saloon, is one of my favorite places. The girls there are generous with their time but I haven't found one I want. The last time I spoke to the manager he mentioned they had new girls coming in this week. Tempters has an agreement with a club in Bozeman to exchange girls every three months to give the clubs variety. Excitement sends shivers down my spine. I can't wait to watch a group of new potential darlings dance so I can consider them for my collection. I'm sure they'll do their thing and try their best to lure me, tempt me, and I'm sure this time, one will win. People don't understand why they are so important to me. I read the papers and the trash-talking about me. Don't they understand it's their fault for tempting me?

My back still holds the scars from my father's humiliation. Dragged in front of his congregation, stripped, and flogged. I never cried because I'd seen the self-flagellation scars on my father's back. He was a sinner just like me. He died knowing his punishment didn't work, because the day I pressed the pillow over his nose, I whispered close to his ear, "I still crave a woman's body and soon I'll have a hundred of them all sexy, and smiling as they wait for me with open arms."

TWENTY-EIGHT

Pushing the crime scene images, the disgusting video of the murder, and what followed in the cabin far from her mind, Beth headed for her apartment. The grime and stink of the crime scene clung to her, even with the coveralls, and she needed to scrub it away. When she'd suggested going undercover, she'd seen the concern in Styles' eyes, so agreed to get cleaned up and then head back out to find the next two possible suspects and shake them down. Her head should have been in the game, centered on the case, but the moment Wolfe had received the phone call informing him another body had been found near Billings, her heart had picked up a beat. Jackson was on the move again and killing women. He was so sure of himself, she'd bet he was using the same scam to get the women into his van. Since his acquittal, he figured he was untouchable—and why not? The kills were so random because he didn't need to plan anything. All he had to do was pin a flyer to a noticeboard and wait for the next victim to call him. If it was a man, he'd only need to say the position was taken and send them on their way. The workers in the roadhouses likely saw him come by frequently to post flyers because he used the noticeboards to get handyman jobs and posted them all over three towns around Billings. How easy would it be to place two notices. No one would look twice. His plan was ingenious, but she could use it to her advantage. Trying to work out which roadhouse he'd use next would be the key because once the current case was over, Beth would only have a day or two before someone noticed her missing.

As she used the hairdryer, she sketched out a plan to take out Levi Jackson. Transport was essential and she'd need to be seen somewhere away from the murder scene at the time of Jackson's death. She'd make sure people would see her, get a motel room, and gather a few things from local stores to give her an alibi. She'd leave her phone switched off in her vehicle. It could still be traced to prove both her phone and car were miles away from her victim. If Styles suddenly decided to hunt her down, which she doubted, she'd talk her way out of any suspicion by hinting at meeting someone at a bar or something. In fact, she could easily set up something like that before she caught the bus. The lack of available women around the mining towns would make chatting to men easy. She'd get into her disguise, buy a burner, and take the bus to the roadhouse. It would be hit and miss. If she arrived and didn't find a notice offering a room and a job as a ranch hand, she'd take the next bus back and then wait a couple of days. If a case came in, she'd have no choice but to work it with Styles. She'd wait for Jackson to kill again and recalculate the odds of where next he'd probably set his trap.

Dragging her mind back to the current case and Styles' insistence to interview suspects after they'd grabbed something to eat, she gathered her hair in a ponytail and pinned it up. She covered her hair with a woolen cap and would wear sunglasses when interviewing suspects in the Cassie Burnham and Vicki Strauss cases because if she planned to go undercover, she'd be dealing with a very smart killer. He might recognize her even with a disguise and she didn't plan on dying anytime soon.

Heading back to the office, the smell of pizza filled the elevator. She smiled. Trust Styles to order a pizza to save time. She walked into the office to find Styles and Ryder on the phone, two empty open pizza boxes on his desk, and a closed one on hers. She nodded to them and opened the box to grab a slice. From their conversation, they were hard at work hunting down suspects. The microchip they'd taken from the camera had been entered into evidence by Wolfe, but when she checked her mail she had a copy of the video in her inbox. She had no reason to watch it again and, instead, searched the files for Levi Jackson's kills. The murders weren't linked to him in any files since his acquittal, and the local press had given the files a name: The Roadside Strangler.

It was fortunate that the call had come into Wolfe in their presence. Any suspicion of her scanning the files could be covered by professional curiosity. Biting back a smile, Beth read the initial statement from the first on-scene officer and the person who'd discovered the body. Crime scene photographs taken by the first on scene showed a very familiar MO. The body of a young woman was partially covered with branches and lawn clippings. She had no doubt the killer was Levi Jackson and did a search for roadhouses near bus stations in the local area of running water. Next, she accessed the CCTV camera outside the roadhouse and hacked into the files. She saw a young woman get off a bus and look around bewildered before going inside. Beth ran the video forward almost an hour before the woman came out and headed toward what she imagined was a parking lot. If Natalie Kingsley, the woman who survived Levi Jackson, had given an accurate statement, she had met Jackson in the parking lot outside the roadhouse. It was the same scenario and one he used over and over because it worked. Beth nodded, convinced this was Levi Jackson. He'd played out this scene so many times before, and after being caught once on a CCTV camera, he'd never allow it to happen again unless he planned it. It was obvious to her trained eye the roadhouse and surrounds had been reconned to gauge the sweep of the camera in order to hide Jackson's van. Beth sighed as the young woman waved and then disappeared out of sight. *No doubt into Jackson's van and a ride straight to hell.*

"Beth." Styles pushed away from his desk. "We've found a couple of possible suspects and they're in town now. We'll split up. Cash has asked a friend to go with him to talk to one of them. We'll take the other."

Folding a slice and wrapping it in a paper towel, Beth pushed the box of uneaten pizza into the refrigerator. She laid the slice on the counter and pulled on her coat. "I'll eat on the way." She pushed a bottle of water into her coat pocket and followed him out the door. "Who have we got?"

"Joseph Crenshaw." Styles led the way into the elevator. "He's been known to visit the clubs and he was seen in Outlaws the night Cassie Burnham went missing. He's a carpenter but more of a jack-of-all-trades. He gets calls to pick up donations for the local charity, so moves all over. The furniture he recycles, the rest goes to the local thrift shop. His wife runs the recycled furniture store in town, and he splits a portion of the profits with a local charity. He's happily married with three kids—but that hasn't stopped a man killing." He turned to Beth. "His workshop is out back of the store. I called the gun and ammo store next door and asked them if they'd seen him around today, and Jim, the manager, said he could hear him working in his shed."

"My guy is Rowdy Bright." Ryder checked his notes. "Rowdy is a driver and delivers cold goods to neighboring towns. He often stays over to collect another load to bring back and frequents the clubs in the four neighboring towns. He does round trips three times a week, so matches the times the victims went missing."

Taking in all the information, Beth nodded. "Okay, let's see what they have to say." She looked at Ryder. "It's great you've managed to deputize someone as backup even for a day. You've seen the kind of man we're dealing with, so keep your distance and don't spook him. Keep the questions general as if you're bored."

"Yeah, I have the general idea." Ryder rolled his eyes and led the way from the elevator. "I'll call when I leave. Bright is at Outlaws, at the bar, so I'll ask him to step outside."

"Maybe ask TJ to do that?" Styles shrugged. "Walking into a bar in uniform will get undue attention."

Beth swallowed a bite of pizza and stared at them as she walked from the building. "You've deputized TJ?"

"He was the only person I could trust not to spread information on the case all over town." Ryder shot her a glance. "He's respected in town. People won't want to mess with me with him backing me up." His lips curled into a smile. "TJ has a reputation much like Styles. If you get my meaning?"

Nodding, Beth hurried to Styles' truck. The wind was cruel and came in hard wintery blasts. "Good luck! We'll all meet at your office when we're done."

"Sure, that works for me." Ryder climbed into his cruiser and headed out of the parking lot.

Looking at Styles, Beth raised both eyebrows. "You never told me about TJ's reputation. He seems such a nice guy, really friendly and helpful. I like him."

"And I figured you could profile a person or see them for their true self in an instant." Styles grinned at her. "TJ is ex-military as well and fit. I know it's hard to believe but you're not the only rattlesnake in town. He might look like a teddy bear, but trust me, that guy can fight like a grizzly."

TWENTY-NINE

Beth Katz confused Ryder. He shook his head, not quite sure what to make of her. When he pulled up outside Tommy Joe's Bar and Grill and TJ slid into the passenger seat, he gave him a rundown on the potential suspect. "So, you go inside and ask him to come outside for a chat. Styles figures I'll spook him if I go into Outlaws in uniform."

"Okay, I can do that." TJ turned to stare at him. "We go back a long way. What's eating at you? You've been angry since Beth came to town. Has she been stepping on your toes?"

Not sure if he should speak his mind, Ryder headed toward Outlaws. "Kinda." He flicked him a glance. "She's prickly and treats me like a rookie. I figure she forgets I'm the law in my counties, not her. The FBI are only in on the case because I invited them. There are only two murders. There's no reason to believe this is a serial killer. Not yet anyway."

"I know the deal." TJ shrugged. "She took some time to thaw with me too. I don't figure she really likes anyone. I haven't seen her interested in anyone yet and she gets plenty of attention. The guys all want to get to know her better. Smart, beautiful, and with a great job, she's a catch."

Not wanting to consider Beth's looks, Ryder turned onto the industrial area and weaved through the backroads to get to Outlaws Saloon. "Maybe she doesn't like men, but that's not my concern. She talks down to me and it's embarrassing. I told her I wasn't a rookie and she has backed off some, but before she was intense. I don't believe she's interested in forming attachments here. I figure she plans to hightail it back to DC as soon as possible. She's a city girl through and through."

"Give her some time." TJ looked at him as they stopped in the Outlaws parking lot. "She's in an unfamiliar environment and all alone. No friends to talk to and they stuck her with Styles. He wouldn't be too pleased having another agent living under his roof either. Man, they must be in close proximity twenty-four/seven and you know he likes to be alone." He shrugged. "I'm not surprised she's a little defensive."

Nodding, Ryder could see his point of view. "Yeah, I guess. I know her main problem: she's used to having things done yesterday and having a big-city team to back her. Maybe that's frustrating for her and she takes it out on me? I don't have the resources for an instant response but I'm doing my best."

"That's all you can do." TJ smiled. "I've seen her nice side. She can be very charming when she turns off the FBI. Maybe tell her how you feel? Give her another chance and I bet a dollar to a dime you'll be best buddies before long." TJ pushed open the door. "Hang five, I'll go and get Rowdy."

As Rowdy Bright walked out of Outlaws, Ryder took out his phone and pulled up the image taken from the video of the killer. The team had averaged his height as six feet and weight at about one-eighty to two hundred pounds. Muscular but not cut like Styles or TJ, this man had some body fat but not a great deal. Wolfe had estimated his age between thirty and forty. The problem was the killer could be any of at least fifty men in town. With his face obscured and no tattoos, scars, or other identifying features, the naked man on the screen, wearing boots and gloves, was practically unidentifiable. The mask or something similar was available at many stores for Halloween. It had become a popular theme of late, so chasing down people who'd purchased the masks would be near impossible, if anyone kept records, which he doubted. He watched Bright's body language as TJ guided him toward the cruiser. Ryder ran questions through his head and, rather than taking notes, activated the recorder app on his phone. He slipped the phone into his top pocket and opened his jacket.

"Is there a problem, Sheriff?" Bright slid into the back seat with TJ beside him.

Ryder looked at him. "Maybe." He removed his phone and slid it onto the console between the seats. "I'm recording our little chat. It's difficult to take notes in the cruiser."

"Okay, whatever." Bright lifted one shoulder and his cheeks colored. "I didn't mean to touch that dancer. It was a mistake. I was pushing bills into her costume and it kinda just happened."

Gathering his thoughts, Ryder turned in his seat to look at him. "It's not about you groping the girls, and they'll ban you if you do it again, but let's cut to the chase, you do know why we're here, right?"

"I've heard talk." Bright leaned back in his seat, his hat in his hand. "I know one of the dancers is missing but I didn't have anything to do with that. I like to watch them but I didn't abduct her or anything."

Narrowing his gaze, Ryder looked at him. "Who mentioned anything about abduction? What makes you think she was abducted? Has anyone mentioned her being taken?"

"Not exactly, no, but a couple of the guys said that two FBI agents interrogated them and mentioned she'd gone missing." Bright turned the hat around in his fingers. "I had a private dance with Cassie last Friday night, is all. She was busy and had a full list of men wanting her to dance for them. Maybe you need to be looking at the others."

Sighing, Ryder shook his head. "We're working through the list, and while we're here, I know you frequent the Silver Nugget Saloon out at Serenity. You were seen there Tuesday night. Is that a regular visit? Do you like to drop by the clubs when you stay over for work?"

"Yeah, me and a ton of miners." Bright looked from one to the other. "Why?"

Ryder shrugged. "Because we need to know who else was there, and as you travel around the counties, you'd recognize people." It was common knowledge around town that one of the dancers was missing. The miners had told everyone and gossip spreads like wildfire in a small town. The murders they'd managed to keep under wraps, and only the killer would know the truth. He watched Bright carefully. "Yeah, we believe someone abducted Cassie Burnham last Friday night and maybe the same person is responsible for Vicki Strauss' disappearance as well. You'd know Vicki, right? You were on her list over at the Silver Nugget. Do you recall anyone who is usually at the club or do you know anyone who travels regular and visits the clubs on certain days like you?"

"I don't know all the miners by name, but some take on odd shifts at different mines." Bright swiped a hand over his chin. "Many come to town just looking for work and pick up the odd shifts. They're not under contract. They're mainly laborers."

The man wasn't telling Ryder anything he didn't already know. "Yeah, that's all well and good, but I need names. As your name is the only one on my list so far, I suggest you stop protecting people and give me the names of anyone you saw in Outlaws last Friday night and at the Silver Nugget last Tuesday, and don't tell me you don't talk to people. I hear you're a social butterfly."

"Darn it, my attention is usually on the girls, but I did sit and wait for both the girls you mentioned and chatted with a couple of the men, yeah." Bright moved around in his seat. "I know Joe Crenshaw, mainly because we cross paths a lot of the time. I play pool with him some nights when we're waiting for our turn, you know, for a private dance. There's no sex involved if that's what you're thinking."

Ryder shook his head. "Go on. Who else?"

"Two miners I know but they hang out with different guys. They stay at the same motel as I do. Some of the others have trailers." Bright chuckled. "People call them snail miners, because they carry their homes with them everywhere they go."

Impatient, Ryder glared at him. "Names and you can go."

"Steve Smith and Jace Conan." Bright looked sheepish. "You ain't gonna tell them I ratted on them, are you?"

Shaking his head, Ryder allowed the implications to filter through his mind. "Did you say all these men had private dances with both Cassie Burnham and Vicki Strauss on the nights they disappeared? Are you sure?"

"Yeah, I'm sure. They were on the list after me. I like to get in early when the girls are enthusiastic and don't smell like the guys they've been sitting on." Bright's eyes flashed from one to the other. "Anything else?"

Trying to make sure he'd covered all the bases, Ryder held up a hand. "One more thing. You move around some, right? Do you know where all the old miners' cabins are located?"

"Some, not all. There's a ton of them all over." Bright raised both brows and smiled. "Looking to buy yourself a secluded man cave? These dancers don't mind a few extracurricular activities." His eyes flashed with amusement. "I guess you'd be in the spotlight if you decided to take a dancer home, right? Being the sheriff and all?"

Annoyed, Ryder shot a glance at TJ, who was grinning like the Cheshire cat, and then back to Bright. "So you've heard talk about people using the cabins for as you say, 'extracurricular activities'?"

"The subject has come up and don't ask me who. Some

places I just won't go." Bright shook his head. "It ain't none of my business."

Waving a hand, Ryder stared at him. "Okay, you can go." He handed him a card. "Any talk, any names you can find for me, call me. Trust me, it will be in your best interests to cooperate." He stopped the recording and waited for Bright to slip from the cruiser and shuffle back into the saloon. He looked at TJ. "What do you think?"

"I'm not a profiler but that guy has always been shady." TJ shrugged. "Give the recording to the FBI. They'll sort it."

Ryder waited for TJ to climb back into the passenger seat. "Okay, your place for coffee and then I'll get back to the office and wait for them. It seems to me Bright is a possible suspect. He ticks most of the boxes. He had opportunity, was there for both abductions, moves around. Has a truck to carry bodies." He sighed. "The only thing I can't work out is motive. What motive would he have for killing women?"

"If you knew that, you'd solve the case." TJ shrugged. "Do you want pie with that coffee?"

Smiling, Ryder nodded. "Sure. Knowing Styles, he'll be working past supper."

THIRTY

The moment Styles pulled into a parking space beside the recycled furniture store, Beth was out of the truck and had her nose stuck to the store window. He let Bear out of the truck and then moved to her side. "See something you like?"

"Oh yeah." She turned to look at him and her smile faded to a frown. "Imagine if I purchased a ton of furniture from here and then discovered he was the killer? I couldn't stay in a place with things he'd worked on all around me. After seeing that tape, it would be a constant memory."

Seeing her concern, Styles shrugged. "There are more stores in Rainbow, and Spring Grove has those handcrafted-goods stores you're looking for. It's close to the res and there are some great Native American furniture stores there you really should consider. Some of the pieces they create are very beautiful. Some have Native American jewelry as well. If you want something special, you should look there. Both regular stores are on Main. I purchased my sofa and those padded chairs in my apartment there, and they delivered them as well."

"Perfect." She turned to look at him eyes dancing. "Do they have a decent motel? There's so much I want to buy, and I like to take my time and see everything. I'll never get to look at everything in one trip. I figured if I could use a motel as a base, I could drive around collecting furnishings. If I get bored with that, which I doubt, I'll go hunt down some nice places to go and paint the scenery. I'm not planning on painting landscapes now but maybe the next time we have some downtime." She met his gaze. "It would be like taking a vacation."

Styles walked past the storefront and headed down an alleyway leading to the back. "That sounds like fun, but please remember the wildlife, Beth. You can't just go wandering off on your lonesome into the forest or along the river."

"I'll be armed." Beth sighed. "I do take notice. I'll carry bear spray and have my weapon with me. I'm not planning on being anyone's dinner."

At the sound of *cluck, cluck*, Styles stopped mid-stride and reached for Bear's collar. "Oh no. Chickens."

"So?" Beth stared at him mystified.

The only thing that terrified Bear was chickens. He had no idea why, but at the sight of one of them, the dog went into full panic mode. He glanced at Beth. "Run back to the truck and open the door for Bear, he'll go ballistic at the sight of chickens. Call him to you and hopefully he won't see them. I'll stay here and wave them away."

As Beth took off, four chickens came around the side of the house, pecking and scratching at the ground. Styles tried to turn Bear back to face the truck, but without warning, the dog stiffened like a day-old corpse. So frightened of the small brown hens, Bear's entire body trembled. The next second, his eyes went wild. Styles hung on to his harness, but the dog was remarkably strong, and as a few chickens wandered across the pathway, the dog suddenly bucked and made a strangled whine. Unable to distract or move him, Styles bent and picked him up and then ran to the truck. Beside it, Beth stared at them wide-eyed. "Grab his blanket." Styles pushed Bear inside and, taking the blanket from Beth, covered Bear and rubbed him, saying soothing words. He looked at Beth. "It's okay, he won't move. We'll have trouble getting him out of the truck when we get back to the office." He sighed. "The vet suggested carrying a tranquilizer for him as we live in a rural area. I usually scope out the area before I let him out of the truck. We cope with it. It's the chickens that sneak up on us that are the problem."

"Wow! You said he was afraid of chickens, but I thought you were joking." Beth shook her head. "Poor Bear. When did this first happen?"

Concerned for his trembling companion, Styles shut the door and shrugged. "Something happened before I got him. I'd say not long before either because he wouldn't have been used as a K-9 with a serious mental issue." He headed back down the alleyway scattering the chickens. "Maybe seeing them triggers the memory of an explosion. He was injured and his handler KIA as a result of an explosion. It might have happened then, I don't know. We just deal with it. It's fine."

"Now I know, I'll scout ahead next time and check out the yards." Beth smiled at him. "I like Bear. I want to help him. Can't we take him to a dog shrink or something?"

Staring at her in disbelief. "I don't figure there's much calling for a dog shrink in these parts, Beth. We're lucky to have a vet and he suggests tranquilizers. I don't want a zombie dog. I'll find another way." He smiled at her. "And thanks. All help greatly appreciated."

The sound of someone using an electric sander came from a large timber construction out back of the furniture store. He glanced at Beth. "Do you want to take the lead on this one?"

"No, you talk to him." She blew out a breath. "I'll do a little profiling and watch for any telltale signs of psychopathic behavior."

As they walked along the alleyway, Styles checked his revolver. When interviewing a suspect, it was a habit to unzip his jacket and make sure his weapon slid easily from the shoulder holster, and although he rarely needed to draw it, having it in plain sight gave an unspoken warning. In truth, he preferred to bring a perp down using hand-to-hand combat skills if possible. Guns, especially his .357 Smith & Wesson Magnum, sure made a mess he'd rather avoid, and the paperwork after a shooting was murder. When they reached the open door, he could make out a man who fit their profile sanding a fine-looking wooden chair. He knocked on the door. "Joseph Crenshaw? FBI Agent Styles and my partner, Agent Katz. May we have a moment of your time?"

"Sure." Crenshaw put down his sander and brushed the dust from his hands on a thick leather apron. "What can I do for you? I haven't collected any stolen furniture, have I?"

Styles explained why they were there. "Does your wife know you frequent the gentlemen's clubs and pay for private dances?"

"She's very understanding, and yeah, she knows." Crenshaw shrugged. "She doesn't like me watching porn at home—she's worried the kids might find it one day—so we made a compromise. It's not like I'm being unfaithful. I'm just watching, not touching, right? She isn't concerned about what I do outside the home. What I'd like to know is how you found out what I do in my spare time? Most of the men there keep it confidential."

Styles nodded. "I'm sure they do. We got the list of bookings for private dances from the managers of the clubs. Your name was on the list and you were at both of the clubs where dancers went missing."

"I haven't got them." Crenshaw shrugged and smiled. "Be my guest, look around all you want. My wife might be okay with me watching strippers, but bringing them home is crossing the line, and having a scantily clad woman cavorting in the family room would be a nightmare to explain to my kids." He chuckled. "Trust me, I'm one of many married men who go to the clubs. In case you haven't noticed the entertainment around town is kinda thin on the ground?" He gave Styles a long look. "I've seen you there too, so don't act all high and mighty. We all need something to dream about, right?"

"We've established you were at the clubs at the times we mentioned." Beth exchanged a glance with Styles and then looked at Crenshaw. "You seem to know the local crowd. Did you notice anyone out of place or acting suspicious?"

"Nope, same people, I guess." Crenshaw shrugged nonchalantly. "I wasn't really taking too much notice of the guys."

"Okay." Beth lifted her chin. "You seem to be on good terms with the dancers. Did they mention anything about being concerned about any of the patrons?"

"I don't figure my conversations with lap dancers is for your tender ears, Agent Katz." Crenshaw turned to Styles and winked. "Right, Agent Styles? What's said in there is between me and the girl."

Clearing his throat, Styles nodded and pulled out a card. "If you hear anything or something comes to mind about either of the missing women, please give me a call."

"Sure." Crenshaw tossed the card on the bench, picked up the sander and went back to work.

Leading the way back to his truck, Styles turned to Beth. "What do you think?"

"He sure has the charm of a psychopath, but I guess from a man's point of view he's living the life. He has a job, a wife, kids, and spare money to push down strippers' underwear." Beth gave him a long hard stare, anger flashed, and her lips flattened. "I wonder what his wife really thinks about having a stripper undulating on her husband's lap? He's a big guy. Maybe she's too scared to say anything?"

Shrugging, Styles stared at her. She was angry and he wasn't quite sure how to deal with her right now. "Maybe but there's nothing we can do unless she makes a complaint." The question hung between them, and once behind the wheel, he turned to her. "Rest assured, Nate and the hospital are very hot on spousal abuse. If he abused his wife, and she went to the hospital or Nate, it would be reported to Ryder and action taken. Ryder would have mentioned it if Crenshaw had been an abusive husband."

"Maybe she's too scared to get help." Beth pushed open the truck door and climbed out. "I'm going to speak with her."

Styles headed after her. "If he is abusive and finds out, it will only make things worse, Beth. The law isn't strong enough to help her. He'll only get a fine, if that."

"Okay, but I'm still going to speak to her. If she needs help, we can get that for her. She doesn't have to stay here with him, does she?" She looked up at him. "Please, Styles. Stay back, because you know darn well she won't say anything in front of you."

THIRTY-ONE

Beth made her way to the front stoop and knocked. The kids had just returned from school and loud voices rumbled down the passageway when a small delicate woman around twenty-five opened the door. The smell of fresh-baked cookies and dogs wafted toward Beth from inside. "Mrs. Crenshaw? I'm Agent Beth Katz."

"My husband is out back." Mrs. Crenshaw frowned. "Is this about that dancer who went missing?"

Surprised, Beth took out her notebook and pen. "Yeah, it just happens it is. What do you know about it?"

"Not much." Mrs. Crenshaw leaned against the doorframe, ignoring the sound of kids fighting behind her. "Joe mentioned it, is all."

Interested, Beth moved a little closer. "What did he say?"

"He travels all around the place, as you know, collecting old furniture and unwanted things from people all over. He hears things or people ask him about gossip, so when he comes home, he tells me." Mrs. Crenshaw leaned in conspiratorially. "They're saying she was murdered for being a whore."

Beth raised an eyebrow. "That's a little extreme don't you

think? I assume you are referring to her perhaps being a sex worker?"

"That's maybe." Mrs. Crenshaw waved a hand dismissively. "What else can you call women who flaunt themselves half-naked in front of married men?"

Beth's attention flicked over the woman, making sure that she had no bruises or proof of abuse, but she seemed fine. "I believe they are known as exotic dancers, and gentlemen's clubs are perfectly legal in this state. There's also no law that says a man can't go and watch the dancers, so I can't imagine a woman being murdered because she works there."

"Really?" Mrs. Crenshaw snorted with laughter. "I know a few wives who would argue with you."

The hairs on the back of Beth's neck prickled. "Do you know who told your husband they figured she'd been murdered?"

"He didn't say and wouldn't tell you if he knew." Mrs. Crenshaw turned around and yelled at the kids to stop fighting. "We have to live in this town. People don't look kindly on those who run to the cops with hearsay."

Obviously, the woman was in great shape. Beth folded her notebook and pushed it back into her pocket. "Okay. Thank you for your time."

Mrs. Crenshaw's husband appeared in the passageway. He came up behind his wife and slid both arms around her waist. She smiled at Beth. "I was just chatting to Agent Katz."

"So, I see." Crenshaw rested his chin on his wife's bony shoulder. "I want my supper early, tonight. I'm going out and don't expect me home, darlin'. There's a few new girls I'm planning on watching and I might have a few beers. Can't risk driving home intoxicated, can I? Nice meeting you, Agent Katz." He pushed the door shut.

"Satisfied?" Styles emerged from a stand of trees and stood feet apart and hands on hips. "See, she doesn't care what he does. As he's around most of the time, she probably enjoys a night alone."

Nodding but confused, Beth frowned. Didn't people get married to be together? What constituted adultery? She'd always imagined fidelity was physical and mental. If someone was in love, why would they consider anyone else? Not ever being in love or having anyone who cared for her in that way left her in the middle of a void of understanding. If she ever found love, she'd want it to be absolute. What would love feel like? How would she know? It was so confusing. She fell into step beside him as they headed back to the truck. "Why get married if you need to go elsewhere for sexual attraction? Surely that comes hand in hand with the person you love, doesn't it?" She looked at Styles. "You've been married. Did you ever feel the need to cheat on your wife, or don't you believe lusting after another woman is cheating?"

"I didn't but that's me." Styles shrugged and gave her a sideways glance. "I guess for some, the magic goes out of a marriage but couples don't want to separate, so look for other means. I've heard of open marriages, where couples do their own thing, have outside relationships. It happens. I'm no expert on marriage. Mine failed, if you recall."

Glad for his honesty, Beth looked at him. "Listening to Mrs. Crenshaw, it seems like many married men go to the clubs and not many of their wives are happy about them drooling over strippers. After hearing that, and if I hadn't seen the killer in action, I might have considered a bunch of jealous women had killed the dancers."

"Yeah, that could have been a possibility. It's obvious Mrs. Crenshaw can't stop her husband going to the clubs and really it's none of our business." Styles slid behind the wheel. "I don't know the answer, Beth. Everyone is different. Whatever works and makes both people happy, I guess."

Unable to imagine having a husband coming home stinking

of another woman, Beth shook her head. *My mother must have endured the same thing, but my father was murdering his lovers.* "I always believed marriage meant being faithful and trusting your partner." She shook her head slowly. "Call me old-school but I don't figure that includes lap dances at strip clubs."

"Aw come on, don't be so judgmental." Styles grinned at her and slipped on his sunglasses. "You don't believe women go to strip clubs or have male strippers at their parties? How do you think their husbands, partners, or whatever feel about that? Is it okay for a woman to watch a guy remove his clothes and not a man?" He turned in his seat to pat Bear and then started the engine. "If you love someone, you wouldn't cheat on them, whatever the inducement."

Beth shook her head. "I'm sure I wouldn't and I wouldn't have a stripper at a party either. Male strippers don't interest me. In fact, they would make me feel uncomfortable." She shot him a glance. "You know, my dad was killing women for years and coming home to my mom after he raped and brutalized them. I often wonder if she had her suspicions and challenged him about it the night he murdered her. He must have shown some signs. I know psychopaths can hide everything with charm, but I figure Mom found something incriminating." She sighed. "That could have triggered him. The cop part of me wants to know the truth about that night and it's likely he'd brag about it to me, but I can't face him knowing what he's done. Thinking about him makes me sick to my stomach."

"Ah... I see. Growing up in foster care and not knowing what happened to your family must have been traumatic. I wish I'd been there. It sounds like you needed a friend."

If he only knew the truth. The nightmares, the cold sweats as my mind replayed every terrifying second. Beth nodded. "It was like living in someone else's life, as if I didn't belong. A friend would have been nice, but I was a loner."

"I can understand why you wouldn't want to relive what

happened. Our brains make us forget things to protect us. Maybe you shouldn't prod the tiger?" Styles headed back to Main. "It's getting late. Is there anything you need to do after we've spoken to Ryder?"

Running the day's events through her mind, Beth looked at him. It was difficult reading him behind the sunglasses. "Apart from bringing the files up to date, if Ryder hasn't found a suitable suspect we can watch, we'll need to call the Little Gem Saloon in Rainbow and speak to the manager. I checked out the webpage. I'll need to start on Thursday night and have my picture up in the foyer. I've noticed they have a list of dancers and what time they're onstage."

"The club is called Tempters." Styles shook his head. "They're classy. A costume is going to be a problem." He waved a hand toward the stores. "Where are you going to get something suitable to wear for pole dancing around here?"

Beth sighed. "You recall those crates that arrived from DC when I sold my apartment?"

"Yeah, I helped to unload them." Styles glanced at her and groaned. "My back is ruined."

Beth smiled at the memory; she'd never heard Styles complain before, but it was ten large crates. "There's a sewing machine, and a stack of material in one of them. I've collected things from all over for my undercover work. I'd planned to make a career out of it after cybercrime. I'll make something suitable to wear tomorrow." She shrugged at his incredulous expression. "Yeah, I'm domesticated. Please don't make an issue out of it."

"You're like a treasure chest. I never know what secret you're going to reveal next." Styles swallowed hard clearly considering something unpleasant. "I hope you're not planning on actually stripping in front of me? That would be taking our professional partnership way too far."

Not sure if she should feel hurt by his need to avoid seeing her naked, Beth shook her head. "Not stripping, no. I pole dance and I don't strip, but I'll need you to take my photo and book me for a private dance."

"What?" Styles dropped his mirrored sunglasses and gaped at her. "No way, Beth. That's not just crossing the line, that's obliterating it."

Laughing at his discomfort, Beth leaned back in her seat as they slowed to a stop outside Ryder's office. "How else do you figure we're going to communicate?"

"What about coms?" Styles stared straight ahead.

Grinning, Beth leaned toward him. "And where do you suggest I hide the power pack?"

THIRTY-TWO

The sun was low in the sky when they left Ryder's office and the wind had picked up again. Beth stared into the distance, scanning the sky above the mountains for clouds. It seemed strange to live in such a windy place without a storm coming. She dreaded her first winter, holed up for weeks with a minimal chance of escaping town. What did happen here in winter? She'd need to ask Styles once the case was wound up.

Before the three of them decided to head out to Tommy Joe's Bar and Grill for supper, they'd discussed the case long and hard, going over every possibility in both cases. The general consensus was that they had enough circumstantial evidence on four men—Joseph Crenshaw, Steve Smith, Jace Conan, and Rowdy Bright—to keep them on the list of suspects. In Beth and Styles' absence, Ryder had sifted through all other possibles and found only one man lined up as perfect for both murders as their four suspects, but he'd been with a woman on the night of Cassie's murder, and after interviewing her, Ryder had considered her to be solid.

The plan to go undercover had its problems, and Styles remained unconvinced as they walked back to his truck. Beth stopped walking and stared at him. "Look, I know Steve Smith and Jace Conan met me when we interviewed them, but they saw me without my wig."

"Exactly, they met you." Styles rubbed the back of his neck. "What if they show at Rainbow? We know they frequent Tempters. I'd bet they'll recognize you again, and if one of them is the killer, he's not going to fall into our trap, is he? If we missed the mark with those guys, then they'll spread the word you're an FBI agent."

Shaking her head, Beth stared at him. It was true, she'd need to bring her A game to fool them, but she'd passed as a man before and she could pass as a stripper. "They won't recognize me. Did you recognize me when I dressed as a sex worker in San Francisco?"

"No, but I wasn't looking too closely." Styles gave her a concerned look. "This is your life on the line, Beth."

Having changed her appearance so many times before, the idea didn't faze her at all. "Okay, I'll leave you to be the judge. If I can't become Crystal the pole dancer, we'll call the whole thing off, but until then, we stick to the plan. Okay?"

"Deal." Styles gave her a lopsided smile. "See, we can compromise. That's a sign of a good partnership." He looked at Ryder. "Do you want to ride with us?"

"Nope, I'll be right behind you." Ryder grinned. "I'm starving."

As she climbed into the truck, Beth allowed the plan to filter through her mind. Unfortunately, TJ would be working at his diner on the nights Beth planned on going undercover. The men figured this was a problem, but she refused to miss the chance of flushing out the killer before he struck again. One call and Styles had obtained a suitable miners' cabin for Beth to call home for a couple of days, and another for Ryder to use overnight. As they walked into Tommy Joe's Bar and Grill and ordered supper, Beth relaxed. The plan was coming into shape and over dinner Beth had time to go over the details one more time to make sure everyone was on the same page, and although Styles and Ryder were skeptical, it didn't matter. Confident she could slide into a role and pass as one of the dancers, Beth would allow them a glimpse of her chameleon side.

Excitement shivered through her. She thrived on danger and the thrill of the chase, but this time if the killer took the bait, she'd control her need to take him out permanently and allow Styles and Ryder to apprehend him. This horrendous killer would slip through her net of personal justice because she must protect her dark-side persona at all costs. In any case, she had other, bigger fish to fry. The moment she could get away from Rattlesnake Creek and head to Billings unnoticed, her sights would be set on preventing Levi Jackson from preying on young vulnerable people. With the brutal Levi Jackson, she'd be totally alone and risking her life, but if she stopped him from killing again, it would be worth it.

She noticed Styles looking at her and placed her steak knife on the plate, realizing she'd been gripping it so tight the imprint of the handle was pressed into her palm. Relaxing her shoulders, she absorbed the ambience in the bar. The soft chatter of voices and chinks of silverware on plates mixed with the click and rolling of balls over the pool tables. She inhaled the smell. It was always pleasant, not stinking of stale beer. She imagined Wez, the chef, kept something delicious cooking all the time. It reminded her of a grandma's kitchen in winter, with comfort food on the stove.

"You're looking apprehensive." Styles pushed away his empty plate and sighed. "Not having second thoughts?"

Shaking her head, Beth pushed the last morsel of delicious steak into her mouth, chewed, and swallowed. It gave her time to create a suitable excuse. "Not about risking my life to catch a killer, no. That's not a problem. It's like riding a bike, yeah? It's only, I've never been onstage before. Where I used to work out, it was just a room with poles and an instructor. Just me and the girls."

She noticed Styles' concerned expression and had a qualm of guilt for lying to him, especially when he'd been so nice to her. Her cheeks heated and she couldn't meet his gaze. Blushing had gotten an immediate reaction from him, which made her feel even worse. In truth, she'd slipped seamlessly into so many characters in her life, being onstage as Crystal the pole dancer would be one of the easier ones.

"You had a pole installed in the gym, right?" Ryder looked way too interested. "Styles mentioned you like to use it to keep in shape."

Beth stared at him until his ears turned red. "Yeah, that and working out with Styles. We practice moves more than strength training. I get all that from the pole. It's harder than it looks. Keeping supple is the key."

"Are you sure?" Styles ducked his head and stared at her. "This is a big deal and I know some situations get you all riled up. To be convincing, you'll need to seduce the audience. You know that, right?"

Beth smiled at him. "Yeah, I know the moves. Don't worry about me. I'll be fine. I can shut people out just like that." She snapped her fingers.

"We'll see. Okay, you'll need some more information." Styles took a pen out of his pocket and drew a map onto a paper napkin. "The layout is different from Outlaws. The dancers leave from a stage door and walk through a small garden area to the parking lot. Ryder will be in TJ's pickup parked on a side road off Main where he can see the stage door. I'll leave just before and be in Beth's new ride. I'll drive straight to the cabin, park in the road behind the cabins, and walk through the backyards to get into position. We'll have our coms. Beth, you'll make sure to attach yours before you leave your ride."

Frowning, Beth stared at him. "What ride? I don't have a ride if you have my truck."

"You'll be in Nate's SUV. It's ambiguous like your truck. There's a ton of them all over the counties." Styles smiled at her. "While you're sewing your costumes, I'll take everything you need to the cabin and make sure it's secure. I'll recon the area around the cabin and find a place to hide. Ryder is going to park outside a cabin a few doors away. He'll walk in the front door—it's unoccupied—and straight out the back and come around and take a position close by. Ryder will be driving in front of you, so as soon as he sees you climb into your vehicle, he'll take off but will keep you in sight. Any problems, you use your com."

Beth nodded. "Got it. I don't figure he'll try anything tomorrow night. He's not an opportunistic killer. He's well organized, so he'll be somewhere watching. I hope I fall into his range of fantasy women. If so, he'll follow me home for sure and see if I live alone. I'll need to stay at the cabin and hope he doesn't break in and try something. It's pretty isolated out there."

"Let him try." Styles grinned at her. "As soon as you turn out the lights, I'll give it a couple of hours and then slip inside. I have a key to the back door. I'll sleep on the lounge. Then Friday night we repeat the same format and see if he bites."

Relieved they had her back, Beth thought for a beat and then shook her head. "That won't work. If he does break in, the best we'll have him on is break and enter. He's not going to risk attacking me with you there, is he? All this will be a waste of time, and he'll know we're onto him."

"The cabin I'm using is only a hundred yards away." Ryder's brow wrinkled into a frown. "Styles can stay with me. It's furnished." He looked at Styles. "Take some extra supplies there when you set up Beth's cabin."

"Okay." Styles rubbed his chin. "I'll leave my backup weapon in the bedside table drawer, just in case you need it.

You'll have your com and I'll keep mine turned on. I sleep light. If anything happens, I'll know and come running. I'm sure you can hold him off until I get there." He glanced at Ryder and smiled. "She fights real hard."

Beth gave an exaggerated shudder. "If he doesn't find a way to drug me first." She pushed both hands through her hair. "I hope you can run fast, Styles. I don't want to be fighting off a killer intent on sewing me to the sofa."

"I don't figure having a permanent smile will do much for your reputation either." Ryder grinned at her and, when she just stared at him, dropped his gaze, ears pinking. "Just sayin'."

Turning to Styles, Beth held up one finger. "Just one more thing before we go? As this may be my last supper with you guys at TJ's, I'm ordering a slice of pie."

THIRTY-THREE

THURSDAY

The day began blustery and cold. Snow clouds grayed the sky. The moment Beth had opened her eyes, time seemed to be moving faster than normal. It seemed to take forever for her to sort through the crates and boxes Styles had carried up to her apartment looking for suitable materials and accessories. Before she started sewing, she needed to become Crystal for the photographs required to advertise her appearance at Tempters. After carrying a barstool from the breakfast bar into her bedroom to use for staging the photographs, she selected a honey-blonde wig, red stilettoes, and a suitable costume. The manager of Tempters had agreed to display them in the foyer and on his webpage along with Beth's performance times, and also shout about her being the new attraction over social media. The killer would be searching for a suitable victim and she'd be sure to get his attention. She spent a great deal of precious time applying her makeup to change her face shape and accentuate her eyes and mouth. Although her blue eyes looked bigger, she selected contacts in a rich turquoise to make her eyes resemble a manga cartoon character. For the final touch, she added clip-on brilliant white teeth. They puffed out her top lip and gave her a dazzling smile. Happy with her transformation, she pulled the drapes together and turned on all the lights in the bedroom. After perching on the edge of a barstool to display her legs, she called Styles from the sitting room. "I'm ready."

His reaction was as she'd hoped. His eyes widened and his pupils dilated. She'd attracted his male animal and he prowled around her almost like a predator. She smiled her best seductive smile and used a deep sultry voice to add to the illusion. "Well, will I fool them?"

"Oh man, that's freaky." Styles gaped at her. "I'm starting to believe you're an alien shapeshifter." He walked around her rubbing his chin. "Wow! You're the real deal. Even up close, I'd never recognize you. Those eyes, holy cow, they're mesmerizing."

Waving him away, Beth kept up the slightly breathless voice but added a dash of sarcasm just so he knew it was her beneath the mask. "Don't get carried away, Styles. Just take the darn photos so I can wash off this makeup and get the costumes made."

"Your voice." Styles shook his head slowly. "It's perfect. It sure doesn't sound like you." He took a ton of images and then showed them to her.

Scanning the images, Beth nodded. "Okay, use numbers five, eleven, and fifteen. They're just what they need and show off my eyes real good. Get them to the manager of Tempters ASAP so he can get them up into the foyer. You don't have much time. You'll need to get my overnight bag and that bag of groceries on the counter and your stuff over to the cabins and then hightail it back here."

"Gotcha." Styles looked around the room. "I've arranged the basics for a night's stay. All you'll need is your costumes and makeup. I'll be back in time to drop them by Nate's place when you're done."

Beth waved him away. "Great! Get at it, the clock is ticking. Don't forget to gas up the vehicles."

As Styles headed for the elevator, she made plans for the rest of the morning. She'd need a few costume changes to cover both nights. The manager of Tempters had surprised her. He was very happy to get a dancer for free for potentially two nights. She'd made arrangements to be onstage for two ten-minute sessions. This was a shorter time than most of the other girls but long enough to get attention. She didn't need to be too exhausted to fight if the need arose. It would be long enough for her to view the crowd for their potential suspects. Her private dance with Styles would happen after her last dance and they'd compare notes in an effort to discover who they might be expecting at the cabin.

After sewing her costumes, she showered and washed her hair. They would have dinner as usual at TJ's before she slipped out and went with Nate. Once there, she'd wait ten minutes and, taking Nate's SUV, would head out to the cabin to transform into Crystal, pole dancer extraordinaire. Tension built as she sipped a glass of wine. Just the one, with a light meal, would relax her. Beside her, Styles checked his watch and gave her a nod. It was time to go. A few seconds later Nate joined them. Beth smiled at him. "Ready to go?"

"Sure." Nate stood and smiled at Styles. "Catch you later."

She slid her arm through Nate's and they went out the back door, climbed into his SUV, and headed for his house. "I'll wait ten minutes and then head out to the cabin. It will take me some time to get there. I'm glad you have GPS. I'm driving blind."

"Just follow Ryder." Nate smiled at her. "He'll keep you in sight, don't worry. He's very reliable."

Nervous tension cramped her belly but she smiled. "That's good to know. Thanks for lending me your ride. I hope you don't have any emergencies while I'm gone."

"It's all good." Nate drove into his garage. "I have a backup plan. Just be careful." He turned in his seat and frowned at her. "Talking about backup plans, I can give you a knockout drug if you get into trouble. You'll just have to stab him with it."

Wishing she could use her hatpin to fix the problem permanently, as it was her weapon of choice, she nodded. "Why not? How long does it take to work?"

"I'll give you fentanyl. So, seconds." Nate climbed out of the vehicle. "Come into my office."

The office was an examination room, a sterile environment with glass cabinets and spotless counters. On one side sat a desk and chairs under a frosted-glass window. Across the room against the wall was a sheet-draped examination table. She looked at him. "It sounds like a good idea but uncapping a syringe might be a problem in a fight. Stabbing him with it and depressing the plunger near impossible. I'll bend the needle or stab myself for sure."

"Ah, give me a second." Nate went to a cabinet and took out a vial of milky liquid and an apparatus. Next minute he turned around and held up a pen. "You've seen these before, haven't you?" He frowned. "Officers use them to inject Narcan or naloxone to overdose victims, or maybe you've seen them carried for anaphylaxis?"

Beth recognized the pen and smiled. "I hadn't thought of using one of these for a knockout drug. You fill your own? How come?"

"It's part of being a doctor in a small town. I'll explain when we have more time." He handed her the pen. "This contains five knockout doses. If you panic and give him too many, it will kill him. I've made it a substantial dose, taking into consideration his adrenaline will be spiking. Aim for bare skin areas or anywhere where the clothing is thin. The thigh is good, neck better."

Feeling the time rushing along gave Beth the sensation of

dropping down in an out-of-control elevator. She nodded. "Got it. I'd better hit the road. Do you have my things?"

"Yeah." Nate led the way into his family room. "On the sofa, and here are the keys to my truck. The one with the green tag is to open the cabin door." He handed them to her.

Beth rummaged through the bags and pulled out her wig. It was all she would need if someone saw her driving through town. She arranged her hair and then fit it on her head. Grabbing up the bag with her costumes and her purse, she smiled at him. "Okay, I'm ready to go."

"Good luck!" Nate smiled at her. "Or should I say break a leg? Styles mentioned you should be in movies."

Nerves curled in her belly but she smiled. "I'll do my best."

THIRTY-FOUR

The drive to Rainbow had been easy enough the first time. It was still light when she'd left for the cabin, and Ryder kept a good distance but in sight the entire way. Leaving the cabin late at night in the pitch black to drive to Tempters was different. Beth didn't know the area, and although she had Ryder's tail-lights to follow, the horrible feeling of being out of control swamped her. It had taken longer to drive to Rainbow than she'd imagined and although Tempters was only a ten-minute drive from the cabins, she couldn't risk running late and so decided to change into her costume before leaving. She'd stuffed her change of clothes into a bag, added her makeup, hairbrush, and the injection pen before hurrying out into the dark. The cabins had no garages and outside darkness enveloped her, almost smothering her.

Apprehension gripped her as she scanned the area. What if she'd been seen leaving town and the killer had already followed her? He could be waiting alongside the road in the bushes ready to ambush her. Pushing fanciful ideas from her head, she used her phone's flashlight, hurried to the SUV, and climbed inside. In the distance, she spotted Ryder reversing from his driveway and slowly moving up the road. She waited and then followed but lost him when he turned onto the highway. She hit the gas in a wave of panic and then sighed with relief when his red taillights bobbed in the distance. It was so dark when clouds covered the tiny slice of moon that, outside of the headlight beams, night enclosed her like an impenetrable wall. Not one house sat alongside the highway, not one reassuring light, nothing. Ahead, heavy white mist spilled from the river to drift across the blacktop, making it glisten in the watery moonlight, and the headlights turned the swirls into ethereal beings reaching out to drag her into the abyss. Maybe they were the ghosts of the victims, waiting for her to join them. She shook her head. "Not tonight. I have an advantage over you. I know he's coming for me."

The signs for the Little Gem Saloon shone like a beacon on the outskirts of town. A flashing sign advertising Tempters with a large arrow sat on the roof. Picturing Styles' map, she headed through the main parking lot and drove around back. The area was lit by pale yellow lights strung around the fence. She parked close to a small area of trees with a path running through it and leading to the stage door. As she reached for the SUV's door handle, the hairs on the back of her neck prickled a warning so strong Beth reached for her phone to call Styles, but then changed her mind. Panicking now would spoil everything. She pulled her coat closer around her and ran along the pathway. Someone was watching her and he was pure evil.

A security guard stood at the end of a small passageway and waved her inside. She looked up at him and used her husky voice. "Hi, I'm Crystal. Where's the dressing room?"

"I'll take you." The man smiled at her. "I'm Tom. The boss told me to keep an eye on you. He added you to the website as soon as your pictures arrived and got a ton of bookings. The tables are full. I hope you put on a good show. You sure look like something special."

Beth shrugged. "I bet you say that to all the girls."

"Nah." Tom chuckled. "Watching the dancers is like candy. A little is fine but too much gives you a headache." He waved her to the dressing room door. "There are lockers along the wall and they all have combination locks. Use them. Don't leave your stuff lying around or it will be gone. The management isn't responsible for any missing property."

Nodding, Beth glanced at her phone for the time. "I've gotta go. I'm on in a few minutes." She hurried inside the dressing room, checked her hair, and touched up her makeup before dumping her stuff into a locker. She took in her surroundings as she waited for the time to tick down. The smell of sweat greeted her, mixed with a variety of perfumes, hairspray, and mentholated salve. Tissues overflowed the metal garbage cans alongside candy wrappers. The other dancers nodded but left her alone. They all looked tired and the conversation was about kids and long hours. Some rubbed their feet and chatted as they sipped coffee. Others sat around half-dressed or stared into mirrors as they applied another coat of thick makeup.

Beth shook her head as nerves trembled her fingers. Darn it. She'd walked into life-threatening situations and faced down some of the deadliest serial killers in the country without as much as a second thought, but going onstage and cavorting in front of Styles sent shivers down her spine. She'd noticed his reaction to her, but then he was only human and she had disguised herself to attract men. She gave herself a mental slap in the face. It was just an act to bring down a killer. Nothing would change between her and Styles. He would act professionally and so would she. She made a mental note to be particularly indifferent toward him the following day. Just to make sure he had no doubt about her acting skills.

She made her way along the corridor and the smell of beer and men's cologne greeted her. Tom smiled at her. "Two minutes."

Two dancers holding bits of their costumes came toward her. One of them looked at her and blinked. Beth smiled. "How's the crowd?"

"Noisy and waiting for you." The woman frowned and wiped sweat from her brow. "The boss has made a big deal about you. I hope you're good or the guys will boo you off the stage. At this time of night most of them have drunk themselves into a stupor and they turn into animals."

A tremor of anxiety shivered through Beth and she nodded. "Good to know."

The music thumped way too loud, and the bass vibrated through her feet as she made her way to the stage. The muscles in her legs trembled as she swung herself around the pole trailing an arm in a welcoming wave to the audience. The moves she'd learned were as familiar as breathing, and she'd danced to this music a million times before. With each slow spin around the pole, she scanned the audience, glad to see her request to have the audience illuminated had been granted. To her surprise, Styles was sitting with Ryder right in the middle of the room. Joseph Crenshaw was sitting with his back propped up against the bar, and along the edge of the room, Rowdy Bright stood with a group of men to one side. Right at the front of the stage, waving dollar bills and grinning like monkeys, sat Steve Smith and Jace Conan. She climbed the pole, wrapped her legs around it, and dropped back, her hair brushing the floor. She met Styles' gaze with one raised eyebrow before executing another move. As she scanned the onlookers, a shiver slid down her spine and raised goosebumps on her hot flesh. All four suspects were watching her closely and there was no way of distinguishing which one was the killer.

Her music slowed and she crawled across the stage. This part of her routine she'd gained from watching online videos. Crawling around to allow men to stuff bills inside her costume wasn't part of her exercise routine but was expected at

Tempters. She slapped away roaming hands and stood to leave, glad when Tom came to her rescue to get her safely through the crowd. It seemed like everyone there wanted a piece of her. Feeling dirty, she dragged the bills from her costume and tossed them onto a counter. She grabbed her bag from the locker and went into the bathroom, locking herself in one of the shower stalls. To think she must repeat the same thing again made her sick to her stomach. How did these woman cope with the foul comments and the groping?

After emptying a bottle of water, she dragged off her wig and hung it on a peg with her bag, stripped off the costume, and took a quick shower, avoiding her face. Just removing the men's touch from her flesh would help. Once done, she dried off, slipped into her next costume and stepped outside. In the bathroom mirror, she pulled on the wig and touched up her makeup. When she returned to the dressing room, the dancer she'd spoken to in the hallway handed her a wad of bills. She nodded to her. "Thanks."

"Why are you doing this?" The woman examined her face. "You're good, but it's obvious you hate being here. It's not easy dancing in front of an audience like those pigs out there. I'm guessing you hate men and are only doing this for the money, right? Can't you use that notion to keep going? Like, 'you can look but you'll never have me' or something?"

Shaking her head, Beth smiled at her. "Oh, I like men just fine, but not those men. Where I performed before, they were a little more restrained. Here, they're like animals, but I'll get used to it. Money is money, right?"

"Yeah, well this is Montana. The men sure are real here, honey." She giggled. "Cashed up most times too." She waved to a coffee pot gurgling on the counter. "Take the weight off and grab a cup of coffee. You'll feel better in no time."

Sighing, Beth nodded. "I sure hope so."

THIRTY-FIVE

Reluctantly, Beth dropped her bag back into the locker, pulled out her phone, and walking to a quiet corner, called Styles. It took him ages to answer and then his voice came down the line. It was quiet in the background and she realized he'd walked outside. "How was I? Think I got the right person's attention?"

"I figure you got everyone's attention. You sure you haven't performed before? Ah... no don't answer that. It's none of my darn business. Sorry." Styles cleared his throat. *"What's up? You sound different."*

When she had a goal in sight as in the permanent removal of a monster, the thrill of pitting them against her was intoxicating. Knowing if this killer attacked her, her response must be to take him into custody took the thrill out of the chase. She had no endgame, no reward, but how could she explain this to Styles? Plainly she couldn't.

"Beth." Styles blew out a long sigh. *"Talk to me. You called me for a reason. What's wrong?"*

Thinking on her feet was one of Beth's attributes. She sighed. "You got it right about my reactions to the men's catcalls and the touching turns my stomach."

"Does it bring back bad memories?" Styles had lowered his voice. *"You can pull the plug if it's too much."*

The small hint of her time in foster care had hit home with Styles and she could hear the concern in his voice. She shook her head. "I'll be fine. I can block it out for ten more minutes. Heck, I didn't believe ten minutes could take so long. Keep your head in the game. There's a ton of distractions and this is a one-time deal. I'm not doing this again."

"I wouldn't expect you to." Styles footsteps crunched on gravel. He must be in the parking lot. *"I'll get back inside. Just so you know, Beth, doing this took guts. You're one hell of an agent and I'm proud to be working alongside you."*

Surprised, Beth stared at her phone unable to believe what he'd just said. He admired her as an agent? She swallowed the lump in her throat. "Thank you. Let's just hope we can catch this guy. I'm looking forward to a few days' downtime after this to set up my cabin."

"We'll take a week." Styles laughed. *"They owe us. I'll see you after the next set."* He disconnected.

Taking down the killer of Cassie and Vicki slipped back into view. Now she had a purpose to walk back onstage again. She must catch their killer tonight and although it wouldn't be satisfying her dark side, at least he wouldn't be killing again and that would do. She'd look forward instead to taking down Levi Jackson at her leisure. She locked away her phone and went to pour a cup of coffee. One more time on the stage and it would be game on.

Back out onstage, Beth twirled to a different tune and surveyed the audience. To her surprise, Joseph Crenshaw and Rowdy Bright were not in the crowd watching her. The other two stage huggers, who'd practically mauled her pushing bills into her underwear, were still there, still grinning. Amused that she'd certainly fooled them with her disguise, she gave them a broad smile. As she twirled, she scanned the room, over and over, trying to pick out anyone looking at her differently. None of the men scowled at her, as reported by one of the strippers from Cassie Burnham's murder case. Everyone was smiling and having a good time.

She finished her routine, pulled the bills from her costume, and followed Tom to the private dancing rooms. When he opened the door and she met Styles' gaze, her cheeks burned. The door shut behind them and she took the offered bottle of water. "Thanks."

"I saw all four suspects earlier." Styles dropped into a chair. "Not now, Crenshaw and Bright have left. Neither are in the bar. That leaves us with the two miners."

Nodding, Beth sipped the water. "Do you figure they're both involved?"

"I guess we'll find out soon enough." He sighed. "I've been made, so I'll head out now. I'll head in the direction of Rattlesnake Creek and then take a back road to double back. Ryder will do the same, so give him fifteen minutes before you leave to get into position. I'll already be at Ryder's cabin by the time you arrive. I'll park a ways away and walk."

Needing to tell Styles about her gut feeling, Beth stared at him. "I was sure someone was watching me when I arrived. Does anyone else know I hired that cabin?"

"The mine's secretary does but they've no reason to tell anyone." Styles shrugged. "They needed to get a bed delivered is all, but they wouldn't have told a delivery driver about you."

She leaned against the wall and sighed. "You hired it under my name, as in Crystal Dreams, so it forms part of my cover story? We don't know how thorough this killer is. One mistake and he'll know it's a sting."

"Yeah, I said I was a travel agent acting on your behalf. It's solid." Styles stood and, taking her gently by the forearms, stared into her eyes. "You've got this, Beth. Trust in your ability. Don't remove the makeup. You'll need to keep up the illusion."

He dropped his hands. "Now let's make this happen before he gets cold feet."

Soothed by his professionalism, Beth nodded. "You got it. Don't forget your com. I'm going to be alone out there." She opened the door and walked back to the dressing room. *Don't let me down, Styles.*

THIRTY-SIX

Dressed in jeans and a sweater and wrapped in a warm coat, Beth walked from the dressing room and ran straight into Tom, the security guard. She smiled at him. It was good to know the manager actually cared for the well-being of his dancers. "Thanks for looking out for me tonight." She pulled the wad of bills from her pocket and handed them to him. "I appreciate it."

"It's my job to make sure the dancers are okay and I'm sure you need that more than me." Tom waved away the money. "I'll walk you to your ride just in case someone wants to get friendly."

Always suspicious, Beth studied his face and then nodded. He wasn't being charming at all, more like businesslike. She followed him outside. "Thanks."

As they emerged from the path between the trees and into the parking lot, the grinning faces of the stage huggers greeted her. Styles and Ryder were long gone and it was just as well Tom was with her or things would have gotten nasty. She glared at Steve Smith and Jace Conan as they moved closer. "What do you want?"

"We saw you looking at us." Conan smiled at her. "We

came all the way from Rattlesnake Creek to watch you dance and we've booked a room at the local motel so we can party."

Continuing to walk toward her vehicle, Beth snorted. "Well, you have yourself some fun now."

"Aw come on, Crystal." Smith came toward her. "It won't be a party without you."

"Move along." Tom moved between her and held out both hands toward the men. "There are more dancers due onstage. Why don't you go and watch them? We don't want any trouble, do we?"

While Tom distracted them, Beth hurried to Nate's SUV and slid inside, locking the doors behind her. She took the com from the glovebox, pushed the tiny battery pack into her pocket, and slid the wireless receiver into one ear. It was invisible under her wig, but she checked her reflection in the rearview mirror just to be sure. Starting the engine, she headed out of the parking lot and onto the dark winding road back to the highway. She tapped her earpiece. "Cash, are you out there?"

"Yeah, you should see my lights as I come out of a side road." Ryder's engine roared in her ear. *"Can you see me now?"*

Relieved to see headlights sweep across the blacktop and taillights moving ahead of her, Beth accelerated into the night. "I see you. I'm right behind."

"Stay back some or it will be obvious you're following me."

Beth eased up on the gas. "Copy."

Trying to ignore the thickening mist and the heavy weight of apprehension, Beth ran possible scenarios through her mind. If the killer had taken the bait, how would he come for her? It was a given he knew his way around a miners' cabin, so gaining entrance wouldn't be an issue. Nervous tension gripped her as she drove off the highway and took the road to the cabins. She couldn't see Ryder's vehicle now, as it had turned well before her, and he'd be parking in his driveway. Knowing the way, she slowed and drove in the opposite direction. Her cabin sat like an empty hearth with no welcoming warmth or lights to greet her. It looked cold and deserted. She pulled into the driveway and the feeling of someone watching her swamped her again. She bent over to retrieve her things and to cover her face in case anyone was hiding in the shadows and could see her speaking to someone. "Is everyone in position? I don't like walking into a dark house. I should've left a light on."

"*We're here.*" Styles sounded as if he was beside her. "*Leave your com open, so we can hear you're okay.*"

Beth gathered her things and looking all around, reached for the door. "Copy."

Shivers brushed her like spiderwebs with each crunching step along the path to the front door. The wind rustled the trees and moved shadows. Could someone be there watching her? Gathering her courage, she pushed down the fear. No one knew she was here. No one had followed her. She'd kept an eye on her rearview mirror the entire journey, so why was she so jumpy? Something deep inside her had triggered her fight-or-flight response and sent her a warning something wasn't right. Fumbling with the key, she found the lock and opened the door. It whined in complaint just to add to the creepy atmosphere. The front door opened up directly into the living room. Swallowing hard, Beth ran her hand down the wall searching for the light switch. Dim yellow light streamed from a dusty bulb hanging from a length of wire in the middle of the room. The fireplace had logs stacked beside it in a bucket and the fire was laid, ready to light. To one side sat a wooden rocking chair, and a threadbare rug covered the floor before a padded deep red sofa. No TV, but a bookshelf held a few dusty volumes. She stood for a few moments, scanning every nook and cranny for a place someone could hide. Behind the drapes, maybe? The heavy drapes were closed and reached the floor but surely, she'd notice a bulge if someone had concealed themselves behind them?

Stepping inside, she kicked the door shut behind her and dropped her things onto the sofa. Being cautious was her middle name and she walked from room to room to ensure the house was empty. It was a small cabin with not many places a man could hide, and yet her attention constantly moved to the shadows. The creepy feeling that someone was watching her remained and she gave herself a mental shake. She needed to keep awake, there'd be no sleeping tonight, not when the feeling of doom surrounded her. Heading for the kitchen, she found the bag of supplies Styles had left on the counter and set up the coffee pot.

"Cough if all is well." Styles' voice came through her earpiece startling her.

Spilling coffee over the counter, she coughed and then froze. Floorboards creaked in the living room and a shiver of fear slid down her spine and curled around her tailbone. Unarmed and without as much as a hatpin to defend herself, she eased away from the counter and turned toward the bedroom. Styles had left his backup weapon in the bedside table. Wind buffeted the house and the old shutters creaked and banged against the wall. *Maybe it was just the wind?*

Moving as casually as possible, Beth walked along the passageway to the bedroom, she closed the door and went straight to the bedside table. When her hand closed around the Sig, she smiled. A P938 BRG Micro-Compact was an excellent choice as a backup weapon and she slid it into the belt of her jeans and pulled down her sweater over it. Sure that the creaks were the wind making noises in an unfamiliar place, she headed back to the kitchen to clean up the spilled coffee grounds. The smell of coffee soon filled her nostrils but so did the smell of smoke. Turning away from the counter, she headed for the living room and stopped dead in the doorway staring in disbelief. The rocking chair creaked back and forth and a curl of smoke rose from the fireplace. A rush of fear gripped her by the throat and she reached for the pistol in the back of her jeans. Before she could grab the handle, pain shot through her head and she fell to her knees with spots dancing before her eyes. The com dropped from her ear and spun across the floor leaving her alone with a serial killer. The weapon was ripped from her jeans and someone shoved her hard in the back sending her face first to the dusty floor.

"Don't move." A man squatted down beside her. "Nice pistol. Too bad you don't know how to use it." He pushed the gun into the belt of his pants and pulled out a knife. He brandished it in front of her eyes, so close she could smell his cigarette-tainted fingers. "This is so much more fun and not so noisy. I've even lit the fire so we can be cozy. Nothing too good for my darlings."

Sickened by his singsong, deluded speech, Beth gritted her teeth. How did he get into the house? Down but not out, Beth shook her head to clear her blurred vision. She had one small advantage: he wouldn't be reckoning on facing someone like her. He was used to women being terrified and trying to get away. Standing and fighting back would confuse him and she'd use that in her favor. She'd faced worse serial killers than him and survived. When he ran a hand over her backside and hummed in appreciation, anger blocked out terror. In one swift movement, Beth rolled onto her back and swung a kick to the man's head. It connected with his hideous zombie mask and sent him sprawling onto the floor. Dizzy, she bounced to her feet and raised her voice. "Nine one one. Nine one one." Her com had been open when it fell from her ear and only time would tell if Styles had heard her call for help.

Right now, she must fight for survival by leaving the FBI agent behind and facing him serial killer to serial killer. Only one of them would survive. She shook her head to stop the room from shifting and stomped on the man's wrist but instead of dropping the knife, his fingers closed tight around it. Not beaten and as strong as a bull, he pushed to his knees, cursing and lashing out with the blade. The eyes that peered at her through the mask were black and unbalanced. His focus was on killing her now and there would be no stopping him. Beth jumped back, tripped over the rug, and sprawled heavily on the floor. The air rushed from her lungs, and gasping she tried to scramble away but his hand closed around her ankle like a vise. His big powerful body loomed over her as he dragged her closer, slashing with the knife. The sharp blade sliced across her stomach, coming so close the cold steel brushed her flesh. She kicked out, slamming him in the face with her heel. As he dropped, she jumped to her feet, lifted one knee and thrust the heel of her boot into his kidney. The strike would have felled most men but not him. As he cried out in pain, his head snapped around to stare at her, the mouth visible through the mask bared in a feral grin.

"Oh, I'm so gonna enjoy killing you." As he slashed the knife at her, he struggled to get his knees under him. "It's gonna be slow and painful. I might skin you alive."

At his threat, Beth's dark side rose like a protective barrier. Her sight sharpened and everything became clear, like an eagle zooming in on its prey from a great height. One mistake now and he would kill her before Styles ran one hundred yards. Murder happened fast, in seconds, and Beth embraced her psychopath and used her instinct to survive. She must attack while he was down, it was her only chance.

Jumping left to right to avoid the blade, Beth rounded on him and aimed a kick between his legs from behind. As he cursed and doubled up, releasing the knife, she straddled his back and heard the breath rush out of him in a groan. After tossing away the weapon, she elbowed him between the shoulder blades, once, twice, and then grabbed his head and slammed his face into the floor. He bucked under her, moaning and it was her turn to laugh. Her vicious blows had slowed him down enough for her to pull the pistol from his belt. She stared at the door. Where the heck was Styles? Ignoring her attacker's threats of disembowelment, she ripped off his mask and gaped at the man with disbelief. *Joseph Crenshaw.*

She pressed the muzzle of the pistol into his ear, so wanting to make him pay. "How do you like it when a woman fights back? Painful, isn't it? You see, in a fight for survival there are no rules. We fight dirty. It's the food chain and right now you're on the bottom. How does that make you feel, Crenshaw? I bet your wife will be so proud when she discovers your taste for the macabre. How did you explain the stink of death on you?"

"Get off me." Crenshaw rolled and cried out as she landed another solid blow to the base of his neck. "Enough, okay?" He held his arms out in front of him in surrender. "Who the hell are you?"

Not taking any chances, Beth pressed the pistol into the back of his head. "FBI. You're through killing strippers. This is the end of the line."

"I'll kill you the second I'm free." Crenshaw's spittle sprayed the floor. "You've got nothin' on me."

Grabbing her dark side by the throat to gain control, Beth lifted her finger from the trigger but pushed the muzzle harder into his head. "Well then, maybe I should save the county a ton of money by accidently blowing out your brains?"

The door burst open. Styles and Ryder, weapons raised and breathing heavy, poked their heads inside and Beth smiled at them. "What took you so long?"

THIRTY-SEVEN

FRIDAY

Styles paced up and down the office. "I'd like to know just how he got inside."

"I guess we'll find out more when we can speak to him." Beth shrugged. "It surprised me too. I cleared the house, and when I heard a noise, I figured it was the wind. Not many can get the jump on me. He hits like a sledgehammer. In the end, we took him down, that's the main thing."

After hearing Beth's threat to shoot Crenshaw, Styles had been ready to find a situation in the cabin, but Beth had surprised him. She sure knew how to talk the talk. What she'd said to Crenshaw, and the malice in her voice, would scare anyone. He cleared his throat. Now in the calm of day, he had questions. "You handled the situation well. In the end, when he threatened you, did you ever want to take him out, Beth?"

"Nah, my finger wasn't on the trigger." Beth shook her head, spilling blonde hair over one shoulder in a fall of silk. "He was whimpering like a lost puppy. I had him beaten. It was just threats, is all, to keep him subdued until you showed. I wanted answers from this guy. When they die during arrest, they leave too many unanswered questions." She frowned. "I was surprised it was Crenshaw, happily married with kids, works for the local charity, father was a minister. It takes all types to commit murder, I guess." Beth leaned back in her office chair. "He's a typical coward. I knew he'd crumble when you arrived and then cry for his lawyer the moment we cuffed him." She checked her phone for the tenth time in a few minutes. "How long does it get to obtain a darn search warrant? We've gathered enough evidence for probable cause. In fact, we have the entire case laid out with a pretty pink bow on top for the DA." She narrowed her gaze. "My problem with the delay is that we don't know if Crenshaw's lawyer has contacted the wife and told him he is in custody. What if she empties the house before we get there?"

Shaking his head, Styles sat on the edge of his desk and looked at her. "Do you figure Crenshaw will want his wife to find his secret stash of trophies?" He rubbed the scar on his chin. "Then again, I guess it could go either way. She'll dump evidence or be angry enough to leave everything for the cops. A woman scorned is a dangerous person."

"I figure raping, murdering women, and necrophilia goes a little past 'scorning' on the cheating-husband scale." Beth chewed on the end of a pen. "I doubt she'll stand by him."

Thinking over cases he'd read or been involved in over the years, he shrugged. "Some women find a man like that irresistible."

"Not me, but then I've seen the murder scene photographs. Let's turn this around. What about men in this situation?" Beth twirled the pen on her fingers. "Do you figure you'd be attracted to a murderess? No, let me rephrase that question. Do you think you could like a woman who kills to protect others?"

Confused, Styles frowned. "You mean like a vigilante or someone in law enforcement?"

"Is there really a difference?" Beth dropped the pen into an old coffee cup and smiled at him. "They both take down dangers to society. Even though one type of killing is inside the law and the other means twenty to life or the needle."

Thinking it over, Styles shrugged. "I guess each case is different. I can't give you a specific answer." He stared at her. "I'm sure you'd have no qualms about a guy who kills for his country, or law enforcement in the line of duty, same with me, but women can be serial killers as well. It's not gender specific. The vigilantes, I agree, are different. Most are driven by things in their past. They want to right a wrong or stop someone from repeating a crime. I can often see their point, as in why they kill. My thing would be trust. Could I trust them not to turn on me in my sleep."

"Same." Beth smiled. "I guess if we're ever faced with a situation like that, we wouldn't be stupid enough to make ourselves targets." Her phone chimed a message. "We have the warrant. Let's go. It's Ryder's jurisdiction and we'll need him to assist."

Styles called Ryder. "We have the warrant. Meet us at the Crenshaw home."

"I was just going to call you. Jerry Blackwood is the attorney representing Crenshaw. He spoke to his client this morning before they shipped him to the Black Rock Falls County Jail. He knows about the warrant application. You'll need to arrange an interview with Crenshaw through him."

Glancing at Beth, Styles nodded. It was what they'd been waiting for. "Yeah, I'll call him once we've executed the warrant. I'm guessing he'll need a ride to Black Rock Falls? Unless that will cause a problem?"

"I can't see it being a problem. Crenshaw is innocent until proven guilty. It's a courtesy for his lawyer, is all." Ryder chuckled. *"I'm sure glad I didn't have Crenshaw here for too much longer. That guy was ranting and pacing like a caged animal. The trip to Black Rock Falls must have been a nightmare."*

Recalling the anger radiating from Crenshaw when Ryder had taken him into custody and the problems getting him back to Rattlesnake Creek late the previous night, he wasn't surprised. Beth had driven her truck with both him and Ryder sitting beside Crenshaw. When they had him safely in Ryder's jail, they'd grabbed TJ and headed back to Rainbow to collect the other vehicles and their belongings from the cabins. It had been almost three in the morning before they'd gotten home. Ryder had left Crenshaw chained hand and foot in his jail cell but slept in his office. He and Beth had gotten a solid six hours sleep and filed the warrant the moment the judge opened his office at ten.

Tired, Styles yawned. "Did you get a couple of hours of shut-eye?"

"Yeah, the moment the prison van arrived I headed off home. I just walked in the office when you called." Styles could hear a rattling of keys. "I'm on my way to the Crenshaw house now."

Styles nodded. "See you there." He disconnected and took the forensics kit Beth handed him. "I sure hope we find his stash of hair. I'm wondering how long he's been killing and how many bodies are out there sitting on old sofas in remote areas. It must be more than two, that's for darn sure."

"I'd say it's more than we imagine." Beth hurried to the door, pulling on her FBI jacket. "How do you want to handle this? We might encounter resistance from his wife."

Unconcerned, Styles shrugged. "Then she'll be cuffed and placed in the back of Ryder's cruiser."

THIRTY-EIGHT

"Are you looking for drugs?" Mrs. Crenshaw stared at Beth from her seat on the sofa. "We don't do drugs, so you're wasting your time."

Beth pulled on examination gloves and stared at her. "Does your husband have a man cave or an office?"

"Yeah, but you can't go in there. It's locked. He won't let anyone go inside, not even to clean." Mrs. Crenshaw sipped a glass of sweet tea and shrugged. "Where exactly have you taken Joe?"

Ignoring her question, Beth cut straight to the chase. "Where is this room?"

"In the loft." Mrs. Crenshaw waved a hand toward the passageway. "There are pulldown stairs just out there, but the room is locked as I said. He's made sure no one can get in."

"Is it booby-trapped?" Styles came to stand by her side.

"Not that I know." Mrs. Crenshaw narrowed her gaze. "Padlocks is all."

"I carry bolt cutters in the cruiser." Ryder hurried outside.

When he returned, they filed into the passageway and Styles pulled down the stairs to the loft. At the top of the stairs, they found a door barred with three large padlocks attached to metal strips reinforcing a wooden door. After Ryder made short work of the locks, he pushed the door open slowly and peered inside. The comment in Beth's throat froze at the sight of hideous images covering the walls. The photographs had been printed from an office printer and each had a corresponding lock of hair neatly tied in a pink bow and pinned to the group. She pulled out her phone and took a video of the entire space, moving slowly along each wall to capture every inch. Beside her, Styles was using his phone to take images of the rest of the room.

Turning, Beth went to a small desk with a computer and printer. She sat in the office chair and booted up the computer. It didn't take her too long to override the password and gain access to the video files. She discovered he had uploaded many of them to a dark website. There were more files than she could have ever imagined. Sickening recordings of a very damaged mind had been very carefully catalogued by date and location. She turned in her seat. "It's all here. The dates and times, how many visits he made. How long he kept them alive before killing them. Every sickening detail."

"How many?" Styles eyes flashed with anger. "So much suffering."

Beth scrolled down lists. "Too many to count right now. We'll hand this over to sex crimes; they can work through it and see if they can find a match in the missing persons files. We've done our part by arresting this guy."

"I'm surprised he didn't gain the attention of the Tarot Killer." Ryder continued to open drawers and collect evidence. "We know he's in the state. He was in Black Rock Falls recently and this guy has been doing this for a long time."

Biting back a smile, Beth shrugged. "Maybe he's busy elsewhere. I'm glad he didn't take him out. I'd really like to hear what Crenshaw has to say for himself. I'm betting Jo Wells will be hotfooting it to Black Rock Falls to listen in on the interview."

"Yeah, we should notify her he's in custody." Styles rubbed the back of his neck and looked at Ryder. "You'll need to ask Mrs. Crenshaw to pack a bag for her and the kids. They can't be here. We'll have to get all this stuff packed up and moved into evidence. I'll call in a team."

"Okay, I'll go and ask her if she has somewhere she can stay for a time." Ryder left the room.

"Tell me more about the dark web. You mentioned he had uploaded them to a site. So do people actually get enjoyment out of watching what he did to the women?" Styles leaned over her shoulder staring at the computer screen.

Beth nodded. "Yeah, I'm afraid every facet of depravity is enjoyed by someone out there, well, many people not just a few. The dark web is their playground, a place they can be safe. The problem is these people are in all walks of life. I mean, I don't think I could name a career that hasn't had a deviant at one time or the other. It probably goes right to the top in many places because this kind of thing is covered up way too often."

"Can we trace any of them?" Styles frowned at the screen. "You're an expert in cybercrime. Have they left any clues?"

Shaking her head, Beth sighed. "That's the beauty of the dark web. It's very difficult unless we find an access point, like someone's computer, to discover these sites in the first place. The people who use them bounce their signal all over the world. They're impossible to find unless they leave a clue to their whereabouts in a photograph or video. We have in the past traced people by a reflection of a building or sign in a window or similar."

This was the last thing she needed to be doing. The Crenshaw case was wrapped up and her anxiety to get to Billings and remove Jackson before he killed another innocent woman was burning a hole in her patience. "I'll download the catalog of video files onto an external drive and place them into evidence. I'll remove the hard drive from this computer and use it to track down others of like mind, but we're talking about possibly months of work and chances are I'll come up empty." She took a hard drive from her bag and plugged it into the computer. "It's going to take a long time to download everything."

"We have time. It's a big house." Styles squeezed her shoulder. "Once we have this case sewn up, I promised you a few days' downtime, maybe a week. I never go back on my word. Is a week enough time for you to recharge?"

Beth liked the word *recharge*. It exactly described the feeling after removing a monster from society. "I hope so, but I won't get the cabin finished in one week. That's not my intention. It's going to be my respite, so I'm planning on going slow and just tinkering with it over time. It's a reason to be visiting towns and buying things or I'd be wandering around aimlessly without purpose." She laughed. "Can you imagine if I'd purchased furniture from the charity shop and Crenshaw had delivered it? I might have ended up sewn to a sofa."

"Maybe, but he knows now you're not a dancer, and from what I can see, they were his favorite." Styles used the mouse to scroll through the image files. "Ah maybe not. Look here at the notation."

Intrigued, Beth turned in her seat to view the screen. "He calls them his 'darlings' and this one isn't a dancer. She's listed as a One B." Beth scrolled through the catalog. "Ah, One B is a sex worker."

"I recognize her." Styles peered at the image of before and after Crenshaw's cosmetic do-over. "Ryder arrested her and normally he'd let sex workers slide if they weren't causing a problem, but she was selling drugs on the side. She was fined and we assumed she left town. From these images, she didn't make it to the bus. That would be where Crenshaw obtained the fentanyl. We knew she was dealing but couldn't find her supply. Crenshaw must have had dealings with her and then killed her." Styles shook his head. "He's been busy over years and in many different states. I hadn't realized he'd moved around so often." He frowned. "Leave this room for the forensic team. We should ask Mrs. Crenshaw some questions and then start on the rest of the house, but I don't think we'll find anything incriminating. Everything we need is here."

Downstairs, Ryder was on his phone making arrangements for Mrs. Crenshaw and her kids to stay at the local shelter. It was run by her church and it would be for only a day or so. Beth sat on the sofa beside her and Styles sat opposite. Beth took out her notebook and pen. "I need to ask you a few questions. You've lived here for some time, I believe, but did Joe move around for his work? Or did he go away on vacation alone sometimes?"

"He moved around with his work all the time." Mrs. Crenshaw shrugged. "People buy our recycled furniture from all over and Joe always insisted on delivering it personally. He was often gone for weeks at a time, dropping things off in different states. He was generous like that, but the deliveries did bring in extra income for us." She teared up. "He liked to go fishing and hunting, so yeah, he went on vacation alone. Not all the time, only in the warmer months. When the snow came, he stayed home."

"Did he bring you gifts? Clothing or jewelry from his trips away?" Styles leaned forward in his chair.

"Oh, he was always giving me clothes and jewelry." Mrs. Crenshaw stood. "Most of the things weren't to my taste but he'd have me dress up sometimes and I did just to please him. Want to see them?"

Beth exchanged a knowing glance with Styles and controlled an involuntary shudder. How close was his wife to becoming a victim? She followed the woman to a hall closet and stared at the boxes of clothes stacked inside. To one side was an ornate jewelry box, overflowing with gawdy costume jewelry.

She looked at Mrs. Crenshaw. "We'll need to take this. Have you packed a bag?"

"Not yet." Ryder walked up behind them. "We'll search the bedroom first." He looked at Mrs. Crenshaw. "Go and wait in the family room. We'll be out of your hair very soon." He gave Beth a long look and lowered his voice to just above a whisper. "Who is going to tell her the charges her husband is facing? She had no idea. I don't figure that's an act."

Wanting to feel empathy for the wife of a serial killer but not buying Mrs. Crenshaw's innocent act, she raised an eyebrow. "I'll speak to her. You go and finish the search. I find it hard to believe she wasn't aware he was doing something weird. Married people get close, so close they can almost read each other's minds. Then there was the smell. We all know the stink of death hangs around. He visited the corpses and she didn't notice?" She headed back to the family room and sat down opposite Mrs. Crenshaw. "It's been a long morning and you'll be moving into the shelter for a couple of days. Do you want to grab something to eat before you go?"

"Yeah, thanks. I'll put on a pot of coffee and make some sandwiches." Mrs. Crenshaw made the way to the kitchen.

It was clean and tidy, almost as if she'd made plans to leave, or was that Beth's suspicious nature? She waited for the woman to sit at the table, accepted a cup of coffee but waved away the offer of food. It seemed inappropriate for what she had planned to reveal. "I need you to prepare yourself for a shock, Mrs. Crenshaw. Have you ever had suspicions things were not right with your husband?"

"Joe? No, why? He's a good man. He helps out everyone." Mrs. Crenshaw ate her sandwich slowly eyeing Beth with a frown. "All this, the search warrant, and arresting Joe must be a mistake. He hasn't gotten as much as a parking ticket."

Blowing out a breath, Beth lifted her chin. "It's no mistake. I'm afraid Joe murdered a woman and he captured it all on video. That's why he keeps his room locked. He has images of the women he killed on the walls."

"I know about the pictures." Mrs. Crenshaw smiled at her. "He loves horror movies and those are just stills. He calls them his 'darlings' and he showed me one day. There's nothing wrong with a man having a hobby. He kept the door locked to keep the kids out. They'd be frightened if they saw them."

Gathering her patience, Beth sipped the coffee. "They're not from horror movies. They're real. He murdered all those women and last night he tried to murder me."

"I don't believe you. He'd never do such a thing and those photographs are from horror movies. Why would he show them to me if they were real?" Mrs. Crenshaw blinked and looked over Beth closely. "You're saying you were with him last night?" Her mouth turned down, "You were alone with my husband? Where?"

Beth cleared her throat. "Yeah. In a cabin in Rainbow around eleven."

"It's all lies." Mrs. Crenshaw's mouth turned into an ugly sneer. "You blonde pretty women are all the same. You're just trying to turn me against him so you can have him for yourself."

"Allow me to explain." Styles strode through the door. "Agent Katz was attacked by your husband. She didn't invite him into the cabin. Your husband has been arrested and is accused of homicide. We have enough evidence to convict him in this state and no doubt other states will be lining up to do the same. You can pack your bags now. Father Paul is coming to take you to the shelter. You can collect the kids from school along the way."

"Stop wasting your time and go and find the real killer." Mrs. Crenshaw glared at Styles. "It wasn't him."

"We'll let the courts decide." Styles handed her over to Ryder and turned to Beth. "We're done here. As soon as Mrs. Crenshaw has left, we'll lock up the place and hand it over to forensics. There's a team flying in from Helena to collect the evidence. It's too big even for Wolfe's team to handle."

Beth got to her feet, rinsed the cups and plate from the table, and followed him outside. She took a few deep breaths of clean mountain air and turned to him. "Did you hear from the lawyer?"

"Yeah, we'll grab some lunch and pack an overnight bag. We get to interview Crenshaw at four this afternoon. We'll stay over at Black Rock Falls. I've booked us rooms at the Cattle-man's Hotel. We can update our files and hopefully have this case tied up and handed over before nightfall. We're staying over because I don't want to risk negotiating the mountains in the dark, especially after getting little sleep last night. You okay with that?"

Beth smiled at him. "That sounds perfect."

THIRTY-NINE

Black Rock Falls

They arrived at the Black Rock Falls County Jail with Crenshaw's lawyer in tow. He was friendly, very professional, and Beth liked him. He walked behind them, and Styles and Ryder kept Beth between them as they walked through the passageway between the cages. They were informed by an apologetic guard this was the only direct route to the interview rooms from the roof. Annoying though it was, it gave Beth an insight into male prison life. The exercise yards like giant animal cages showed groups of men. Each it seemed preferred the company of their own cultural group and all explained without shame what they'd like to do to her. She'd deliberately worn her FBI jacket same as Styles because anything else would make her appear to cower before a bunch of foul-mouthed criminals. They reached the corridor leading to the interview room and Styles turned to look at her. She smiled at him. "Better than being at the zoo, huh?"

"Just don't let them get inside your head." Styles turned to the lawyer, Jerry Blackwood. "We'll be outside when he's ready to talk."

"Okay." Blackwood followed the guard through a door.

One of the guards, motioned them closer. "Agents Wells and Carter are here. They've asked to speak to you." He motioned to another door. "In here."

Glancing at Styles, Beth waited for him to comment.

"I'm okay to have them observe." He stared at her and then at Ryder. "You both okay with that?"

Nodding, Beth followed the guard through the door. She smiled at Carter and Jo. "Nice to see you again. What a case this has been. Have you been following it?"

"Yeah." Jo nodded and her attention moved to Styles. "Hi, Styles, how's that dog of yours?"

"He's fine and spending the night with Nate." Styles grinned at her. "He didn't want to leave me, but he understands the word *kennels* and suddenly decided to go along, although with his head down and tail between his legs. It's only for one night. He'll be fine. Nate loves him."

"I have the same problem, but as luck would have it, Zorro has formed a relationship with Duke." Carter moved a toothpick across his lips. "He's owned by Deputy Dave Kane out at Black Rock Falls. We stay in their cottage from time to time and the dogs get along just fine."

Clearing her throat, Beth looked from one to the other. "Have we got a plan? This is one crazy killer and we need more information. I'd like to know what made him kill for a start."

"That might be difficult." Jo waved a hand to Styles. "Styles should take the lead because this guy has no respect for women. That's obvious by the way he posed them. I'm happy to throw in a few questions but we should have everyone in the interview room. You mentioned in your notes that he acted like a coward the moment Styles and Ryder arrived." She looked at Ryder. "That's if it's okay with you, Sheriff?"

"Yeah, I haven't had too much experience with psychopaths." Ryder removed his hat. "I'll stay outside and watch through the two-way mirror. It will be too crowded in there." He pulled a small recording device from his pocket. "You'll need this for the record."

Beth smiled at him. "Thanks. I was going to use my phone but that's much better."

A guard led them into a small room outside the interview room and as they arrived, Blackwood stepped out.

"He's ready to talk." He eyed them all critically. "I will stop you if any question is inappropriate. Is that understood?"

Rolling her eyes, Beth nodded. "Sure. We're all tired. Can we get this started?"

They filed inside and, Beth took a seat to one side, and Jo sat beside Styles with Carter on her right. Chained to a desk sat Crenshaw. Even though this man hadn't gone to trial, no one was taking any chances and his chains clanked as he surveyed the faces. She placed the recording device on the table and switched it on. She gave the date, time, and who were present in the room.

"We've found the videos and the photographs plastered all over your loft. Your wife gave us the clothes and jewelry you took from the bodies." Styles leaned on the table, hands clenched. "What we'd like to know is why?"

"My lawyer has negotiated a deal if I talk to you. He's told me about the evidence against me, so I figure you'd got me, seeing the chains and all. They wouldn't grant me bail, so I guess this is home now."

"So talk, we're all listening." Styles stared at him.

"Yeah, I'd love to talk about my darlings. They're all in here." Crenshaw tapped his head. "I understand you'll need an excuse why I killed them all. I don't know, it seemed the right thing to do, is all. The first one, I needed someone to be nice to me. Greet me when I came home." Crenshaw wiped the end of his nose, making his handcuffs rattle against the metal loop on the table.

"Did you have a happy childhood?" Jo crossed her legs and looked interested. "Your father was a minister, I believe?"

"He was and I was happy for a time." Crenshaw shrugged. "I guess."

"A time?" Jo raised an eyebrow. "What changed?"

"When I was fourteen, I think, I liked looking at girls—that's natural, right?" Crenshaw seemed to wait for Jo's nod of approval and then smiled. "Not for my pa. He said it was sinful and beat me any time he noticed my eye wandering to a pretty face. The girl next door was so cute, long hair and a dazzling smile. I would imagine her naked and smiling at me. It had gotten the best of me when I started to peek through her bedroom window and watch her undress. It was like a dream until my pa caught me. He took me to church and told everyone what I'd done. Flogged me right there in front of the congregation and did so every Sunday. So, I decided to get me my own girl and hide her away where no one would find her." He sighed and stared into space as if recalling his first kill. "After that, well, I was just on automatic."

"What about your wife? Didn't she smile and welcome you home?" Jo casually took out a notepad and made notes, ignoring him.

"I needed an excuse to move around unnoticed." Crenshaw's mouth twitched into a smile. "No one suspects the nice guy who works for a charity, has a wife and kids, do they? None of you suspected me for years. All that time, I had my darlings out there waiting for me, welcoming me with open arms, saying, 'Here I am. I belong only to you.'"

Suddenly wishing Crenshaw would escape so she could wipe him from existence, Beth snorted. She couldn't help herself. "I'm sure when the truth gets out that I took you down, all five-foot-five and one-ten pounds of me, and you cried for your mommy, no one will ever want you again."

"Trust me, one day I'll get out and come looking for you." Crenshaw smiled at her. "You'll be on the top of my list." He licked his lips. "I love blondes just like you, Agent Beth Katz. Yeah, I know who you are, and you'd make a great addition to my collection."

Beth stood and pressed both knuckles on the table and glared at him. "Bring it on. I've made it my life's work to take down monsters like you." She turned and left the room.

Outside in the small room. She stared at Ryder's astonished expression and burst out laughing. "Oh, that feels so much better."

"He hasn't upset you?" Ryder offered her a bottle of water.

Shaking her head, Beth looked at him. "Nope. I wanted to push him over the edge. He's all talk. He uses drugs and weapons to overpower women. He's nothing but a coward. I'm not afraid of him."

"I am." Ryder rubbed the back of his neck. "After seeing the maniac side of him, I'll have bad dreams for a long time."

The questioning continued but they already had what they'd come for, the why behind the murders. Being belittled and beaten as a child would have been the trigger, and once he'd gotten started he couldn't stop. Beth took a seat and stared through the two-way mirror. The voices coming through the intercom sounded tinny.

"Where did you obtain the fentanyl?" Styles dropped into Beth's seat and raised both eyebrows at Crenshaw. "We know you used it to subdue your victims or more likely anesthetize them."

"It's spread all over and easier to obtain than you figure." Crenshaw shrugged. "That and oxy. If I wanted to deal in drugs, I could get a regular supply."

"How?" Styles frowned. "I personally cleaned up the fentanyl drug ring and they're all in jail."

"I clean out people's homes, right?" Crenshaw waved a hand dismissively. "The majority are deceased estates. You know, old people's places? The family can't take the time or don't care about the possessions. They just want me to empty them. They always want a rush job so they can get the cleaning crew inside and get the property on the market. It's all about money. I guess to make them feel good about not caring, the family donates the contents to the charity and I go in and clear it out. The old folks usually have cancer drugs, pain meds, all types of stuff. It's a treasure trove of drugs." He shrugged. "Ask the local pharmacists. I drop a ton of them by for disposal. I only kept the drugs I needed." He winked at Styles. "Sometimes I got lucky and found a stash of morphine."

"And where are these drugs now?" Styles narrowed his gaze at him.

"In my truck, inside the gun locker." Crenshaw shrugged. "I'm a responsible citizen. This thing with my darlings was a distraction, is all. When you look at the facts, you'll see they made me do it. I'm not responsible for my actions. I'm a law-abiding citizen. Ask anyone."

"Do you recall where you left the bodies of your victims?" Jo glanced up.

"You have my files. It's all in there. Where, when, how I felt at the time." Crenshaw shrugged. "I don't recall after a week or so, so I make notes on each one." He smiled. "The videos are something, huh? Do you know how much I can sell them for?" He chuckled. "You look at me like I'm a monster, but there are thousands out there just like me. We all share the same fantasies. It's just some of us act on them; others, well, they wait for the rest of us to share our stories."

"Do you think about the women you killed?" Jo stared at him.

"At the time, yeah. They become an obsession. I can't get enough of them but as soon as I do another, I forget them." Crenshaw tried to lean back in his chair, but the chains impeded him. "That's why I take the movies. In winter it's difficult to get around, so I watch the videos to take the edge off."

"Have you ever wanted to kill your wife?" Jo inclined her head. "Do you love her?"

"I like her. She understands me. I don't love her. I don't love anyone. I only have strong emotions toward the women I take. Is that love? Who really knows what love is anyway?" Crenshaw chuckled. "I've come close to killing my wife once or twice. In winter, as I said before, it takes a ton of control to not grab a stripper. I wanted to take one home at one time but then thought better of it. Instead, I play games with my wife. She dresses up for me, you know, like a dancer in all that skimpy underwear, and allows me to apply her makeup. The last time it was difficult and took all my willpower to stop myself from killing her."

"What do you think made you stop?" Jo crossed her legs and leaned back in her chair. "What was different that time?"

"The only thing that comes to mind is she enjoyed me roughing her up." Crenshaw shrugged. "She giggled and I really like my darlings to be struggling and afraid of me."

"So, dominating women and making them afraid is your fantasy?" Styles cleared his throat. "If so, why drug them?"

"Watch the videos." Crenshaw stared at him. "Look at them when they know what I've done to them. When they realize they're never gonna leave the cabin and I'm the last face they'll see. Being dominant, as you call it, is power. They have no choice. They belong to me."

"Getting back to your wife." Jo's brows furrowed. "So you didn't try to kill her but you came close, right? What happened next? How did you control yourself that time?"

"I went straight out to find a stripper and she lasted two

beautiful weeks." Crenshaw shrugged. "I discovered they last much longer over winter and the snowplow attachment I purchased for my truck meant I could go to more places and find more abandoned cabins."

"I'm just about done here." Jo folded her notebook. "Are there any more questions?"

No one said a word.

"Okay, that's all we need." Styles stood and turned off the recorder. "Thanks for your cooperation." He nodded to the lawyer and stood to one side to allow Jo to walk ahead of him and then collected Ryder's recorder.

When the group came through the door, Beth looked from one to the other. "Do you figure he'll plead guilty?"

"Yeah, he appears to be resigned to the fact." Carter stood hands on hips. "I'd say he'd do a plea bargain of some type. I doubt he'd want to be extradited to a state with the death penalty. Plead guilty and he'd get life in Montana."

"He's an interesting case and very obliging. He seemed to enjoy speaking about the murders. I'd have spent more time on the specifics, but I doubt his lawyer would have allowed it. I'd really like to know more about why he sewed them to the sofa." Jo leaned against the table. "I'll keep him in mind for a follow-up interview and go in-depth with him some time in the future."

Beth frowned. "I figure it was to keep them from fighting back and leaving marks on him when alive and to keep them in position, as in 'greeting him with open arms,' when they died."

"You could be right." Jo looked at Styles. "Did you give the lawyer a ride to the prison?"

"Yeah, but he's making his own way back." Styles pushed his Stetson over light-brown wavy hair curling at his collar and smiled. "I guess he'll be staying in town for a time to represent his client. I imagine it will be chaos here once the press gets a hold of the story." He walked away to talk to Carter.

"Do you have a minute?" Jo led Beth to a quiet corner. "I'd like a word."

Stomach flip-flopping, Beth swallowed hard. Had Jo profiled her? Had she let her guard down during the interview? She summoned her charming side and smiled at her. "Sure. What's on your mind?"

"I have your father on my list of serial killers I'm planning on interviewing." Jo met her gaze. "I won't include him if it's going to become an issue between us. I understand you have dissociative amnesia about the night your mother died and you've never visited your father."

Heart thumping, Beth sucked in a breath. "That's right. The fact that he exists after what he did disgusts me. I'm glad I don't have his name. I don't even recall using a different last name and that's fine by me. Having him in my life has been a burden. People look at me differently as if it's my fault he's a lunatic." She stared at the ground, trying hard to keep the dark side from rising and showing in her eyes. "I don't care if you interview him, Jo. Maybe you can find him an excuse for killing my mom and all those women, but I'll never forgive him."

"There's never an excuse for killing, Beth." Jo touched her arm. "If ever you need to talk about your concerns, I'm always here and it will be in the strictest of confidence."

Nodding, Beth allowed the panic to drain away and cleared her throat. "Thanks, that's very kind of you and I'll keep that in mind." Relieved, she turned blindly away and almost stumbled into Carter. She grasped his arm and smiled. "Ty, where are you holing up tonight?"

"We're staying at the Cattleman's Hotel." Carter turned amused green eyes onto Beth. "I hope y'all will join us for supper? They have a fine restaurant on the premises. We booked a table for eight."

The idea sounded just fine to Beth. She turned to Styles and Ryder. "What do you say?"

"Yeah, sounds good." Ryder grabbed his recording device from the counter.

"Sure, but can we make it an early night?" Styles rolled his shoulders. "It's been a tough few days and we're exhausted. We'll need to update our files for the handover to the sex crimes team."

"Sure." Carter smiled. "Next time you're in town, we'll have a guys' night out. You need to let your hair down sometime. All work and no play... well, you know the deal."

"I sure do and, thanks, I'll look forward to it." Styles turned to Beth. "Are you happy to take Monday and Tuesday for some downtime? I'm going fishing and no one is going to stop me."

Beth's mind went straight to Levi Jackson. At last, she'd have time to slip away unnoticed. She nodded. "Yeah, Monday and Tuesday would work for me."

"Great!" Styles tipped his head toward the door. "Let's get out of here."

Beth smiled. "I thought you'd never ask."

FORTY

MONDAY

"If you need to contact me, message me." Styles pushed his Stetson firmly on his head and smiled at her. "I'll check my messages when I get into range. The bars are sketchy where I'm going. If it's an emergency, use your satellite phone to reach me." He gave her a long look. "Not work, right? The Snakeskin Gully team is bored stupid, so get them to handle any situation that comes up." He paused a beat. "But if it's personal, call me anytime."

Beth nodded. "I'll be fine. I'm only driving to a few towns and staying overnight. I'll be looking at stores and driving. My phone will be off. I'll turn it on if the sky falls." She waved him out of the office door. "Go fishing. I'll be leaving right behind you. I just need to book a room."

She waited for him to walk into the elevator and headed for her computer. It was just after six and she'd planned on an early start. She'd need to perform a magic trick and be seen in several places at the same time, but not where she was actually heading. *Complicated* wasn't the word she'd use, but she'd managed similar situations many times before and they all just needed careful planning. She'd estimated by carefully analyzing Levi

Jackson's MO that he murdered twice in the same area and then moved on, which meant, he'd be hunting for another victim out of Running Water. It was in his comfort zone and the last place the cops discovered a body. She figured it was a ninety percent chance, Jackson had left his flyer offering a free room for work at his ranch in the Running Water Roadhouse. The position was perfect and right beside a bus station, the same as all the other scenarios. She just needed to get there and insert herself into the game before some poor girl was lured to her death.

Surreptitiously during the investigations into Joseph Crenshaw's killing spree, Beth had been making plans. She'd accessed the dark web to obtain the necessary tools of the trade she'd need using reliable criminal associates. Yes, she had many untraceable "friends" who had no idea of her true identity and all accepted untraceable cryptocurrency as payment. Her wealth had tripled over the last year when she'd destroyed a catfisher preying on vulnerable women. The master of deception hadn't fooled her and he'd have slipped by unnoticed by her, but he wasn't happy to take just their money—he took their lives as well. His millions had become hers with a stroke of a key, to add to her substantial offshore accounts. Via the dark web there was really little she couldn't buy.

With Levi Jackson firmly on her radar, she'd used the final week of the previous investigation to make a deal for a nondescript pickup under the name of Tim Burke and would pay cash on delivery. The vehicle would be housed in an old warehouse she'd purchased under another false identity. The place was padlocked and the keys secreted behind a loose brick. She would change the padlock. The building was an easy walk from the Rainbow bus station, and with buses twice daily to and from Spring Grove, it offered the perfect transport option.

She'd made a booking at the motel in Spring Grove in her name and asked for an end room. This was a practice she always used, as it was easier to slip away unnoticed through a side window. On arrival she'd make a big deal about visiting the local stores. Styles had zoned out when she'd explained the reason for staying over and then added her intention to head out to visit the Native American furniture and goods stores. This excuse would give her a good timespan to get back and forth to Running Water and hopefully become Levi Jackson's next potential victim. After extensive research into Running Water and the surrounding counties, she'd planned everything, including booking a motel room under her alias, close to the roadhouse. If she needed to clean up after her encounter with Jackson, a motel used by thousands of travelers would be perfect. All motels accepted cash and her ID would pass scrutiny. As Tim Burke, she'd become one of many faceless travelers drifting through town.

She double-checked her computer, deleting all signs of her activity, and headed for her apartment. Everything was packed, her disguises and weapons. Excitement thrummed through her mixed with a little twinge of fear. The latter kept her on her toes and stopped her becoming complacent. Levi Jackson was a strong man and, from the condition of his victims, brutal and malicious. She'd need to bring her A game and hope it was enough. First, she'd need to set up her alibi. Beth must convince everyone she'd spent her downtime in Spring Grove. Making sure her presence was known would be the key to success.

A little after eight, she arrived in Spring Grove and headed straight to the motel, checked in, and asked what stores were in walking distance. Asking for recommendations and telling the woman at the counter how she loved to spend hours wandering through towns and buying small pieces of craft had set the scene. Her mention of exercising at daybreak offered a valid excuse, if for some reason she wasn't in her room the following morning. It was a crucial part of her plan. The woman could identify her if necessary and recall their conversation. There had been no choice but to leave her truck in plain sight. She'd leave her phone as well. Both could be tracked, which was another added security, and could prove she was in town the entire night. She had an untraceable burner purchased in another state with her to use in Running Water.

In the week previously, Beth had checked out the entire area around the motel and roadhouse in Running Water online and found no CCTV cameras anywhere. It was a safe place for her to move around unnoticed. On arrival at the motel, she unpacked her things from a huge suitcase, left toiletries in the bathroom, messed up the bed, and dampened the towels. The bus left at ten, which gave her time to potter around the local stores buying things. Making sure, should any suspicion be thrown her way, she'd have a solid alibi. No one could possibly be in two places at the same time—but they weren't the Tarot Killer.

Keeping one eye on the time, Beth purchased a few things, retelling her story of fixing up her cabin as she went. Being noticeable and using her charismatic personality made her memorable. Days ran into each other in the slower way of living in small towns, meaning the actual day she'd been there would be confusing, so she used her credit card to buy the items. The date stamp would prove when she'd been there. She slid her phone under the seat of her truck and locked it. Both vehicle and phone would track her movements and she needed to be electronically in Spring Grove for at least the next twenty-four hours.

The next phase slotted into place as she changed her appearance into Tim Burke. She applied appropriate makeup to change her face shape, carefully added a mustache and goatee. The thin shaggy wig, ball cap, plaid padded jacket, jeans, and scuffed boots would fool anyone. Her other disguise she'd use to kill Levi Jackson. Her weapons and other essentials she packed in a duffel. She checked all around the room, left a half-full to-go cup of coffee beside the bed, took the phone off the hook, and climbed out of the bathroom window. Looking all around, she pushed on sunglasses and headed for the bus station. Adding a thick Southern accent, she purchased a ticket with cash and climbed onto the bus heading for Rainbow. She sat at the back, took the window seat, hunched down, and became anonymous. Her stomach tightened. If all went to plan, in a few hours she'd be facing down Levi Jackson, in possibly a fight for her life.

FORTY-ONE

Rainbow was holding a festival of some kind or maybe a street fair, with stalls carrying all kinds of different items from antiques to cookies. From the bus, she made her way to the gas station. The mechanic was selling the Ford pickup. She asked for him by name and was sent round back to a small parking lot, used for vehicles awaiting repair. She walked around the pickup with the FOR SALE sign resting against the windshield. Moments later a man wearing coveralls, with a rag hanging out of his back pocket, walked toward her smiling.

"Tim Burke?" The mechanic grinned. "Man, I could set my watch by you. I see you've found the truck. It's only five years old and reliable. My son is selling it. He joined the Army."

Nodding Beth moved around, peered inside, and looked at the engine when the man popped the hood. It looked clean. It was overpriced but had low mileage. "Is it gassed up, ready to go?"

"Just as I told you in my email." The man held out the keys. "Start it up and see for yourself. It's sound. I serviced it myself. It's like new."

Wanting to get away but acting as if she hadn't made up her

mind, she made him an offer of two thousand less but in cash. It sounded like a good idea and men liked to haggle. "What do you say?"

"One thousand less and that's the best I can do." The man's expression was pained.

Nodding, Beth opened her rucksack. She had wads of bills in five-thousand-dollar bricks. She handed him a pile of bills and then took ten bills from another brick and added them to his pile. "Okay, give me the paperwork and a receipt for the cash. I don't want the cops pulling me over and sayin' this vehicle is stolen."

The transaction took a few minutes and Beth slid behind the wheel and drove away. Time was ticking and she needed to check out the warehouse and change the lock. She found it easily enough. The key was behind the brick and inside the place was clean and dry. She could hide the truck inside and access it when necessary. Everything was going to plan and the entire process took only twenty minutes. She smiled as she drove away and turned the pickup onto the highway and then followed the signs to Billings. It was a nice day, not too windy and the sun shone on the open vistas. There could be nothing more spectacular than driving through Montana. The blacktop stretched out before her, snaking its way onward in a never-ending trail. Traffic was reasonable, mainly eighteen-wheelers and delivery vans moving cargo from one town to the next. The pickup had a GPS, but she used the one on her burner. She didn't need anyone knowing where she'd gone after leaving Rainbow. All bases must be covered, take nothing for granted, and watch your back was her mantra.

She cruised through Running Water, past the roadhouse and the bus station, scoping out the area before turning around and pulling up to purchase some gas. She wandered into the roadhouse. In her disguise, no one took a second look at her as she perused the noticeboard. Her heart skipped a beat when she noticed the flyer. She had no doubt it belonged to Levi Jackson. The man was so confident he'd left flyers advertising his handyman and gardening service on the same board. She paid for the gas and drove around some, getting a feel for the area. After hunting down a suitable place to dump Jackson's van after she'd put out the trash, she noted the position of the motel and headed down Main.

Moments later, she slid into a parking space outside a greasy spoon. Hunger gnawed at her belly and she needed to be strong and rested before slipping into her new persona. She'd thought long and hard about her look and studied Jackson's previous victims, making her disguise as close to them as possible. Although none of the murders were attributed to him, she could easily identify him as the killer from his trademark moves. All of the bodies found dumped in the three surrounding towns were his victims. She had no doubt and her vendetta against him would be justified one way or the other later tonight. If he took the bait. She checked her watch, noting the traveling time between Rainbow and Running Water, and went inside, ordered, and then took a seat to wait for her meal to arrive.

The roadhouse had CCTV cameras on the gas pumps and the roadhouse door. That wouldn't be a problem for her dressed as a man, but when she disguised herself as his next victim, Jackson might be watching the roadhouse via the camera feed. CCTV cameras were easily hacked but was Jackson that smart? Anything was possible for a killer who posted stories of his kills on the dark web. He would be watching the bus arrivals for sure and searching for potential damsels in distress. She had the bus schedules on her phone and checked them once again. Timing would be crucial. She'd need to slip into the group of passengers alighting from the bus and walk with them to the roadhouse. As she ate her meal, the thrill of the chase mixed with a stranger emotion she hadn't encountered before: regret. If she failed, Styles would discover her true identity and she would have let him down. The tarot card, wrapped in its sterile container, was in her duffel along with her hatpins and she still carried the fentanyl pen Nate had given her. If she died tonight, Styles would carry some of the blame. His career would be over. They'd say he'd covered up her identity. She stared at her reflection in the window and met her familiar eyes. *I will not fail.*

FORTY-TWO

Beth pulled up outside the motel and walked inside, making her stride wider than usual. The man on the front desk didn't even request an ID, and just snatched up the bills before sliding a key across to her without more than a sidelong glance. He'd given her an end room as requested, and after leaving her ride outside the door, she went inside. The room was clean but old and held a slight smell of disinfectant. She dumped the duffel on the bed and went to the bathroom. It was cold inside and the tattered wings of dead moths caught in a flyscreen over a large bathroom window fluttered in the breeze. With ease, she lifted out the screen and tried the window to see how wide it would open. To her surprise it slid outward on greased sliders, leaving plenty of room for her to slip out. The side of the motel led to a grassy mound covered with bushes. It was all she needed to slip away into the darkness.

She went about carefully removing her disguise. She'd need it for the trip back to Spring Grove and packed it neatly into plastic containers. Once back in Rattlesnake Creek, she'd add the clothes and boots to a carton of garbage and incinerate them. Should Styles question her, which she doubted, she'd say it was garbage from the cabin. She checked the time. The bus wasn't arriving for three hours. After taking a long hot shower, she locked the bathroom window and crawled into bed. She set the alarm on her phone and went to sleep.

Waking in darkness to the eerie music on her phone, Beth sat up. Excitement sizzled through her and, instantly fully awake, she went to the bathroom and washed her face. She stared at her reflection in the mirror and grinned. It was time to begin the elaborate transformation. Jackson had a hankering for country girls, sweet and innocent, young and poor. Her kit held everything she needed and she went to work using makeup techniques to change her appearance. Satisfied with the new shape of her face, she added a shoulder-length dull brown wig. Her full lips turned down and gave her a sad expression. It would fool anyone. She'd chosen her clothes with care, jeans and a sweater. The boots she'd purchased years ago from a charity shop were worn but had sturdy heels. She needed good heels to fight. Footwear could save her life. She added a woolen cap and thrust two hatpins in either side. These weapons ensured her wig wouldn't be torn off in a struggle and produced an almost bloodless kill. They were perfect. She ran a finger over the silver tops and tingles surged up her fingers.

After shrugging into a brown hip-length jacket, she twirled around to see her reflection in the bathroom mirror. The dull country girl had emerged from her cocoon. She went to her rucksack and removed the container holding one of her tarot cards. Using the dark web, she'd had them made in the UK and collected them during a vacation. Machine-printed and packed like rare baseball cards, each in individually sealed packets, meant they were untraceable, with no prints and no record of them being manufactured. She smiled and turned the card over in her hand. Like millions of others, Beth used the dark web to her advantage. It gave surfing the net a whole new meaning. The cards she'd stashed in a variety of places, making them accessible when necessary. Criminals she trusted could always access them and anything else she needed. Her network of highly paid associates was reliable. All of them knew the penalty if they crossed her, but funnily enough, not one had ever tried. She'd seriously considered using them to purchase her undercover truck and the warehouse, but time was limited. Going forward, she'd make sure she had more time to organize things, so she didn't place herself in danger of being on a suspect's list.

Suddenly concerned, she scanned the room. She'd need to leave some of her things behind, at least the car keys, clothes, and disguises. Deciding the chances of being disturbed by housekeeping at this time of night were practically zero, she slid her things under the bed. After hanging a DO NOT DISTURB sign on the doorknob, she turned out the lights. She grabbed her duffel, slipped out of the bathroom window, shutting it to leave a small gap, and disappeared into the darkness.

The night was crisp and a cloud of vapor drifted from her mouth. Glad of her leather gloves, she kept to the shadows, rounded the bus station, and slid between two parked buses. The next bus arrived in minutes, and in a squeal of breaks and huffing sounds, the doors opened and people streamed out. Keeping her head down, Beth merged into the crowd. Most of the passengers came down the steps, shoulders slumped as if tired. Some went to waiting vehicles or a person's open arms, others trudged to the roadhouse. She kept in step with the last group and went inside, glad to join the line for a hot beverage and whatever was on offer at ten at night. When she reached the counter, she ordered a large skinny latte and fries. When she paid in cash, they gave her a number to display on her table. She headed for a table near the noticeboard, placed her number on it, and then joined a few people staring at the noticeboard. Most were hunting down rides with truckers. A list written in chalk detailed the times of departure and destination. Her attention zeroed in on Jackson's flyer. If someone was watching her, she needed to be convincing and bent to read it slowly. Heart thundering, she reached out and plucked the notice from the board. Her fingers trembled as she stared at the final line. *Interested? Call Bill.*

Mixed emotions surged through her. She'd been right about everything. She'd found Levi Jackson and now all she needed to do was become his next victim.

FORTY-THREE

The roadhouse buzzed with conversation and the chinking of silverware as Beth stared out of the window. Without being obvious, she scanned the parking lot for Jackson's signature white van and almost missed it. Parked in the shadows of the trees surrounding the perimeter, it was barely visible. Her meal arrived, and after adding extra sugar to her cup, she sipped her coffee, her gaze on the flyer. It was crudely made and printed on regular paper. She pulled out her phone and, trembling with expectation, called the number. It answered on the fourth ring.

"You got Bill. What can I do for you?"

Trying to keep her voice calm, Beth used her little girl voice. "I'm calling about the room. Is it still available?"

"You sound very young. You haven't run away from home have you, sweetheart?"

His voice was sugar sweet, manipulative, and charming. Recognizing him as one of her own kind, Beth smiled to herself. "No I'm eighteen and I can do what I please. My pa owned a ranch. I know this job is probably for a man but I'm a good worker and I need a place to stay. Will you give me the chance to prove I can work hard?"

"As I've had no takers, I'll give you a week to prove you have what it takes. It's getting late, you'll need to come now. I'm not planning on staying up past midnight for you."

After reading the statement of Natalie Kingsley, the victim who'd escaped, Beth could almost hear Jackson's words before he spoke them. She blew out a long sigh for his benefit. "I came on the bus. I don't have any way of getting to your ranch at this time of night."

"Then it's just as well my wife needed a hot apple pie from the roadhouse or I wouldn't be close by. I just reached my van." He sounded breathless. *"Come out front and I'll give you a ride. What are you wearing?"*

Beth smiled. "Brown coat, black hat, jeans. How will I know you?"

"I'll flash my lights." He disconnected.

Running Natalie Kingsley's statement through her mind, Beth stuffed the last few fries into her mouth and washed them down with coffee. She noticed her hand tremble slightly and gave herself a mental shake. He wouldn't kill her until he'd raped her, which gave her time to take him down, but if he restrained her, she wouldn't be able to use her hatpin and would be at his mercy. From Natalie's description of Jackson, he was strong and heavy, so that usually meant muscular. How could she prevent him from getting her inside the van? Fighting in a restricted area would be suicide.

Pushing down a wave of uncertainty, Beth walked through the glass doors to the roadhouse and scanned the parking lot. Her eyes came to rest on the flashing lights of the white van she'd noticed previously conveniently waiting outside the range of the CCTV cameras. Legs heavy and heart pounding like a military tattoo, she hurried across the parking lot. The van window buzzed down and a man in shadow poked out his head.

"The door is open. Jump in. It's getting cold." Jackson's teeth flashed as he grinned.

Beth ran around the hood, opened the door, and jumped in. Immediately, Jackson grabbed her duffel and threw it into the void behind his seat. She checked his features and had no doubt it was Jackson. This man must be dumb to keep calling himself Bill when he abducted women. If another one escaped and told the same story as Natalie, he'd have been in jail by now. How the investigators had allowed him to slip through the net was mind-blowing.

Beth fastened her seatbelt and sat back waiting for him to speak. When he said nothing, she turned to look at him. "How far is your ranch?"

"Not far. There's a dirt road through the woods a couple of miles away. I'll take a shortcut to the cabins. That's where we keep the ranch hands." Jackson smiled at her. "Do your parents know you're out here on your lonesome?"

Shaking her head, Beth gave him a sideways glance and went back to checking out the cab for weapons. "I'm all alone now but I do okay."

As the van chewed up the miles, her mind was working overtime. She could see the scenes described by Natalie playing out like a well-rehearsed drama. Jackson wasn't as smart as she'd imagined. He'd not only used the same name on the flyer, but was following the exact MO. The last murders happened in secluded places, wooded areas, and there was no lack of them in this county. She sighed. Perhaps he figured if his plan worked, why change it? Or was this all part of his reoccurring fantasy? Maybe not, because young women weren't his only targets. He'd murdered mothers and young children as well. The sick freak.

Without warning, the van turned sharply and bounced down a dirt road cut between trees. As the headlights illuminated a way ahead, she spotted picnic tables and a small building containing bathrooms. Through the trees, moonlight reflected on fast-flowing water. A light mist drifted across the trail, giving the forest a spooky feel. This must be a popular rest area for travelers. Acting dumb, Beth looked at him when he stopped the van. "Why are we here?"

"The back of the cabin is through those trees. We'll need to walk from here." Jackson slid from his seat and opened the sliding door to the side of his van. "Grab your things."

Natalie's statement flashed through Beth's mind. If she went into the van, he'd hit her from behind, overpower her, and restrain her. That couldn't happen. Trembling with uncertainty, she went around the back of the van, the opposite choice to Natalie, and stood staring at him. From the light inside the van, she made out his confused expression followed by a flash of anger.

"Get your bag." Jackson scowled at her. "You don't expect me to carry it for you, do you?"

Fear gripped Beth by the throat. He was bigger and more powerful than she'd imagined. It would take all her skills to come close to defeating him. Without warning, he lunged forward and grabbed her around the waist and tossed her inside the van. Face down in a muddle of stinking sheets and pillows, Beth had no time to take a breath before he tossed her over to face him as if she weighed nothing. Instincts raging, she pushed down the overpowering need to fight back. He was so strong and what he wanted was for her to struggle. Acting passive should throw him off guard. She went limp and just stared at him gasping for breath.

"You know what this means, don't you?" Jackson leered at her. "All alone in the woods with a man. You know what I want, don't you?"

She'd confused him but it wouldn't stop him. The violence would start very soon. He needed a reaction, to fuel his fantasy. The fighting and struggling was all part of it. He'd have many ways to make her scream and fight back. She'd need to be strong just long enough to take him out. She looked at him and shook her head. "No, what do you want?"

"You're making me angry." He slapped her face and sat back on his heels waiting for a reaction.

Not reacting and not showing she cared when people abused her had been the only weapon she'd possessed as a kid. Abusers fed on negative responses. Levi Jackson was no different. He'd not get a whimper from her no matter what he did.

"What's wrong with you?" He slapped her again and pinched her breast.

Blood trickled into Beth's mouth, the metallic taste coating her tongue. Pain shot through her chest bringing back memories long hidden. Her dark side rose like an avenging angel. No way was this monster ever going to restrain her. The second he reached for her left hand she reared up, pulled out a hatpin, aiming for his ear—and missed. The pin barely pierced his neck and he snapped back, screaming with rage. She had one second to escape. Scrambling for the door, Beth jumped from the van and bolted along the dirt road, moving deeper into the forest. Seconds later, Jackson was behind her, roaring like a raging bull.

Fit and very fast, Beth ran along the path blindly into darkness. The uneven trail was a nightmare to negotiate. Shrubs and vegetation reached out to snag her clothes, slowing her down. Her big jacket was a burden and she stripped it off as she ran. The heavy breathing and curses were gaining on her and in desperation, she left the path and zigzagged between trees. Right behind her branches cracked, and a heavy weight slammed into her as he tackled her to the ground. The air rushed from her lungs. She gasped for air as terror gripped her. He was so strong and tossed her over like a rag doll to face him. This was what it was like to be a victim.

"That's better." Jackson smiled down at her. "I like a good

chase." He grabbed both her hands and pulled them together over her head. "This is gonna be so much fun." One hand fumbled at his waist.

He's going for his knife. Time seemed to slow as her instinct to survive kicked in. Gasping for breath, she glared at him. She had one more chance to spoil his fantasy, one more chance to kill him before he sliced her up. That's how it went. She'd read all the details of his kills. His face was close to her, his hot cigarette-tainted breath brushing her cheek. "You had the mothers. Why did you kill the kids?"

"What?" Jackson stared at her confused.

Trying to gather her strength, Beth needed time to act. "I know about the women you raped and murdered, but why the kids?"

"How did you know?" Jackson shook his head like a dog dispelling water, his eyes dark pools of surprise above her.

She'd destroyed his fantasy and his mood changed from frantic to puzzled. Beth tensed her muscles. "I know everything about you and what you did. I've read what you posted on the dark web. I've seen the crime scene images. If I'm going to be part of your trophy collection, at least tell me why you killed the kids?"

"A mother will do anything to save her kid." Jackson laughed and shook his head as if he couldn't believe what he was saying. "Killing them in front of them made them fight harder. I like it when they fight back." He shook his head. "You figure you know about me and yet you came along? I've heard about women like you. You want a bad boy? Bad boys get you killed."

Playing dumb, Beth shook her head. "No and I didn't know it was you until you attacked me. I've read about the murders and checked them out. I'm a hacker, is all."

"If you figure keeping me talking will make me go easy on

you, think again." Jackson grinned at her. "I'll just kill you slower. I have all night."

Any doubts that Jackson was the psychopathic killer she'd been hunting vanished in that second. Pinned and helpless, she'd become like all his other victims. Gripped in an uncontrollable rage to find justice for the women and children he'd murdered, her dark side kicked in with a burst of adrenaline. *Do something now or die.* In a fight for her life, she reared up and headbutted him square on the nose. He bellowed in pain and the grip loosened on her hands.

"You bitch." He held his face rocking back and forth.

Scrambling to get away, Beth's feet slid in the damp fallen leaves covering the forest floor as she ran weaving between the trees. When darkness surrounded her and the dense forest offered sanctuary, she dropped, panting at the foot of a tree shrouded in bushes. In the distance, she could hear him, cursing and stumbling after her. Her psychopath side, the hidden part of her that gave her the strength to hunt down monsters, slipped away. Suddenly transported back to her childhood, it was the night the man she'd loved, her father, had changed her forever. Terrified, shocked, and in fear of her life, she'd witnessed him murder her mother, slicing and stabbing. He'd laughed as he cut deep, offering no quick death. He'd made sure she died in excruciating pain. In Beth's mind the time was now. Every second played out the recurring nightmare. The image of her mother's terrified eyes as she fought for life, her screams of agony, and her last words to her as she died.

"Run."

A new reality closed in around her as she relived the memory. Instantly a defenseless little girl, she could see the blood dripping from the cutthroat razor and smell her mother's blood. She'd ran into the woods to escape her father. Reality and memory merged, and Beth couldn't find a way back to the real world. Trembling, with sweat streaming into her eyes, she rolled into a ball unable to move. Terror had her by the throat. The sound of a man searching the forest, the heavy footsteps, and breaking of branches came closer. He was coming. Coming for her.

FORTY-FOUR

Sweat ran between Beth's shoulder blades in an annoying tickle, and her lungs ached with each ragged breath. The dark forest spun around her and damp leaves brushed her face. She shook her head as reality slid firmly back into place. It had happened before, the shifting of time, as her mind thrust her back to that night. The memory never left her and talking to Styles had brought it back to the surface, not in a dream this time but right now, when she needed all her skills to survive. It was a vulnerability no one could know existed. Heart pounding, as Jackson moved through the bushes, she rammed the memories deep into the recesses of her mind and forced her legs to move. Rising up, she exploded from her hiding place and darted from behind the tree. She needed to attack from behind and ran in a semicircle in an attempt to get behind him.

As she'd crossed his path, he'd glanced her way. She'd underestimated Jackson. Enraged and pumped with adrenaline, he was on top of her in a few long strides. His thick hand closed around one arm and her head jerked back as he spun her to face him. Beth raised one knee to his groin but he turned away and she kneed him in the thigh. Gasping, she stared into wild eyes.

Spittle running down his chin, glistening in the moonlight, as he cursed her. She punched him hard in the face. "Let me go."

"Yeah, keep fighting, make me work for it." Jackson suddenly grinned. "I knew I'd make you scream." He raised the knife in his hand to show her. "This is gonna be fun."

His stinking breath washed over her, and out of options, Beth drew back her fist and slammed a punch into his throat. As his eyes widened, and as he gasped for air, she lifted her knee and this time connected. Wrenching her arm from his grasp, she pulled out the hatpin and drove it deep into his ear. As he howled in agony, she dragged it out. When his head fell forward, exposing his neck, she plunged the hatpin into the base of his skull severing his spinal cord, instantly paralyzing him. Twitching, Jackson made a gurgling sound, spittle dripped from his fixed grimace. His eyes rolled back in his head and he fell heavily on top of her.

Panic gripped Beth as Jackson pinned her beneath him. He twitched in the last throes of death and it made her sick to her stomach. She gagged as the stink of his bowels and bladder relaxed. Gasping for air, Beth pushed at him using her knees and hands. After many attempts, she finally managed to roll him onto his side and wiggle out from under him. She checked his pulse and was horrified to find him alive. *What does it take to kill this guy?*

Under her fingers his heart thumped weakly and then missed a few beats before it stopped. She sat staring at him for a long five minutes before checking him again. Nothing. Breathing a sigh of relief, she removed the pin and wiped it on his shirt. She'd need to search the van for the other one. Leaving evidence behind would see her behind bars in no time. Suddenly exhausted, she pressed her back against a tree, and sat for a time dragging in deep breaths. This kill had been brutal and slipping away from Styles unnoticed had been more difficult than she'd imagined. When her heart rate returned to normal, she took out the tarot card and, sliding it from the wrapper, pushed it deep into Jackson's open mouth. It was over and Beth flopped back on the damp leaf-strewn ground staring at him. "That's payment for all the women you've murdered and their innocent kids."

She wanted to punch the air and scream out that the Tarot Killer had removed another monster from society, but exhaustion dragged at her. Standing slowly, she pulled her phone from an inside pocket and using the flashlight, checked all around the body for evidence. Any fabric or hair from her found on his body would come from her wig or from clothes she'd destroy. She'd been wearing gloves and they'd go into the incinerator too, just in case his bodily fluids had contaminated them. Using the thick dead vegetation and fall leaves on the ground, she covered all signs of activity. Walking slowly, she made her way back along the trail, and collecting her coat along the way, she pulled it back on. The cold wind cut through her clothes, chilling her damp flesh now she'd stopped running. It seemed to take forever before she reached the van and finally retrieved the hatpin and her duffel.

Exhausted, she climbed into the driver's seat, and turned the key hanging from the ignition. The van refused to start. She leaned back in the seat and thought for a beat. Maybe in her rush she'd forgotten to do something. She checked everything and tried again moving the shifter back and forth. Sighing with relief when the engine roared into life, she turned the van around and moving slowly, followed the dirt road back to the highway. When the lights of the roadhouse came into view far in the distance, she searched for the small off-road area leading into the forest where she'd decided to leave the van. After dumping the van, she kept to the edge of the forest, staying in the shadows. It was some ways from her destination and looked farther in the dark. She couldn't risk being seen by passing traffic and so she made her way across open land, stumbling in the dark until she reached the motel. All was quiet as she slipped back inside the window. She stared at herself in the mirror for a long while before stripping off her clothes and bagging them with care. She sprayed her gloves with Lab Clean and used the fluid to remove all traces of DNA from her hatpins. After taking a long hot shower, she crawled into bed.

The feeling of elation had leaked away on her run across the lowlands. Exhaustion had her by the throat. She stared at the ceiling, covered her face with her hands, and allowed the tears to fall. She couldn't remember the last time she'd cried. Keeping emotions locked away had become a way of life. Perhaps working with Styles was making her soft. No one had complimented her before or encouraged her and she wished he could have been there backing her up. It had been a frightening encounter. She'd underestimated Levi Jackson and come close to becoming his next victim. If she'd failed to stop him, he'd have killed again and again. Like so many killers out there, the undetectable or uncatchable, she had become the only force to stop them. Beth dried her tears and straightened. She had a job to do, her father's debt to pay. The Tarot Killer must not fail—not ever.

FORTY-FIVE

TUESDAY

The chill in the early-morning breeze invigorated Beth as she stepped down from the bus at six the following morning at the Spring Grove Bus Station. Disguised as Tim Burke, Beth kept her ball cap pulled low over her eyes and made her way to the back of the motel. It was very quiet at this time of the year, as only a few miners occupied the rooms on weekends. Glad to see the window ajar as she'd left it, she climbed inside and checked all around. The security lock was still on the door, the phone was off the receiver, and nothing had been touched. She dragged out her suitcase, and after spraying her clothes with Lab Clean, dropped them into garbage bags along with the duffel and pushed them inside. She washed the makeup and glue from her face, added her usual cosmetics and dressed in her normal clothes. She added a gold snake bracelet she'd purchased the day before, opened the door to the motel, and packed her things into the back of her truck.

By seven, her stomach growled with hunger. It had been a long night but she still needed her cover story. She'd purchased a few nice items the previous day but to validate her weekend, she needed a few more things. First, being seen in town was a priority. She dropped her key at the office and drove to the diner. She'd noticed a furniture store close by and lingered outside looking at the window display. The store opened at eight-thirty, so she had some time to fill. As she went to turn away, she noticed a red truck pull up behind her ride. She blinked in astonishment as Styles climbed out and walked toward her grinning, with Bear loping along at his side. She turned to look at him. "Have the fish all gone on vacation?"

"Nope. I fished all day yesterday and woke before dawn." He scratched his cheek and looked at her sheepishly. "I couldn't sleep last night. I had this weird feeling you were trying to contact me. Your phone is off. Did you know?"

Shaking her head, Beth stared at him. "I did mention it would be off so I could get some undisturbed downtime."

"Yeah, you did, but I always go with my gut, so I tracked your phone. You know as an agent it's on my app?" He looked chagrined. "Well, I called the motel an hour ago."

Stomach clenching, Beth waited for the third degree. She'd taken every precaution by placing a DO NOT DISTURB sign on the door and removing the phone from the receiver. Had they opened the door to do a welfare check on her and found her missing? No, that couldn't have happened as the security lock on the door was still in place. She lifted her chin and met his inquisitive gaze. "And?"

"You sure make long calls." Styles inclined his head. "Were you calling overseas or something that early in the morning?"

Relieved, Beth blew out a sigh. "I just knew you'd be calling me for something, so I took the phone off the receiver so I could get some peace. You recall? Like we agreed?"

She placed her hands on her hips and took in his apologetic expression. In truth, she had needed him last night and somehow he'd sensed her danger. How extraordinary. No one had ever cared about her before. This would sure take some getting used to. "So, you came out to see if I was okay?"

"Yeah." Styles smiled. "I guess I did. I feel kinda stupid now but better safe than sorry."

Beth nodded. She had to say something and smiled. "Thanks, that's very thoughtful of you."

"Maybe it's just as well I came by. I see you have a bruise on your cheek." Styles moved closer to stare at her face and cupping her chin ran the pad on his thumb over the bruise under her left eye. "Right here. How did that happen? It's going to be black in a day or so."

How could she tell him that in a struggle for her life, a notorious serial killer had slapped her? Grasping for any silly excuse, Beth shrugged. "Really? Yesterday, I found a dime store and they sold secondhand furniture out back." She shrugged. This part of her story was true. "I lifted down a chair from a pile and the darn thing smacked me in the face. I didn't think it bruised me. At the time, I was too busy looking at stuff to care."

"This is why you need me along. Not because you're incapable of lifting down chairs but because I'm much taller and can reach things for you. And I just happen to like shopping. Just don't tell the guys. I have an image to protect." He chuckled and indicated to the diner. "I'm starving. Are you planning on eating anytime soon?"

Beth nodded. "Yeah. I was heading that way but a nice table and chairs in the store caught my eye."

"Well, how about I come along with you today?" He led the way to the diner and indicated to the woman at the counter that Bear was a K-9 with a handler, and they sat down and stared at a plastic-covered menu. He looked at her. "If you purchase the table and chairs, I could help you unload them and you could show me around your cabin."

Mind reeling with foreseeable problems if Styles needed to check up on her all the time, she smiled and added a good dose of her psychopath's charm. "It's really sweet that you worry about me, Styles, and yes, I'd love to have company today. You know your way around the towns better than I do, but just like you, I need some alone time to unwind. Some *me* time."

"I understand. We work close every day and I need to chill out alone sometimes as well. It's just that you're a city girl." He shrugged. "That's not saying you'll get into trouble. It's just that things happen to women alone out here."

Beth considered what he'd said. "If you're that concerned, I'll check in when I'm away from my apartment overnight. I'll send you a message when I get back to my motel so you'll know I'm okay."

"That works for me." Styles ordered a stack of pancakes and bacon. "It's still early. You mentioned visiting the Native American stores on the res. Why don't you leave your truck here and I'll give you a ride. We'll be back by nine and you can check out the furniture next door."

Smiling to herself, Beth added the fixings to the coffee the server had just delivered. How perfect was this? With Styles as her alibi, she was safe—this time.

The week had flown by and Beth had spent her time following up and supplying additional information on the Joseph Crenshaw case to the DA. She'd sent in all the information on his dark website to cybercrime in the hope some of the creeps accessing it might be found. How many of them were serial killers? How many of the comments she'd read about murders had been true? She could only hope that some new whiz kid in cybercrime could track them down.

With the forest wardens across the state and local mining leaseholders being made aware that old cabins in remote areas might be dumping grounds for bodies, reports had been coming in from all over. The discovery of skeletal and mummified remains of women in the areas specified by Joseph Crenshaw proved to be not the only evidence of his crimes. One of the cabins had been covered by an avalanche fifteen years previously. It had been uncovered after a particularly hot summer. The body of a woman wearing heavy makeup had been discovered inside. She'd been murdered. The brain stem injury was exactly the same as Crenshaw's other victims. The woman was identified as a missing sex worker and matched an image of one of his darlings from his files. The search was still proceeding for more victims. It was a massive case and counties were lining up for their chance to prosecute Crenshaw.

Beth had no reason to see Crenshaw again, but she'd spoken to Agent Jo Wells recently about the case. Jo had found the man interesting and was keen to speak to him again. She could use his willingness to talk about what made him tick to add to her book of serial killers' reasons for murder. Beth smiled to herself. She'd believed Jo Wells would be a threat. Her knowledge as a behavioral analyst was outstanding, but to really understand the mind of a psychopath, Beth had the advantage—after all, it really did take one to know one.

Her mind drifted back to her shopping excursion with Styles. She'd spent an enjoyable day with him and his assistance unloading furniture at the cabin had been welcome. They'd spent a nice couple of hours just walking along the sandy banks of Rattlesnake Creek, throwing sticks for Bear and talking about life in general. It was a beautiful place to live and as they walked Beth turned in circles taking in the vista. Rattlesnake Creek's water ran fast, weaving through huge boulders as it made its way downstream. It roared by and whitewater waves caressed the wide sandy riverbank, leaving behind streams of white foamy bubbles that cast tiny rainbows across each one. The bubbles appeared to change color as she walked by, and mesmerized, she bent to examine them.

The river originated from triple waterfalls set high in the mountains, the Three Fork Falls, clearly seen in the distance surrounded by a constant cloud of water vapor. Pine trees followed the river on one side and the forest climbed up the mountain, the green tops stopping short of the snowcapped mountain peaks. Rattlesnake Creek was opposite the forest and nestled into a valley between mountain peaks, one of many scattered all through the base of the mountain range. The town itself along with many of the old mining areas had its history depicted in the historic buildings. Rattlesnake Creek had maintained them and they stood proud as the reminders of the Old West.

Tucked in among the mountains and accessed by roads hewn out by hand, the mines both old and new had found a new life in the last few decades. With the increase in the price of gold, gemstones, copper, and other precious metals, this part of the Montana Rocky Mountains was thriving. The idea of exploring everything this area had to offer thrilled Beth. She'd always wanted a rustic cabin in the woods, filled with genuine antiques. Finding them, or using her search for them as an excuse to be away from town when necessary, had become an exciting possibility. Oh yeah, Rattlesnake Creek was the perfect place to live, that was for darn sure.

Her cabin still needed two beds and a refrigerator, and she'd recently ordered them online. She'd purchased the essentials: a coffee pot, cups, plates, silverware, two nice stuffed chairs, and a wooden kitchen table and four chairs. All had been stacked in the back of their trucks and Styles had unloaded them and given her advice on where he considered they should be placed inside the cabin. She still needed a closet and dresser to keep a few spare clothes. The next shopping expedition for other items would be her excuse to be away from her apartment next time. After that, she'd use hunting down art supplies and vanishing into the forest searching for scenery to paint as an excuse to be missing. She had thought about this long and hard and, after searching the net, had found some images online of the surrounding area to paint. Of course, when she went hunting down psychopaths, she'd hardly have time to paint as well. She'd chosen acrylics as her medium and could spend some time painting at night. Acrylic paints dried fast and she'd take the finished pictures and some unfinished ones as well to the cabin well before she needed them, just in case Styles came snooping. She'd set aside one of the bedrooms as her studio. The room had a window that let in the sun. It would be perfect and would fool anyone. She stared at Styles working at his desk and sighed. *Well, maybe everyone.*

As if sensing her looking at him, Styles looked up and smiled.

"Do you recall, a recent case where the women were found murdered and covered with lawn clippings? A guy by the name of Levi Jackson was charged when a woman claimed she'd escaped from his van after he tried to murder her and he walked. I've always believed there was more to that case than met the eye. He fit the profile. Everyone said so."

Coming close to becoming Jackson's victim and what the cops' reaction would be to finding his body had been at the front of Beth's mind for a time. Right now, she needed to hide that particular fact from Styles. Feigning disinterest, Beth sipped her steaming cup of coffee and set it down. She nodded. "Yeah, I remember reading about that one. It went to trial. He had a great attorney and walked. If I recall, the defense based its case on the fact he admitted to picking her up for rough sex and after paying her let her out at a gas station. They had CCTV footage of her getting willingly into his van and leaving it. The defense established she was a sex worker. The case on the murdered women and kids is ongoing. Why?"

"They found Levi Jackson murdered by the Tarot Killer. He had a tarot card stuffed halfway down his throat." Styles stared at her. "He was discovered in the forest out at Running Water. The murder weapon was a sharp instrument, like a long needle. One puncture wound was found in the ear and one to the base of the skull. His brain stem was obliterated. As usual, no trace evidence was discovered. They did find a garbage bag filled with lawn clippings in his van—just like the ones used to cover the bodies of the other victims. He was a handyman and traveled around through the three counties where the bodies of the other victims were found—and guess what? The lawn clippings and branches found on his last victim matched those from his own yard." He leaned back in his seat. "It gets even better. A flyer in the back of the van offered a room for a few hours' work at a ranch. The instructions were to call 'Bill.' The number was the same as the burner phone found on his body."

Trying not to smile, Beth put down her coffee. "Really? That's incredible."

"This was exactly the same info the sex worker gave them. Go figure? Problem was, even if they'd found new evidence, they couldn't retry him, not with the double-jeopardy law, but he did the murders, that's for sure." Styles shook his head. "The other strange thing is they found his van miles away from his body. It was in the forest with the keys in the ignition. This is where it gets interesting. The guy had two phones, a burner in his pocket and a regular phone in his glovebox. When they traced his regular phone and his ATM withdrawals, they discovered he'd been in all the places the murders occurred."

Leaning back in her chair, Beth raised both eyebrows. "Wow! It makes you wonder how many more serial killers are free because of the double-jeopardy law. Surely, they could have charged him for one of the recent murders? They had evidence, didn't they?"

"They suspected him at first because he left flyers seeking work as a handyman on noticeboards in roadhouses and other counties around Billings. He came under the persons of interest list as he regularly moved through the murder areas." Styles scratched his head. "I can only imagine because he admitted to picking up the woman at the roadhouse and returning her alive, they believed him, especially once it was established that she was a sex worker, as he'd stated. She was on file for numerous arrests." He stared at her. "How does the Tarot Killer see what we don't? How is he getting his information and how the heck is he taking out serial killers all over the state without anyone catching him?" He flicked a pen in the air and caught it. "He makes us look like amateurs."

Reaching for her cup, Beth shrugged. "Seems to me he's just taking out the garbage. Think about it, Styles. This Jackson guy was a violent criminal. He raped and killed women and their kids. He preyed on the weak and vulnerable. If we'd hunted him down, we'd have likely had to catch him in the act to prove our case, right? I mean after walking free from his previous case no one was touching him. I figure I'd have needed to go undercover with you as backup. If I recall, he's a big guy. How would you have stopped him raping me and then slicing me up?"

"I'd have shot him. Most likely killed him." Styles shrugged. "I would have protected you. You know that, right?"

Nodding, Beth met his gaze. "Yeah, by killing him."

"I've never been known to be subtle." Styles leaned back in his chair staring at the ceiling and then dropped his gaze back to her. "Don't say this makes me the same as the Tarot Killer, Beth, because we're miles apart."

Enjoying his reaction, Beth sipped her coffee, eyeing him over the rim. She loved his enthusiasm in their discussions. It was no holds barred. "How so? He's off the streets either way."

"Agreed, but I carry a badge." Styles smiled at her and pushed to his feet.

There was the hero slipping out again, and amused, Beth nodded trying to be serious. "So, what's next on the agenda for Agents Katz and Styles?"

"The sky's the limit." Styles stared into space and then looked back at her. A slow smile curled his lips. "How about we take down the Tarot Killer once and for all?"

Good luck with that. Beth chuckled. "That sounds like a plan. When do we start?"

A LETTER FROM D.K. HOOD

Dear Readers,

Thank you so much for choosing *Shadow Angels* and coming with me on the second book of my new series, Special Agent Beth Katz.

If you'd like to keep up to date with all my latest releases, just sign up at the website link below. We will never share your details and you can unsubscribe at any time.

www.bookouture.com/dk-hood

Writing about a serial killer in the guise of an FBI agent has been a thrilling challenge, and in this story, I was able to show you both sides of Beth Katz: as a dedicated FBI agent fighting crime and in her alter ego as the Tarot Killer, where she uses her psychopathic insight to hunt down unstoppable monsters. Teaming her with the unpredictable Dax Styles has given me so many angles to explore in future storylines and it will be great fun to share the stories with you.

If you enjoyed *Shadow Angels*, I would be very grateful if you could leave a review and recommend my book to your friends and family. I really enjoy hearing from readers, so feel free to ask me questions at any time.

You can get in touch on my Facebook page, Twitter, or through my websites.

Thank you so much for your support.

D.K. Hood

www.dkhood.com
dkhood-author.blogspot.com.au

 facebook.com/dkhoodauthor
x.com/DKHood_Author

ACKNOWLEDGMENTS

To #TeamBookouture. So many people work behind the scenes to bring my books to publication, far too many to mention, but my heartfelt gratitude goes out to all of you.

Many thanks to my readers' continued support and friendship, with special mention to Mina Soares, Tara McPherson, Martha Brindley, Linda Hocutt, and Susan Sanchez Purvis.

Made in United States
North Haven, CT
26 May 2024

52962404R00161